HIGHLAND HEROINE

BRIDES OF THE HIGHLANDS
BOOK 3

KIRSTEN OSBOURNE

ARE YOU SIGNED UP FOR DRAGONBLADE'S BLOG?

You'll get the latest news and information on exclusive giveaways, exclusive excerpts, coming releases, sales, free books, cover reveals and more.

Check out our complete list of authors, too!

No spam, no junk. That's a promise!

Sign Up Here

www.dragonbladepublishing.com

Dearest Reader;

Thank you for your support of a small press. At Dragonblade Publishing, we strive to bring you the highest quality Historical Romance from some of the best authors in the business. Without your support, there is no 'us', so we sincerely hope you adore these stories and find some new favorite authors along the way.

Happy Reading!

CEO, Dragonblade Publishing

Additional Dragonblade Books by Author Kirsten Osbourne

Brides of the Highlands Series
Highland Heart (Book 1)
Highland Home (Book 2)
Highland Heroine (Book 3)

$$\cdot \!\!\! -\!\!\!-\!\!\!-\!\!\! \text{❈} \!\!\!-\!\!\!-\!\!\!-\!\!\! \cdot$$

CHAPTER ONE

The Highlands, 1555

THE TORCHLIGHT FLICKERED over McAfee Keep's great hall, where Moira McAfee weaved through tartan-clad nobles and clan members. Banquet tables overflowed with roasted meats, fresh bread, and ale as laughter reverberated off stone walls decorated with ancient weapons and colorful banners.

Moira's red hair shimmered, braided with silver and emerald beads, her stride exuding confidence. She acknowledged each guest.

"Moira," her father, Duncan, beckoned from the head table. "Join old Angus MacNab."

She approached the elderly warrior, whose face softened into a grin. "Ye grow more like yer mother every day," he rasped affectionately. Angus was her mother's uncle, and one of the few ties she had to the woman who had died giving birth to her.

"Thank ye, Angus," Moira replied, discussing details of that day's hunt while sensing tension beneath the festivities. This celebration was an act of defiance—they were still here and strong despite the coming conflict.

Moving away from Angus, Moira overheard two clansmen conversing in a shadowy alcove by the hearth. "Ye ken the Gordons will be here in a day or two," one whispered apprehensively.

"Aye, and the Stewart army with them. And we all know there are others, even if we dinnae know who," the other muttered, hand on his dirk. "Laird Stewart's ambition ensures they'll strike soon." He shook his head. "Why would a man think he should be the ruler of all the Highlands? We have Queen Mary for that!"

"Let us hope our defenses hold," sighed the first clansman, glancing at the keep's sturdy walls. "We've prepared as best we can."

"Prepared, aye," agreed the second. "But will it be enough?"

The laughter and merrymaking continued unabated around them, but Moira's mind raced with strategies and contingencies. She'd been told she would not be allowed to participate in the battle, even though her ability with a sword was greater than any of their army. She was a lass, and that meant she had to stay behind.

Moira walked to her father across the great hall, her red hair a blazing contrast to the sea of tartans. Conversations hushed as she confronted Duncan, her father. "We cannot stand idly by!" she insisted, her eyes locked onto his. "Think of how much help the three of us could be. Fiona shoots an arrow like no other, and Ailis throws her knife better than anyone in the Highlands. Father, ye must allow us to help with the battle!"

Duncan met her gaze with calm authority. "Restraint is not always a weakness. Provocation is what the Gordons and Stewarts seek."

"Must we wait for another abduction or worse before we act?" Moira countered. Both of her sisters had been kidnapped by the men who would soon attack. Surely that had shown her father that things must change. If things went like they seemed to, she would be next, and she would not tolerate a kidnapping well.

"We must protect, not just retaliate," Duncan replied, his eyes darkening. "They don't have the burden of protecting women and children in their attack. But I must protect all the women and children in McAfee territory, be they McAfees, Sinclairs, or Stewarts."

Ailis intervened gracefully. "There is no way to avoid this

battle without losing our way of life. We love the Highlands, and it is therefore our duty to protect them."

Fiona placed a calming hand on Moira's shoulder. "We must consider the cost of aggression on our people. Think of the lives that will be lost. Ours and the enemies." Fiona always seemed to speak with reason. While it was a quality Moira usually admired about her eldest sister, she wasn't pleased to have her sister siding against her at that moment.

"But Fiona," Moira pleaded, "can we afford the cost of inaction? Laird Stewart plans to take over all of the Highlands. He says it's the right time with the queen away in France. We cannae allow him to become our ruler."

"Then we will respond with precision and unity," Fiona assured her. "But we will go into nothing blindly." She pressed a hand to her flat stomach. "Besides, I'm with child, and I will not put the babe at risk."

"Unity," Ailis said. "Our strength has always been in standing together, not rushing apart."

Duncan looked at his daughters. "My daughters, your passion is vital. Ye each have a part to play in protecting this keep and dealing with our wounded. We cannae risk losing ye all to battle."

The debate softened as understanding flickered between them. Moira recognized her father's wisdom, while he acknowledged her fierce spirit.

"Let us watch and wait," Duncan finally said. "And if the morrow brings battle, we shall face it as one large united army."

Moira nodded reluctantly, her resolve turning into a silent vow: she would be ready to defend her home and family with all the ferocity of the Highland blood that ran through her veins.

MOIRA NAVIGATED THE bustling celebration, her red hair vivid against the stone walls. An uneasy tension lay beneath the revelry as she sought Granny's chamber.

Inside, the matriarch sat by the fire, her silver hair seeming to glow by the flickering flames. She looked up from an old tome.

"Granny," Moira said, approaching her. "Father won't agree to allow me to fight. I want to be there, helping the men." Granny was really only her sister Fiona's grandmother, but she and Ailis had always been treated as her own.

"In times of danger, ye must trust yer instincts," Granny replied, her eyes steady.

Granny's words echoed in Moira's mind as she gazed into the crackling hearth. The matriarch's wisdom had always guided her, but now Moira felt torn between duty and desire. She yearned to stand alongside her clansmen, to prove her worth as a warrior and protector of the Highlands. But more than that, she wanted to help. Help the cause, help her people, and help all those who would come after them.

"But what if me instincts are leading me astray?" Moira asked, her voice barely above a whisper. "What if me desire to fight blinds me to the greater good of our clan?"

Granny reached out, her weathered hand gently cupping Moira's cheek. "Ye have a fire within ye, lass. 'Tis a gift, not a curse. Trust that it will guide ye true, even in the darkest of times."

Moira leaned into Granny's touch and drew strength from the love and the wisdom she found there. "I fear for our future, Granny," she confessed. "The Stewarts and the Gordons threaten everything we hold dear. How can we face such formidable foes and emerge victorious?"

Granny's eyes sparkled with a knowing light. "We have faced trials before, mo ghràdh. The McAfee clan is strong, and our spirit is unbreakable. Ye dinnae need worry about losing. We will be victorious."

Moira nodded. It seemed Granny knew the outcome of the battle that hadn't been fought yet. Moira said a quick prayer that Granny was right this time, as she'd always been in the past. "I will do whatever it takes to protect our people, Granny. Even if it means defying Father's wishes."

The matriarch smiled, a hint of mischief playing at the corners of her lips. "Sometimes, lass, the greatest acts of bravery are those that go unseen. There are many ways to fight for what ye believe in, and not all of them require a sword."

Moira's brow furrowed as she considered Granny's cryptic words. The chamber door swung open before she could press further, revealing a breathless Ailis.

"Moira, come quickly!" Ailis urged. "Fiona has discovered something that might change everything."

Moira exchanged a knowing glance with Granny before following Ailis out into the torch-lit corridor. As they hurried through the keep, the sounds of the ongoing celebration faded into the background, replaced by the pounding of Moira's heart.

They found Fiona in the armory, hunched over a weathered map spread across a wooden table. Her brow was furrowed in concentration as she traced her finger along the parchment.

Fiona looked up as Moira and Ailis entered, her eyes filled with a mixture of excitement and trepidation. "I've discovered a hidden passage." She tapped a spot on the map. "It leads from the armory, beneath the keep, and emerges in the forest beyond the walls."

Moira leaned in, studying the faded ink. "How did ye find this?" she asked, her mind racing with possibilities. She had never even heard whispers about a hidden passage in the keep.

"I was searching through our ancestors' journals," Fiona explained. "Great-great-grandfather Angus McAfee mentioned it in passing, as a last resort should the keep ever fall."

Ailis ran her fingers along the stone wall, searching for any sign of the hidden entrance. "If this passage truly exists, it could change the course of the impending battle."

Moira nodded. "We could use this passage to our advantage," she said, excitement building in her voice. "Imagine if we could sneak out a small force, undetected, and launch a surprise attack on the Stewarts and their allies from behind. It would look suspicious if one of the McClain men led the group, so we shall lead it ourselves!"

Fiona's eyes widened. "It would catch them completely off guard. They'd be fighting on two fronts, with no idea how many of us there truly are."

Ailis chewed her lip thoughtfully. "But Father would never agree to such a risky plan. He's adamant about keeping us safe within the walls of the keep."

Moira's gaze hardened with determination. "Then we don't tell him. We gather a trusted group of warriors, slip out under cover of darkness, and take matters into our own hands." She was certainly not above acting in secret to help her people.

Fiona sighed dramatically. "I must stay. I have to protect the bairn I carry." She looked at Ailis.

Ailis shook her head. "I'm one of only two healers. I must stay as well unless we want any man who is wounded to be at greater risk of death." While Moira and Fiona had a very basic understanding of how to heal, Ailis had studied under her mother's mother, and she was quite skilled in the ways of treating wounds and sicknesses.

The sisters exchanged glances, the gravity of their decision written on each of their faces. Fiona's eyes reflected a mixture of concern and resolve, while Ailis' jaw tightened with determination. Moira knew that this plan would test not only their loyalty to their father but also their bond as sisters.

"We cannae do this alone," Ailis said, her voice barely above a whisper. "We'll need help from those we trust most."

Moira nodded, her mind already sifting through potential allies. "Angus MacNab would follow us to the gates of hell if we asked. And Tavish, the stable boy—he's quick and clever, and knows these lands like the back of his hand."

Fiona's brow furrowed. "What about Alisdair McClain? Me husband's support could prove invaluable."

"He would be missed by the enemy, and they would know

something is afoot," Ailis said. "Alisdair must lead the men if we hope to win. And without Lachlan and Brodie at his side, we would be found out immediately."

Moira paced the armory, her mind whirling with the weight of their decision. She knew that defying their father's wishes could have dire consequences, not just for them, but for the entire clan. And yet, the thought of sitting idly by while their enemies marched on McAfee lands filled her with fierce determination to help.

"We cannae let this opportunity slip away," she said, turning to face her sisters. "If we succeed, we could turn the tide of this war before it even begins."

Ailis nodded slowly, her green eyes reflecting the torchlight. "Aye, but we must be cautious. One misstep, and we risk not only our own lives but the lives of those who follow us."

Fiona placed a gentle hand on Moira's shoulder. "And what of Father? If he discovers our plan, he'll be furious."

Moira met Fiona's gaze, her resolve unwavering. "Father will understand, in time. He taught us to fight for what we believe, to protect our clan at all costs. This is our chance to prove ourselves, to show that we are every bit as capable as any man." She sighed. "But as much as I ken ye want to join us, the bairn ye carry is more important. And Ailis is right about staying behind to heal any who are injured. I am the only one of the three of us who can go. And I will lead the men well."

Ailis sighed, the weight of their decision heavy on her shoulders. "Aye, but what if ye fail? What if our actions only bring more suffering to our people?"

Moira's eyes flashed with determination. "We willnae fail. We carry the strength of our ancestors in our veins, and we will not let them down." There could be no failure. The clan had always held strong, and they always would.

Fiona nodded, her blonde hair glinting in the torchlight. "Then it's settled. We will gather our allies, and Moira, ye will lead them as they slip out under cover of darkness, and strike at the heart of the enemy. I wish I could go, but ye must wield yer sword while Ailis and I stay behind." She laid a palm against her still-flat belly.

MOIRA'S SHADOW STRETCHED along the stone walls of McAfee Keep as she searched for her father, Duncan. Her steps echoed in the hallway leading to his study. She pushed the door open forcefully, finding him hunched over scattered parchments on an old oak table. She had no desire to defy her father's wishes. Instead, she would reason with him—warrior to warrior.

"Father," Moira began, her voice unwavering. "I need to be part of our defense."

Duncan looked up, his eyes reflecting the firelight. "We've already had this discussion. Ye are me daughter, not a warrior."

"Ye *taught* me to be a warrior," she retorted. "And I won't stand idly by while our kin fight for their lives." She crossed her arms over her chest, refusing to give in to him.

"Moira, it's no' yer place—"

"Is it me place to wait for death or dishonor?" she interrupted. "I've planned and prepared defenses."

He rose from his chair slowly. "And what of the danger?"

"Better than most," she said confidently. "Ye trained me to lead and protect our lands. Let me do so." It made no sense that he didn't want her to fight when he'd raised her to be a warrior, not a simpering maiden.

The laird studied Moira before sighing and nodding. "Very well but promise me you'll guard your life as fiercely as our lands."

"I swear it," she replied with determination. She wasn't certain if her father had merely acquiesced because she begged, or because he believed she could help. Either way, Moira was thrilled she would have the chance to fight in a real battle and not just compete in games.

The clan had gathered in the great hall, waiting for news. As Moira stepped onto the dais, all eyes turned to her.

"We stand upon the precipice of war," Moira declared. "I vow before ye this day—I will fight beside you."

Their fear was replaced by determination as they cheered in agreement. Moira's promise was more than words. It marked her transformation into one of their leaders, ready to defend her clan—and all the Highlands—at any cost.

◆—————❧—————◆

CHAPTER TWO

T HE CLAMOR OF battle disrupted the tranquil Highlands all
around McAfee Keep. Stinging smoke and the scent of blood
filled the air as she assessed the destruction.

The clash of steel jolted Moira from her paralysis. Her red
hair, heavy with sweat, clung to her brow amidst the chaos. Fury
brewed within her as she clenched her jaw, each scream
tightening her resolve.

"Protect them," she whispered, her words cutting through
the turmoil. This vow ignited an inner fire that mirrored the
world around her—fear and doubt ceased to exist as she
embraced her Highland warrior heritage.

She hurried downstairs from her bed chamber to check if all
the women and children were safe. When she saw the huge
crowd of people, she knew that if all hadn't made it to safety,
most had. There was no time to go to every cottage in the village
to make certain all women and children were safe.

Her hand wrapped around her sword's hilt, its familiar weight
steadying her thoughts. The love for her kin fortified her
determination, transforming it into unbreakable armor. Losing
those dear to her was a price too high, regardless of war's costs.

"Stewart will rue the day he decided to target us with his
deceit," she muttered as she set off to find the men she had
chosen to be part of her sneak attack from behind.

Each step solidified Moira's intent—to stand as her family's
shield and her clan's spear. The invading Stewarts would face in

her the relentless fury of the Highlands—undaunted, untamed, and poised to strike. Why they thought they could control the Highlands, she didn't know, but she was ready for them. Her people would remain the same and always fight against those who wanted to change them.

She thought back to the evening before, when she'd worked to solidify her plans. Moira had stood in the great hall of McAfee Keep, surrounded by her family and the three McClain brothers: Alisdair, who had married Fiona; Lachlan, who had married Ailis; and Brodie. Alisdair paced before the hearth, and his brothers leaned against the walls, expressions grim.

"Yer plan is madness, Moira!" Alisdair boomed. "Women should nae be fightin'—" He shook his head. "Ye did not ask permission before ye made your own plan."

"Me father has given his permission. Would ye have me sit as our home burns?" Moira cut in, eyes blazing. "Clyde Stewart will nae stop until all in the Highlands serve him."

"We cannae underestimate Stewart," Lachlan said. "But we must act wisely—not just with rage."

"Rage may be what saves us," Moira replied. "We've fought too hard to cower before such a man."

Brodie spoke up. "If Moira believes she can fight, then I trust in her blade." He glanced at the youngest of the three sisters. "I dinnae like the idea of her fighting any more than anyone else does, but I ken she can do it and do it well."

Alisdair's fist struck the table. "We protect our own but dinnae throw lives away on pride and folly."

"This is about survival," Moira insisted. "Our clan and family—it's who we are. If I can wield a sword to protect that, then so be it."

The room fell silent.

"Ye speak of defying norms, lass," Alisdair said softly. "But are ye prepared for danger?"

"Better to face danger with courage than to live in fear," Moira declared. "I stand not behind ye but beside ye. We will fight—for the Highlands, for McAfee, for all that we hold dear." Backing down was not an option they could take. Their way of life depended on it.

The matriarch of the clan, Fiona's grandmother, stood listening. "May the spirits of our ancestors guide yer blade," Granny murmured from the shadows.

THE AIR FELT heavy as Moira entered the ancient armory of McAfee Keep. Her fingers brushed over cold steel, selecting a familiar broadsword. It was one that had been made for her, lighter than a man's sword, making it easy for her to do damage to the enemy. As she gripped it, her father handed her a round targe shield adorned with their crest.

"Thank ye," she replied before securing the shield and donning chainmail, leather bracers, and greaves. Her father had required one of his men to make it for her when she'd proven so skillful with her sword. Her sisters didn't have the same protection she had, but they would not need it. Their skills were with long-distance weapons.

"Ye've chosen well," Granny McAfee said proudly.

Her father nodded toward the gathered clan members. "Choose yer companions."

Moira selected seasoned warriors known for their tenacity and grit. "Through the secret passage, we strike from the shadows," she commanded. "The Stewarts think they can crush us, but they don't know the strength of the McAfees. They don't know the fury they've unleashed."

The small band followed through a narrow tunnel that led them behind enemy lines.

"We'll strike from the shadows, catch them unawares. They'll never see us coming." She turned, fixing her gaze on the distant keep where Clyde Stewart no doubt watched the chaos he had wrought. The man was a coward, and she couldn't imagine he would be on the battlefield. "And when we're through, the Stewarts will learn the true meaning of Highland vengeance."

With a rallying cry, Moira led her band of warriors into the fray, their footsteps swift and silent as they skirted the edges of the battle. They moved like ghosts through the shadows, the cloak of night aiding their stealthy approach.

As they neared the rear of the Stewart forces, Moira signaled for her fighters to spread out, each taking position to maximize the element of surprise. She crouched behind a gnarled oak, her breath slow and steady as she waited for the perfect moment to strike.

It came with a sudden shift in the wind, the smoke from the fires briefly obscuring the Stewarts' line of sight. Moira let out a fierce battle cry, leaping from her hiding place with her sword drawn. Her warriors followed suit, descending upon the unsuspecting Stewarts like a Highland tempest.

The clash of blades sang through the night as Moira moved within the chaos, her sword a blur of deadly precision. Each strike fueled her resolve, each fallen foe a testament to the unyielding spirit of the McAfees.

Around her, her warriors fought with equal ferocity, their faces etched with grim determination. The Stewarts and their allies, caught off guard by the sudden onslaught, struggled to mount a coherent defense.

Moira pressed forward, scanning the fray for any sign of Clyde Stewart. She knew that to truly break the Stewarts' resolve, she would need to strike at their leader. A flicker of movement caught her eye, and she turned to see a figure apart from the battle, sword in hand. He stood well behind his men.

Moira shook her head. The man needed a better vantage point than the Sinclair Keep, but he was unwilling to put himself in danger. He was a coward who pretended to be a great leader, worthy of ruling all the Highlands.

She moved toward Clyde Stewart until he stood before her,

his dark eyes glinting with malice. Moira's grip tightened on her sword as she faced the devilish man, who had brought such destruction upon her clan.

"Moira McAfee," Clyde spat. "I should have known you'd be leading this pathetic attempt at resistance." Clyde had once considered her a pawn in his game to subdue the Highlands, but he'd learned she was more than that. Much more.

Moira's lips curled into a snarl. "You underestimate the strength of the McAfees, Stewart. It will be your downfall."

Clyde snickered, a harsh, grating sound that echoed across the battlefield. "Your clan is finished, McAfee. The Highlands will be mine, and there's nothing ye can do to stop me."

With a roar of fury, Moira lunged forward, her sword clashing against Clyde's in a shower of sparks. The force of the impact reverberated through her arm, but she held firm, her gaze locked with Clyde's.

Around them, the battle raged on, the cries of the wounded and dying mingling with the clang of steel. But for Moira, the world had narrowed to this moment, this confrontation with the man who threatened everything she held dear.

They traded blows, their swords a whirlwind of deadly intent. Clyde was a formidable opponent, his strength and skill honed by years of conquest. But Moira had the fury of the Highlands in her veins, the unyielding spirit of her clan driving every strike.

Sweat poured down her face, mingling with the grime of battle. Her muscles burned with exertion, but she pushed through the pain, her focus unwavering. She would not let Clyde's blade slip past her defenses. She would not fail her clan, not now, not ever.

With a final, desperate surge of strength, Moira aimed a devastating blow at Clyde's sword arm. Her blade found its mark, slicing through leather and flesh alike. Clyde let out a howl of pain, his sword clattering to the ground as he clutched at his wounded limb.

Moira pressed her advantage, the point of her sword coming

to rest against Clyde's throat. "Yield," she growled, her chest heaving with exertion. "Yield, and I may yet spare your miserable life." He didnae deserve to live, but she wouldnae be the one to kill him. That would be left to the men in charge.

Clyde glared up at her, his eyes burning with hatred. For a long moment, he seemed poised on the brink of defiance, his jaw clenched in a silent snarl. But as Moira's blade pressed more firmly against his skin, drawing a thin line of crimson, Clyde's resolve crumbled. "I yield," he spat. "I yield, damn you."

Moira held her position a moment longer, her eyes boring into Clyde's, ensuring his submission was genuine. Satisfied, she withdrew her sword, though she kept it at the ready. "Call off your men," she commanded. "The battle is over."

Clyde's face twisted with barely contained rage, but he complied, bellowing the order to his troops. Slowly, the sounds of combat began to fade, replaced by an eerie, expectant silence.

Moira turned to survey the battlefield, her heart heavy as she took in the toll of the conflict. McAfee and Stewart alike lay unmoving on the blood-soaked ground, their lives cut short by the folly of men's ambition. But as her gaze swept over her warriors, battered but unbroken, a fierce pride swelled within her chest. They had stood against the tide of Stewart aggression and emerged victorious, their Highland spirit undiminished.

Moira's attention snapped back to Clyde as he struggled to his feet, his wounded arm clutched tightly against his chest. "This isn't over, McAfee," he snarled, his voice thick with pain and fury. "You may have won this battle, but the war for the Highlands has only just begun."

Moira met his gaze unflinchingly, her sword still poised to strike. "We'll be ready, Stewart. The McAfees will never bow to your tyranny, no matter the cost."

With a final, venomous glare, Clyde turned and limped away, his retreating form swallowed by the smoke and shadows. Moira watched him go, her heart still pounding with the thrill of battle, the weight of victory tempered by the losses they had suffered.

"Moira!" someone called in a familiar voice. She turned to see her sister Fiona rushing toward her. "Moira, are ye all right?"

Moira embraced her sister fiercely, the relief at seeing her alive and whole overwhelming all other concerns. "I'm fine," she assured Fiona, pulling back to look her over for injuries. "And you? How do ye fare?"

Fiona managed a weary smile. "I think it was harder for me to watch the battle from above than it would have been to take part in it. Ailis is safe as well, helping tend to the wounded."

Moira nodded, a weight lifting from her shoulders at the news. But even as relief washed over her, she knew their trials were far from over. The Stewarts' defeat was a significant victory, but it was only the beginning of what promised to be a long and arduous struggle. She would never understand men's need to rule over others.

"We must fortify the keep," Moira said, her mind already racing with the tasks ahead. "Shore up our defenses, gather supplies, tend to the wounded. The Stewarts will return, and we must be ready."

Fiona's expression grew somber, the gravity of their situation settling upon her. "Aye, sister. We'll stand strong, as we always have. The McAfees will endure."

Together, the sisters made their way back to the keep, their steps heavy with the weight of responsibility. Around them, the warriors of the McAfee clan began the grim work of gathering the wounded and dead so they could be either treated or given a warrior's burial.

Moira scoured the men on the ground, trying to find one man in particular—Brodie McClain. He had personally worked with her on her sword fighting, and she thought a great deal of him.

She didn't see him there, and she breathed a sigh of relief. Her family was safe and so was Brodie. She hated that they'd lost men, but the people who were most important to her were safe.

CHAPTER THREE

LEAVES CRUNCHED UNDERFOOT as Moira led Brodie away from the keep, her red hair escaping her braid as if it had a mind of its own. They walked through the field where the battle had taken place, arriving at a clearing, surrounded by ancient pines.

"Here," Moira whispered, stepping into the open space. She looked around for the enemy and realized Brodie was doing the same.

Finally, Brodie nodded. "Aye, perfect for quiet."

"Quiet isn't what I need!" Moira exclaimed, pacing with pent-up frustration. "I should be training alongside our clans!" How could he not understand her need to be part of the defense?

She clenched her fists, tensing up with duty instilled by her family and McAfee lineage.

Brodie stepped closer, offering silent support. "Ye are a warrior, Moira. Yer family knows this—'tis the enemy who should fear being unaware. Ye've trained for years to become as strong a swordswoman as ye are. No one thinks ye are less than what ye are."

His words sought to ease her worries without dismissing them, grounding her in the face of uncertainty.

"What use is a warrior who can't wield her sword when it matters most?" Moira asked, seeking solace in his gaze. Surely, he would understand that as a warrior himself.

"When the time is right, yer little band of warriors will attack again. Strength lies in knowing when to draw your blade and when to wait. Ye did good at the last battle by taking the Stewart's army unawares." Brodie replied, closing the gap between them. "If ye try the same thing again, it will be expected. Yer time will come. And when it does, nothing will be able to stand against ye."

"I've not always been certain of me place in this world," he admitted quietly, the words weaving a new layer into their bond. "I'm the son of a laird, but I'm the third son, and only the seventh son will inherit. I need to make me own way."

Moira watched him and saw something raw and unguarded in his eyes, a side of Brodie few had seen.

"Growing up among brothers who wielded claymores effortlessly, I fought with them, but I always felt that I wasn't strong enough," he said, bending a fallen twig. "It took years to discover different kinds of strength."

Moira had a hard time believing anyone could beat this man. He was like a rock, carved from a Highland mountain. "Is that why ye lurk in shadows, McClain?" Moira teased, but her heart filled with respect for him.

"Perhaps I know when to bide me time," Brodie replied with a half-smile before stepping closer. "And you? Are ye an eagle, ready to swoop down on your prey?"

"A wolf," she said boldly. "Loyal to her pack and ready to defend it." As she grinned at Brodie, she was struck by his handsomeness. Perhaps that was why she was drawn to him so completely.

"A fine match we make—a serpent and a wolf," Brodie chuckled.

"But the serpent must be swift to keep pace," Moira challenged.

"You underestimate the cunning of the serpent," he retorted playfully. "He may surprise ye with his speed." His arm moved quickly, pulling her to him and looking down at her.

All at once there was nothing in Moira's world but Brodie.

His eyes, dark and intense, held her gaze captive. In that

moment, the world fell away, and all that existed was the space between them, charged with an electric current that set Moira's heart racing.

Brodie's hand, calloused from years of wielding a sword, gently cupped her cheek, his thumb tracing the delicate line of her jaw. Moira's breath caught in her throat as he leaned in closer, his forehead resting against hers.

"Moira," he whispered, his voice rough with emotion. "I've fought it for so long, but I can no longer deny what me heart desires."

She trembled in his embrace, her own feelings threatening to overwhelm her. "Brodie, I..."

He laid a gentle finger across her lips, silencing her for just a moment. Then he lowered his head and brushed his lips lightly across hers before finally just leaning in and capturing her mouth with his.

Moira melted into Brodie's kiss, her lips parting beneath his as a soft moan escaped her throat. His strong arms encircled her, pulling her flush against his hard body as the kiss deepened, becoming more urgent, more demanding.

Moira threaded her fingers through Brodie's thick, dark hair, holding him to her as if she feared he might disappear like a figment of her imagination.

When they finally broke apart, both breathing heavily, Brodie rested his forehead against hers once more, his eyes closed as he savored the feel of her in his arms at last. "I have wanted to do that for so long," he murmured roughly. "But I never dared hope..."

"I never dared hope either," Moira whispered, her voice trembling with the depth of her feelings. "I thought me duty to the clan would always keep us apart."

Brodie's hand slid down to the small of her back, holding her close as if he couldn't bear even an inch of space between them. "I would have waited forever for you, Moira."

Moira's heart soared at his words, a joyful laugh bubbling up from her throat. "And I'd have waited for you. We've wasted too much time denying ourselves."

She leaned up and captured his lips once more, the kiss filled with promise and a newfound sense of freedom.

The troubles of the clans, the machinations of their enemies, all faded away. In this moment, nothing existed beyond the circle of their embrace, the mingling of their breaths, the racing of their hearts.

When they parted once more, Moira gazed up at Brodie, her eyes shining. This day hadn't turned out as expected, but she was thrilled.

He took her hand in his, raising it to his lips to press a fervent kiss against her knuckles. In that fleeting moment, the weight of impending battle lifted as they found solace in shared laughter in the middle of the Highlands' wilderness.

The wind carried the scent of pine and earth as Moira led Brodie deeper into the forest. Their footsteps softened by the moss-covered ground.

"I was raised among warriors," Moira began, her voice steady. "My da' never treated me any differently than the other warriors. It's only been since we've been full-grown that he's worried about our safety.

"Granny was just as fierce," she continued, touching the rough bark of a tree. "She taught me to be strong, like the oak."

"You carry their strength within you," Brodie replied, admiration in his tone.

"Sometimes, I wonder if it's enough." Her gaze met his, searching. "The world outside doesn't always value what we McAfees hold dear."

"Then let them be blind," Brodie said firmly. "You've no need to prove yourself to those who cannot see."

Moira unsheathed her sword—a sleek blade that gleamed silver against the green backdrop. "Come now, let's see how well ye handle that sword, McClain," she challenged, her tone shifting to playful competitiveness. He had helped her to hone her skills, and she had beaten him at sword fighting at the last Highland Games. Of course, she'd beaten *everyone* at the last Highland Games, thanks to his help.

"Are ye asking for a dance or a duel?" Brodie asked, drawing his own weapon with fluid grace.

"Perhaps a bit of both," she teased, assuming a fighting stance that was elegant and formidable.

They circled each other before striking. Their swords sang as they collided, echoing through the trees. They moved together, building trust and understanding between them.

"Ye're holding back," Moira accused lightly.

"Wouldn't dream of it," Brodie countered with a grin. "Just enjoying the view."

They broke apart, panting and laughing. There was shared exhilaration in their eyes and recognition of each other's skill and camaraderie forming with each clash of steel.

"Ye fight with the heart of a lioness," Brodie admitted, lowering his sword.

"And ye, Brodie McClain, have the stealth of the serpent ye claim to be," Moira responded, her smile softening.

Moira paused on a moss-covered stone, catching her breath. The crisp Highland air stung her lungs, but it felt refreshing.

"Tell me, Brodie," she asked, "what dreams do ye have for the future?"

Brodie leaned his sword against a tree and joined her. "I dream of peace," he said sincerely. "And ye, Moira?"

"I wish to be judged only by me courage and skill as a warrior," Moira replied.

Their conversation flowed naturally, discussing childhood escapades and hopes for clan unity. Each word strengthened their bond—a future where McAfee and McClain stood united as kin.

"Yet," Moira confided, "I fear I'll never be seen as more than a girl playing at war."

Brodie turned to her. "Moira, yer mettle outshines many who call themselves warriors. Don't let others' views blind ye to the respect ye've earned."

"Thank ye, Brodie," she said with a warm smile. "For seeing the warrior in me when others may not."

"Always. Now, shall we?" He gestured to their swords.

Together, they returned to training, now infused with a deeper understanding—an unbreakable bond forged in steel and solidarity.

After their training session, Moira sat on a rock and felt the sun bearing down on her. It was almost winter, but the sun still warmed her. She leaned back, fiery hair cascading over rough bark.

"Peaceful," Brodie whispered.

"A rare thing." Moira sighed, eyes lingering on the glistening water. "Especially with another battle looming."

"Perhaps moments like this remind us what we're fighting for," he said, dappled sunlight playing in his gaze.

"It's possible," she replied, her eyes connecting with his.

Brodie produced a handmade necklace from his pouch—a braided leather cord supporting a wooden pendant carved with interlaced swords and a shield symbolizing unity and protection.

"Ye made this?" Moira asked, voice filled with admiration.

"With me own hands," he confirmed proudly. "I hope it brings ye protection."

She draped the necklace around her neck, sensing its significance. Expressing gratitude, she met his tender stare, feeling an unspoken connection deepen between them.

Moira fastened the necklace, the wind carrying distant sounds to their Highland sanctuary. In silence, their bond deepened amidst nature's serenity.

As the pendant's warmth mixed with the Highland breeze, Moira turned toward Brodie. Their gazes locked, and time seemed to pause.

"Moira," he whispered. He reached out, tucking a curl behind her ear, his touch sparking a flame within her.

Leaning into his caress, she felt his hand trace her jaw before resting at her neck. The air between them crackled, charged with pent-up passion.

"Our siblings have married one another. I would like to court ye. Not because they've married but because I feel that we are meant to be," he murmured, truth reflected in his deep brown eyes.

Driven by fierce determination, Moira closed the gap between them. Their lips met in an intense kiss that swept them up like a crashing wave. She tasted highland mist and sun warmth on his skin as their bodies melded together.

When they finally parted and reality returned, they faced their situation—two warriors from different clans bound by duty yet connected by powerful love.

"Moira," Brodie said firmly, "whatever may come, I pledge myself to ye."

Pride and resolve filled her chest. "And I vow to ye, Brodie, that naught will tear me from yer side. In battle or in peace, we are one."

"Side by side," she echoed.

"Until the end," he affirmed.

As dusk set in, Moira and Brodie found comfort in the wilderness surrounding them. "Standing on the precipice of another fierce battle, yet all I can see is ye," Moira whispered.

Brodie's thumb traced circles on her hand. "And I can't imagine standing here without ye, Moira. Ye've given me hope where there was only strategy and survival."

Their eyes locked, and for an instant, the world around them stilled.

"Ye know we must return soon," Brodie said softly.

"Aye," she replied with a nod. "But for now, let us just be Moira and Brodie—just two souls intertwined by fate."

He pulled her close, wrapping his arms around her in a tender embrace. She rested her head against his chest, listening to the steady rhythm of his heart.

"Whatever tomorrow brings," Moira murmured against his

tunic, "I will carry this moment with me."

"And I will carry it as a guiding light," Brodie replied, his breath warm against her ear.

They stood together in silence, sharing resolve and mutual understanding. As nightfall enveloped the land, they reluctantly loosened their embrace. Their hands lingered upon each other before exchanging a look that conveyed unity.

"Come," Brodie said, offering a small confident smile. "Let us return to face what may come, knowing that together, we are unstoppable."

Moira nodded. She didn't want to return and give up her private time with him, but she knew he was right. Hand in hand, they walked back toward their clans and toward a future of both peril and promise.

CHAPTER FOUR

As DAWN LIT up the Scottish Highlands, Moira McAfee strode across the dewy heather, mist clinging to her cloak. Beside her, Brodie McClain surveyed the land with practiced focus.

"Are ye ready for what lies ahead?" Moira asked, eyes fixed on the distant mountains.

"Always," Brodie answered, calm in the face of potential dangers.

Entering the shadowy forest, their path snaked through the underbrush. Moira led confidently, her red hair ablaze against the green. They journeyed until the sound of rushing water grew louder.

A narrow bridge formed from fallen tree trunks spanned a churning river below. "Carefully now," Moira warned, studying its unstable structure.

The bridge creaked and swayed but they advanced together— a shared goal binding them as they navigated this wild terrain.

The heavens unleashed a torrent, turning the path beneath Moira and Brodie into a treacherous mire. The storm's raindrops pelted them with relentless force.

"Och, what a lovely morning," Moira remarked, her voice barely audible over the wind tearing through the trees.

"We should find cover," Brodie replied, concern lacing his amusement.

As they darted toward a large tree, its thick branches promised refuge from the onslaught. Pressing their backs against its trunk, they huddled against the elements. Moira felt the rough bark biting into her skin.

Brodie leaned in close without encroaching upon Moira's independence. She was strong within life's storms—both literal and metaphorical—in the Highlands.

Peering through the veil of rain, Moira spotted ancient stones on a nearby hillock. "Look there, Brodie."

He discerned the shapes amidst the grey curtain. "Aye, the old stone circles hold whispers of our ancestors."

"Let us listen," Moira urged, her adventurous spirit reignited.

They ventured forth despite the ground resisting underfoot. As they drew closer to the circle untouched by chaos, each monolith stood as a testament to the Highland way—stoic and enduring.

"Imagine the tales they could tell," Moira murmured, reaching out to touch history itself.

"Aye," Brodie agreed, his voice filled with reverence. "May they speak of peace."

Within the stone circle, the storm outside vanished as time seemed to pause and echoes of the past called.

Moira traced the intricate carvings, her eyes narrowing, trying to decipher the ancient symbols. A shiver ran down her spine unrelated to the dampness on her skin. The etchings told a story—one lost to time and memory—but their meaning was elusive.

"Look at this, Brodie," she exclaimed. "These must be me ancestors' tales… battles fought, alliances forged. Sometimes it is hard to believe that our land wasn't always Christian."

Brodie stepped closer, examining the grooves in the rock as he tried to unlock the stone-held narrative. He glanced around cautiously before replying, "Aye, they may well be. But old tales can be perilous as well as enlightening."

Before Moira could respond, a low growl echoed through the trees. She turned sharply toward it, reaching for her sword hilt. Shadows at the forest's edge morphed into wolves with tense bodies ready to pounce.

"Back to back!" Brodie commanded, unsheathing his blade.

Though Moira's heartbeat quickened, her grip on her weapon was steady. They positioned themselves back-to-back within the stone circle.

The wolves advanced with hungry yellow eyes.

"Remember what we've been taught," she said firmly. "Strike true and stand firm."

"Always," Brodie replied, his calm presence balancing her fiery energy.

They moved in sync—two clans united in survival. As the wolves lunged, battle erupted amidst history's whispers. The stones stood silent witness to an eternal struggle between man and nature.

Swords clashed, their metallic ring echoing through the Highland air. Brodie's blade parried a wolf's lunge, while Moira's swift strike sent another assailant retreating.

"Watch your left!" Moira cried out. The two fought in sync, instincts honed from years of training. As they battled, the wolves' numbers dwindled until the few remaining fled into the forest, leaving behind only heavy panting and two warriors standing back-to-back.

Moira and Brodie locked eyes briefly before sheathing their weapons. "Let's keep to the open paths," Brodie suggested. "The wolves are cunning, but we'll see them coming in the clear."

"Agreed." Moira nodded, still exhilarated from battle. As they continued through the forest, they shared tales of their ancestors—stories of valor that shaped their people's hardened souls.

"My father spoke often of a battle that took place near Dun Troddan," said Brodie with reverence.

"And Father would recount a battle that took place near Inverlochy," Moira added.

"Before me father became laird, the lairds had fought no battles in several generations. Father decided it would be best for the laird to train and fight with his men, and I know Boyd plans to do the same as Father."

Their footsteps fell into a steady rhythm as each story forged a connection transcending clan boundaries. "Perhaps it is time for new tales to be told," Moira mused. "Ones that speak of unity rather than discord."

Brodie met her gaze, the weight of her words settling between them. "Aye, Moira. Perhaps it is."

The Highlands' craggy cliffs and heather-strewn hillsides converged around them as they ventured further into the wilderness. Moira's boots found purchase on the uneven terrain, attuned to subtle shifts within nature.

"Over there," Brodie pointed toward an inconspicuous opening in the cliffside, half-concealed by ivy and stone.

Moira's pulse quickened as she approached the hidden aperture. With a nod to Brodie, they lit torches and cautiously entered the cavern, its air filled with the smell of damp earth. Moira led the way, her torch revealing undulating contours.

"Look at this," Brodie murmured, gesturing to a collection of artifacts nestled in a natural alcove.

Crouching beside the relics, Moira examined fragments of pottery etched with intricate patterns; a rusted dirk telling tales of battles fought; and smooth stones adorned with symbols teasing recognition.

"Imagine what Granny would say if she saw these," Moira said, thinking of Fiona's granny and her troves of lore.

"Aye," Brodie agreed, studying an ornate brooch. "The history of yer clan might be locked within."

Together, they examined each artifact in hushed tones, conjuring images of ancestors who might have sought sanctuary or strategized within the very same cave.

The torchlight flickered, casting a stuttering glow on the jagged walls of the hidden passage. Moira peered into the darkness ahead, breath misting in the cold air.

"Are ye certain we should press on?" Brodie's voice was steady, though concern tightened around his eyes. His hand rested lightly on his sword.

"Think of what may lie in the heart of this mountain," Moira replied, her green eyes reflecting both fear and determination.

Taking a deep breath, they ventured further. The passageway twisted and narrowed until cool dampness pressed against their outstretched hands. Finally, it opened into an underground chamber. Faint light filtered from above, casting a glow over faded frescoes and a sprawling mural depicting a ferocious battle.

Brodie traced the outline of a fallen warrior etched into the stone. Beside him, Moira hesitated to touch the depiction of chaos and valor. It wasn't the clashing swords or cries of fallen warriors that captured her attention but the familiar faces staring back at them across centuries.

"This fascinates me." Moira pointed at two figures in the mural's center, locked in combat yet bound by kinship. "All the clans of the Highlands united against a common enemy. That's what we need to make happen now. I wish I knew how to get all the leaders to see what Clyde is trying to do."

Brodie studied the scene. "Aye, together against a common enemy. Perhaps we should send missives to the lairds of the clans we are not seeing in battle. They may be willing to help us turn the tide."

"I wish we could show this to the leaders of the clans aiding us. There is still a great deal more arguing than allied clans should have." Moira's thoughts tangled with the revelation, her loyalty to her clan now bound with a need to uncover the deception.

"If only I could paint…" Brodie said, grinning at her.

"Don't look at me," Moira replied. "I never learned to make pretty art. But I can swing a sword with the best of men."

He laughed softly. "You certainly can."

The ground trembled beneath Moira's feet, a low growl echoing through the cavern. Dust danced in the torchlight as Brodie gripped her arm firmly.

"Moira, we must leave, now!" His words cut through the panic with another rumble vibrating through the chamber.

She nodded, scanning for an escape. "This way," she called, indicating a narrow crevice hidden by a fallen boulder.

Their breaths came in harsh gasps as they clambered over rocks and debris, the passageway constricting around them with every urgent step. The roar of collapsing stone spurred them on with desperate haste.

"Keep moving!" Moira shouted over the noise, barely audible. She felt Brodie close behind her, his presence grounding her.

Ahead was a tight squeeze leading upward to daylight. "It's our only chance," she muttered and hoisted herself up with practiced agility. Brodie followed quickly despite the danger.

As Moira breached the surface, the sounds of the cave's demise peaked. They emerged onto the grassy land just before the earth groaned one last time.

They lay there briefly, covered in dust, silence enveloping them except for their labored breathing.

Moira looked at Brodie, her eyes meeting his steady gaze. Bound together by shared history rather than clan or feud, she asked with raw concern, "Are ye hurt?"

Brodie shook his head and sat beside her. "Nay, thanks to you."

Dust clung to Moira's red curls as they strode down the path through the Highlands, a reminder of the cave's near collapse. Each step brought them closer to navigating the world with their newfound burden. The air was brisk, scented with pine, while verdant flora swayed gently in the breeze. The beauty of their surroundings contrasted with the tumultuous history they had unveiled—a history that bound all the clans together unexpectedly. If only they were still united as they had been in the mural.

Moira's determination grew at every thought about their discovery. She glanced at Brodie, whose contemplative silence weighed heavily. He scanned the horizon like one searching for guidance. "We must encourage all our allies to join together with all of their allies against the Stewarts and theirs. I believe our army could be much stronger if we would send emissaries to the clans who are not yet part of the war."

Their journey back consisted of shared glances and nods—affirmations of their bond and purpose. As they neared Moira's ancestral home, she resolved it would become a bastion of change.

"Only the beginning," she repeated softly. They exchanged a nod and walked to the keep together. She was not looking forward to him returning to McClain land.

CHAPTER FIVE

Moira followed Brodie through the dense trees, the wind weaving a chorus above them. She brushed back her red hair, eyes taking in the endless Highlands. She couldn't imagine a more beautiful place to live.

Brodie led them to a secluded glen, sunlight dappling the ground and patterns dancing in the breeze. Moira breathed in deeply, happy to be outdoors where she belonged. Other women may be happy hiding in the keep, but she was not. This was truly where she belonged.

"Have ye ever seen such splendor?" Brodie whispered, gesturing toward the landscape, wilderness reflecting in his brown eyes.

"Every day when I wake up, I see the beauty of the land we love," Moira replied.

They reached a hill overlooking the McAfee castle grounds. The imposing structure stood watching over them. Brodie stopped, all around him at the land.

"My father is the seventh son of a seventh son," he said. "Our lineage stretches back to Norman lands and a distant ancestor came to England with William the Conqueror." The magic of his bloodline lingered unspoken. He wanted to tell her more, but he wasn't sure how she would react. It had been a closely guarded secret for a long time, and the idea of sharing it, even with Moira, was frightening. There were rumblings of the persecution of witches, and though he and his family knew they were not witches, he truly wasn't certain how others would react.

Moira smiled. "Ailis is certain she saw Boyd disappear. That must be from the magic running through his veins," she said with a laugh.

He just grinned, unwilling to confirm or deny what had happened with their siblings a couple of months before.

A breeze stirred Moira's hair as she met Brodie's gaze. Their conversation was lost to the wind, leaving behind only their shared glance.

"When I was young, I felt the weight of expectation," Moira whispered, stepping closer. "Being the youngest, there was much to prove." She confessed her doubts about living up to her family's legacy or carving her own path. "I always felt like less than me sisters because me mother was Father's third wife and not his first. He never treated me differently, but it was always right there in the back of me mind."

In the Highland stillness, Moira wasn't afraid to reveal her insecurities.

Brodie reached out and touched her arm, his eyes shimmering with empathy. "Ye are not alone in your fears," Brodie said. "It is not the absence of fear that defines us, but how we face it."

Moira's breath faltered as Brodie stepped forward, the warmth between them palpable. His quiet strength separated him from his kin, a gravity that connected their spirits.

Their eyes held fast, two souls conversing without words, each glance an unspoken promise. The wind carried ancient songs of the Highlands, whispering of entwined destinies.

Compelled by something beyond his ken, Brodie leaned in and their lips met in a passionate collision, forged by the wild landscape. Untold stories and uncharted futures were hinted at by this joining of courage and hope.

The world narrowed to the point of connection, urgency leaving no room for doubt. Moira's hands felt the steady drum of Brodie's heart against her palms, syncing with hers in an eternal dance.

It was not a gentle joining but one of fierce belonging—they were both too fierce about everything in life for it to be any different. The kiss sealed truths under the watchful eyes of towering peaks and sheltering sky.

As they parted, breaths mingling in the cool highland air, the profound reality of their bond settled into their hearts like the vast glens before them.

Time seemed to pause, granting them an eternity in a heartbeat. Moira's senses were heightened, acutely aware of Brodie's body against hers. Their heartbeats joined in a powerful symphony resonating deep within her bones.

Inhaling his scent of pine and earth, she wove her fingers into his hair, pulling him nearer. They moved as one, two spirits dancing to ancient Highland rhythms. Surroundings faded away, leaving only the press of Brodie's lips.

His hands traced her arms all the way to her shoulders, and then her neck. He was always surprised by how soft this woman's skin was when she was so fierce in every other way.

Their lips parted, warmth lingering between them. Foreheads pressed together, the world's sounds seeped back in—the rustle of leaves and whispering wind. Moira's heart raced, her eyes locked with Brodie's brown pools holding unspoken secrets.

Her cheeks flushed, and newfound vulnerability washed over her. "Brodie," she began softly before faltering, hesitating to expose her inner turmoil.

Surrounded by Highland majesty, Moira stood at a crossroads. Her heartbeats shook the walls she'd built around herself, crumbling them to dust.

"Ye ken what I feel for ye," she whispered, fiery hair catching the light like courage, "is something fierce and wild." Her fingers traced Brodie's jaw—the touch spoke of trust forged through battle. "It scares me more than any blade or arrow ever could."

Her admission filled the air as they stood among the windswept hills. Moira waited, not as a sister or warrior, but as a woman venturing into her own heart's unknown territory.

Brodie's eyes ignited with joy, reflecting the fiery hue of

Moira's hair in twilight. He reached for her hands, his voice resonant. "Moira, ye've given me a gift greater than any Highland treasure."

The words wrapped around her like a comforting embrace. She felt the thrum of life where their fingers intertwined.

In that confession lay the end of uncertainty. They stepped into each other's arms, hearts pulsing to an ancient melody woven into the land itself.

As Brodie held her securely, Moira nestled into his shoulder, closing her eyes to savor their embrace. The wind whispered through the heather and pine as if in reverence to their bond.

"Whatever may come," he murmured against her hair, "we'll get through it together."

His words wrapped her in certainty. Here, in Brodie's arms, she found sanctuary.

Moira's fingers slipped from Brodie's grasp, lingering briefly on his calloused hands. "Time will not wait for us," she whispered, her voice strong yet vulnerable.

Brodie nodded, his eyes focused on her face. "Aye, Moira, we ken what must be done."

They stood side by side, gazing toward the horizon where her home lay hidden among the peaks and valleys. Thoughts of secret meetings, whispers of rebellion, and delicate alliances filled their minds.

"I want ye to be careful in battle," he said. "Stay in the keep if at all possible."

She sighed. "Ye and everyone else think I need to be cosseted, but I dinnae. I am strong."

As they walked back to the keep, she felt a sense of tranquility wash over her. She was happy to have this man at her side.

The warmth of Brodie's touch lingered on her skin, counteracting the night's creeping chill. A shiver tingled down her spine—not from cold but from uncertainty and the allure of the battles to come.

Torchlight flickered in the distance, guiding her toward home while reminding her of their divided worlds. With each step, she pondered Brodie—his calm brown eyes, his expressive voice, and the way he regarded her with complete sincerity.

Her heart surged as she clutched the intricate tartan fabric over her chest. Resolution filled her stride, showcasing her unyielding courage and determination to fight for what mattered most.

Pausing at the crest of a hill overlooking Clan McAfee grounds, Moira allowed herself one fleeting moment to dream—a future where Brodie stood patiently beside her, combining his keen mind with her fiery passion to face Highland intrigues together.

CHAPTER SIX

THE WIND RUSTLED through the thicket behind McAfee Keep as Moira patrolled, her red curls dancing in the brisk air. Her gaze swept over the familiar rugged landscape when a shadow emerged from a cluster of trees. Hand on her dirk, she narrowed her eyes.

"Lucas Gordon," Moira said icily. "What brings ye here?" Lucas had caused Moira and Ailis a great deal of misery while they'd been at his father's keep for the Highland Games.

Lucas raised his hands. "Moira, I come in peace. Clyde Stewart has gone mad and is pushing us toward a disastrous battle. I seek amnesty and a place among yer ranks."

Doubt flickered across Moira's face but she nodded, leading Lucas to the great hall where Alisdair McClain awaited. Lucas recounted the discord within the Stewart Clan and revealed an attack planned two days away.

Lachlan McClain scowled. "I dinnae trust him."

Brodie weighed in, "Serpents can provide valuable information. We might use what he knows to our advantage."

Alisdair considered this. "Speak, Lucas Gordon, and know that deceit will cost dearly."

Tense silence filled the room as Lucas divulged the names of allied clans. The complex web of Highland alliances shifted constantly; one thing remained constant: determination to protect clan and kin at all costs.

After Lucas had finished speaking, Alisdair said, "Please wait outside this room while me brothers and I discuss whether ye can be trusted."

Lachlan shook his head as soon as Lucas was out of earshot and the door was closed between them. "I dinnae trust the man. He needs to go back to where he came from."

Alisdair frowned. "I think yer missing the greater picture in your distrust. It would be one more man fighting for us, and we may be able to get more information from him. Things he dinnae think to tell us."

Brodie nodded, his expression thoughtful. "Aye, Alisdair has a point. If Lucas is telling the truth, we cannae afford to ignore the information he brings. The Stewarts' plans could end us all."

Lachlan's scowl deepened. "And if he's lying? Leading us into a trap? We'd be fools to trust him so easily."

Brodie was the one who answered. "We dinnae have to trust him completely, but we can use what he knows. Keep him close, watch him carefully. If he proves false, we'll deal with him then."

Alisdair frowned, weighing their options. "Brodie is right. We'll grant Lucas amnesty for now, but he'll be under constant watch. We cannae risk the safety of our clans."

He turned to Lachlan whose jaw was clenched, his eyes flashing with reluctance. "Aye, brother. We'll do as ye say. But mark me words, I'll be watching him like a hawk. One false move, and he'll feel the bite of me blade."

Alisdair nodded solemnly. "Understood, Lachlan. We must be vigilant." He frowned. "I will have Moira watch our new guest. Her instincts are sharp, and she knows him better than most."

Moira's lips pressed into a thin line, but she inclined her head. "As ye wish, Alisdair. I'll make sure he doesnae step out of line."

With the decision made, Alisdair called for Lucas to be brought back in. The young man entered, his eyes darting between the brothers and Moira, trying to gauge their expressions. Alisdair stepped forward, his posture straight and imposing.

"Lucas Gordon, we have decided to grant ye amnesty…for

now. But know this," Alisdair's voice grew stern, "ye will be under constant watch. Any hint of betrayal, and ye will face the consequences."

Lucas bowed his head, relief and gratitude etched on his face. "Thank ye. I swear on me life, I will not betray yer trust."

Lachlan scoffed under his breath, his hand resting on the hilt of his sword.

"Moira will be watching ye closely, Lucas. Dinnae think for a moment that yer past actions are forgotten," Alisdair said. "I ken ye dinnae want to feel her blade."

ALISDAIR ENTERED THE private chamber, halting all conversation. Fiona, Ailis, and Duncan turned toward him, faces full of anticipation and concern.

"Lucas Gordan will join our ranks. He'll stay in a tent with the others," he announced.

Moira expressed her disapproval. "Ye trust him enough for that? How do ye ken he's not a spy for the Stewarts?"

"His knowledge has been valuable," Alisdair replied. "We must use every tool to protect our lands." He paused for a moment. "And ye, Moira, are assigned to watch him, and make sure he does nothing to undermine me authority."

Moira's eyes widened at Alisdair's words, a mix of surprise and indignation flickering across her face. "Ye want me to be his keeper? After all the grief he's caused us?"

Ailis stepped forward, her brow furrowed with concern. "Alisdair, are ye certain this is wise? Lucas has proven himself untrustworthy in the past. What if this is another one of his tricks?"

Fiona placed a gentle hand on her sister's arm. "Aye, Ailis has a point. We cannae afford to let our guard down, especially now with the Stewarts plotting against us."

Duncan, their father, stroked his graying beard thoughtfully. "Alisdair, lad, I trust yer judgment. But we must be cautious. The safety of our clan must come first."

Alisdair nodded, his expression solemn. "Aye, I understand yer concerns. But we must use every advantage we have against the Stewarts. Lucas's information could prove invaluable in the days to come."

He turned to Moira, his gaze steady. "I ken it's not an easy task, Moira. But yer the best one for the job. Yer instincts are sharp, and ye ken Lucas better than most. If anyone can keep him in line, it's ye."

Moira's jaw clenched, her eyes flashing with a mix of frustration and resignation. "Very well, Alisdair. I'll do as ye ask. But mark me words, if he steps out of line, even for a moment, I'll not hesitate to put him in his place."

Ailis sighed, her shoulders slumping as she met Moira's gaze. "Just be careful, sister. I dinnae want to see ye hurt again because of Lucas's schemes."

Moira softened, reaching out to squeeze Ailis's hand. "Dinnae fash yerself, Ailis. I'll not let him get the better of me. If he tries anything, he'll feel the sharp end of me dirk."

Fiona stepped forward, her voice calm but firm. "We must stand united in this. The Stewarts will seek to exploit any weakness or division among us. Moira, ye have our support in watching over Lucas. But remember, ye dinnae have to face this alone."

Duncan nodded, pride shining in his eyes as he looked at his daughters. "Aye, Fiona speaks true. We are stronger together, as a family and as a clan. Trust in each other, and we'll weather any storm that comes our way."

Alisdair clapped a hand on Duncan's shoulder, a small smile tugging at his lips. "Well said, Duncan. We'll face these challenges together, just as we should."

Moira took a deep breath, squaring her shoulders as she met the gazes of her family. "Aye, ye're right. I'll not let Lucas, or the

Stewarts, divide us. I'll keep a close eye on him and make sure he stays true to his word."

As they all dispersed, each to their own duties, Moira couldn't shake the unease that settled in her stomach. Watching over Lucas would be no easy task, given their tumultuous history. But she was determined to prove her worth and protect her clan, no matter the cost.

BRODIE AND LACHLAN joined the group as they went to address the clan's warriors in the courtyard.

"Me brothers," Alisdair thundered, "the Stewart forces will descend upon us in two days' time."

A collective murmur swept through the crowd.

"We will meet them with Highland strength. Our swords will sing the song of freedom!" Alisdair declared, igniting their spirits.

The warriors roared in approval, raising clenched fists.

"We fight not just for victory but for our way of life!" he continued, silencing the crowd once more.

Another wave of affirmation rose from the men. Brodie began strategizing while Lachlan stood beside his brother. United in purpose, they prepared to defend their homeland with honor and freedom intact.

As Alisdair's speech ended, he raised his arms. "Tonight, we gather in strength," he proclaimed. "Tomorrow, we feast within these walls as brothers in arms."

IN THE BUSTLING kitchens of McAfee Castle, Moira kneaded dough with intensity while Fiona moved from pot to pot, tasting and seasoning.

"Careful, Moira," Fiona chided gently. "We need that to rise."

Moira flashed a smile. "It will be the fluffiest bread they've ever tasted."

Ailis remained in the infirmary, lending her steady hands and calming voice to those who needed it most.

Granny McAfee entered the kitchen, watching her grand-daughters work with pride. "Ye both know this feast is more than food for the belly. It's nourishment for the soul, a reminder of what we're fightin' to protect."

"Thank you, Granny," Fiona replied softly. "We'll make sure this feast is one to remember."

"Let's give them a night of joy and laughter," Moira said. "For tomorrow, we may dance with fate, but tonight, we feast!"

The sisters resumed their tasks in the bustling kitchen, rich with the aroma of roasting meat and baking bread. Camaraderie and shared purpose filled the air alongside anticipation for a memorable feast amid the shadows of war.

In McAfee Keep's candlelit great hall, Moira danced with Brodie to the energetic beat of bagpipes and drums. Their lively reel was accompanied by laughing and clapping kilted figures.

"Ye've truly outdone yerself with this feast, Moira," Brodie shouted over the music, his eyes twinkling with mirth.

"'Twas a clan effort," she replied, breathless from the dance. "We all needed a night such as this."

As one song ended and another began, Lucas Gordon approached Moira with an unexpected request for a dance. She accepted, curious about his sudden change in demeanor.

During their dance, Lucas whispered an apology for his actions during the games. Moira eyed him cautiously before responding, "Apologies are easy, Lucas. It's actions that carry weight."

"Then let me coming here be the first step in proving me

sincerity," he said earnestly.

After the dance, Moira informed Brodie of Lucas's apology.

"There's a struggle within him," Brodie observed. "He's not sure he's done the right thing by joining us. He doesnae mind running from the Stewart, but he minds betraying his own father."

"Can we trust him?" Moira asked, still wary.

"Time will tell," answered Brodie. "For now, we must watch and wait."

Dancing together again, Moira found comfort in Brodie's quiet strength and considered the possibility of unity if Lucas sought genuine redemption.

As the last notes of the piper's tune faded, Brodie McClain stood in the shadows, his mind anticipating the challenges ahead. He watched Moira and Fiona clear the remnants of the feast, their laughter contrasting with his silent strategizing.

Under the cover of dawn, Brodie convened a secret meeting in the war room. The men who'd decide the clan's fate gathered around a map-laden table: stern Alisdair, sword-ready Lachlan, and conflicted Lucas Gordon.

"Lucas," Alisdair began, "name the clans that stand with yer father."

With hesitance and an inward struggle, Lucas named each supporting clan; each one sending ripples through the listeners.

Brodie listened intently and stepped forward as Lucas finished. "There are undecided clans who value honor. We must reach them before Clyde Stewart does."

Lachlan's skepticism showed. "Ye have a plan?"

"We send emissaries to the unaligned clans offering truth and kinship," Brodie answered. "I'll see to it myself."

Alisdair nodded. "Time is a luxury we dinnae possess."

With determination, Brodie mentally listed which men would serve as envoys. His plan was set; now he just needed to sway the tide in their favor.

CHAPTER SEVEN

D AWN'S FIRST LIGHT cast its golden fingers over the rugged Highlands as warhorns shattered the morning stillness. Brodie's heart thrummed, a rhythm echoed by the pounding hooves of enemy steeds. The Stewarts charged, but the McClains and McAfees, along with their allies, stood ready, anticipating a silent, deadly promise.

Brodie surveyed the prepared defenses and his brothers-in-arms. Their strategy had been crafted under cover of darkness to outmaneuver the Stewarts' expectations.

Moira held back her forces within the keep. Her absence on the battlefield would be their unexpected advantage. Brodie knew Moira's mind was strategizing, her resolve unshaken amidst adversity.

The battle roared as metal clashed against metal. Brodie moved through the fray with lethal grace, his sword an extension of his will. A Stewart soldier lunged toward him, but Brodie sidestepped and delivered a swift counterstrike that felled the man.

"Stay focused!" he shouted above the din, locking eyes with a younger clansman who seemed momentarily dazed. The youth nodded and plunged back into the melee.

As skirmishes raged around him, Brodie predicted enemy strikes before they landed. He ducked a swinging claymore and dispatched another adversary with an upward thrust.

The Stewarts kept glancing behind them, expecting to be

flanked. However, no attack came from the rear, allowing the McClain and McAfee alliance to press forward relentlessly. Without their anticipated pincer move, the Stewarts' lines crumbled under sustained onslaught.

Amidst carnage, Brodie thought of Moira. Her unpredictability granted them the upper hand. He envisioned her within the keep's walls, intellect sharp as the blade she wielded. Her fiery resolve ignited respect in Brodie that blossomed into something more potent.

The cacophony of combat was all-consuming, and Brodie fought with singular clarity. Each swing, each dodge moved them closer to victory and peace. Today, Brodie shone as bright as any warrior on the field, leading the charge that inspired courage in his comrades.

As the sun cast long shadows, Brodie's arm ached from his sword's weight, his breath labored. Spotting a standard-bearer rallying the enemy, he surged forward, cutting down anyone in his path.

Heaving the banner to the ground, its insignia muddied, the Stewart allies' morale shattered. The second battle ended quicker than the first, their hopes dashed on the Highland terrain.

Brodie and his brethren stood victorious but weary, faces etched with exhaustion and bloodstained hands. Breathing in fleeting peace, they knew greater challenges lay ahead.

The remaining Stewarts retreated into the mist toward Sinclair territory. Weary yet resolute Highlanders dealt with war's aftermath. Brodie helped carry wounded comrades inside McAfee Keep.

"Gently now," he grunted as they laid an injured clansman among others. The air filled with the scent of blood, sweat, and herbs.

Moira moved among them, her red hair a flame against pale bandages. She passed clean linens to Ailis, who skillfully tended to the wounded.

"Will he be all right?" Moira whispered.

"Rest easy," Ailis replied while tying a bandage. "He'll walk again and have a tale to tell at ceilidhs."

Moira scanned the room, her gaze landing on Brodie seated on a bench. Ailis approached him, needle and thread in hand, to tend to his deep cut. The crimson-stained tunic sleeve emphasized how danger had caught up with even the stealthy Brodie.

"Your arm," Ailis instructed gently but firmly, beginning her work on the wound.

Brodie nodded stoically, his eyes betraying the pain. Moira resisted the urge to rush to him and offer comfort. Instead, she watched with gratitude and concern.

"Ailis, your healing hands are a blessing," Brodie whispered, glancing at Moira before returning his attention to Ailis's focused face.

"Stay out of trouble next time, McClain," Ailis teased as she finished patching him up.

Moira's cheeks flushed as Brodie thanked Ailis and stood flexing his newly stitched arm cautiously. He locked eyes with Moira, an unspoken understanding passing between them—an acknowledgment of life's fragility and their shared emotions.

As twilight painted the land in hues of purple and gold, Moira stood beside Brodie, their hands barely touching as they watched the sun dip below the horizon. With each moment together, their bond solidified and tempered by past trials and those yet to come.

BRODIE, HIS ARM aching beneath fresh bandages, stood before Laird Duncan McAfee's door. He knocked on the heavy oak, the sound echoing through the stone corridor.

"Enter," came a steady voice from within.

Brodie entered and found Duncan at a table covered with maps and documents. The elder man lifted his eyes from his work, regarding Brodie with an assessing gaze.

"Good evening, Laird McAfee," Brodie said, his voice urgent. "I've come to discuss an important matter."

Duncan nodded and gestured to a chair across from him. Brodie remained standing—a statement of the gravity of his request.

"Speak your mind, son," Duncan spoke evenly.

"I seek your blessing to marry Moira—immediately," Brodie declared. "I understand tradition but cannot face what may come without her as me wife."

Silence filled the room, charged with unspoken fears and impending battles. Duncan leaned back in his chair, examining Brodie intently.

"I hoped for new alliances with me daughters' marriages. Yet they seem destined for McClains," Duncan mused.

He looked at Brodie thoughtfully. "But I see how ye regard each other. No man should stand against that—not even a father."

Brodie waited for the deciding words.

"You have me consent," Duncan said firmly, nodding. "Wed her. May it bring joy in these dark times."

"Thank you, Laird McAfee. I am forever in your debt," Brodie replied, relief washing over him.

"Take care of her," Duncan advised sternly. "Together, face whatever storms lie ahead."

Brodie bowed deeply and left the chamber, heart filled with the prospect of a union forged not only in passion, but also shared purpose amid their turbulent world.

BRODIE ENTERED THE infirmary, eyes locked on Moira as she tended to the wounded. Her red hair was pulled back, dirt smudged on her cheek emphasizing her pale skin. She was a comforting figure in the dim hall.

"Moira," Brodie said, approaching her. She looked up, eyes connecting with his. "Can we speak?"

Understanding the urgency, Moira nodded and joined him in a quiet corner.

"I've spoken with your father," Brodie started.

"And?" Curiosity danced across her face.

"He's given us his blessing. I want ye to be me wife, Moira. Before the next battle, I need to know we belong to each other."

Moira's eyes displayed a storm of emotions before determination took over. "Ye need to know?"

"Aye," he affirmed with conviction.

Her voice softened yet remained resolute. "My feelings for ye are strong, Brodie McClain." She touched his bandaged arm lightly. "They won't go away."

"Then ye'll marry me?"

"Aye, I will marry you. Before the next battle, ye shall have your wish."

Gratitude swept over Brodie as he held her hands between his own. "Thank you, Moira."

"Let us face what comes together, as husband and wife," she replied, gripping his hands firmly.

THE GREAT HALL of McAfee Keep was alive with the sounds of gathered clans, the lingering aroma of roasted meats mixed with the earthy scent of peat smoke filling the air. At the center, Brodie's heart pounded fiercely. As Moira entered, her fiery red hair catching everyone's attention, all whispers ceased.

She approached Brodie like a Highland legend, tartan draped over her shoulder. They exchanged vows before the clan, steady voices heavy.

Cheering erupted and bagpipes played, marking their union in a time of strife. Though the ceilidh began joyously, Brodie and

Moira only had eyes for each other and slipped away into the shadows.

In their modest wedding chamber, they stood close by the fire's warmth. A kiss spoke of battles fought and joys discovered while fingers traced lines across skin and stirred embers kindled in adversity.

"Ye are mine," Brodie whispered reverently against her skin.

"And ye are mine," Moira responded softly, guiding him to bed with care for his fresh wound—a testament to their fragile peace.

The tension between them was palpable as they sat across from each other at the small table. The flickering candlelight cast dancing shadows across their faces, highlighting their raw, undeniable attraction.

She took a sip of her wine, her lips lingering on the edge of the glass just a beat too long. He couldn't help but watch, mesmerized by the way her tongue darted out to catch a stray droplet. He shifted in his seat, feeling a sudden, insistent heat low in his belly.

He leaned forward, closing the distance between them. "You know what I want to do to ye right now?" he murmured, his voice low and rough with desire.

She raised an eyebrow, a teasing smile playing at the corners of her mouth. "Tell me," she breathed, her eyes locked on his.

He reached across the table, taking her hand in his. His thumb traced slow, deliberate circles over her knuckles, sending a shiver down her spine. "I want to show ye just how much I want you," he said, his voice barely above a whisper.

She bit her lip, her breath catching in her throat. "Is that so?" she whispered back, her own desire rising to meet his.

He nodded, his eyes never leaving hers. "I want to kiss ye until you're breathless, until you're begging for more," he continued, his voice growing more urgent. "I want to explore every inch of your body, to discover what makes ye moan, what makes ye tremble."

She let out a soft gasp as his hand moved up her arm, tracing the curve of her shoulder before coming to rest on the nape of her neck. "And what if I say no?" she asked, her voice barely audible.

He leaned in even closer, his lips just a hair's breadth from hers. "Then I'll spend all night convincing ye otherwise," he murmured, before finally closing the distance between them and capturing her lips in a searing kiss.

The newlywed's passionate embrace deepened as Moira ran her fingers through Brodie's dark hair. His strong hands roamed her body, tracing curves he had only dared dream of touching before tonight.

Moira pulled back slightly, cheeks flushed. "Careful, me brave warrior," she whispered with a playful smile. "You're still healing."

"For you, me bonnie lass, I can endure anything," Brodie murmured, gently kissing the soft skin of her neck. Moira sighed with pleasure, tilting her head to give him better access.

Their wedding clothes fell away piece by piece until there was nothing left between them but heat and desire. Brodie gazed at his new wife in awe, marveling at her wild beauty.

"You're perfect," he breathed reverently.

Moira smiled, a blush coloring her cheeks. "As are you, me husband," she whispered, her hands exploring the hard planes of Brodie's chest, mindful of his bandaged wound.

Brodie gathered her in his arms, the warmth of their bare skin igniting sparks of passion. He kissed her deeply, pouring all his love and longing into the caress of his lips. Moira responded with equal fervor, her body molding to his.

Gently, Brodie laid her down on the bed, hovering over her. His dark eyes glittered with desire in the firelight. "I've dreamt of this moment," he confessed huskily.

"As have I," Moira breathed, pulling him down for another searing kiss. Her fingers danced over his back, tracing the scars that told stories of battles past.

Brodie pressed his body against hers, the heat between them rising with each fervent caress. His lips traced a path from her mouth down the graceful column of her neck. Moira gasped as he found a sensitive spot, arching into his touch.

His hands skimmed over her breasts, thumbs brushing her peaked nipples as she shivered with pleasure. Brodie took his time worshipping her body, paying reverence to every freckle and curve.

Moira's own hands were not idle. She explored the hard planes of his warrior's physique, fingertips gliding over ridged abdominal muscles that quivered at her touch. Lower still, she grasped him, stroking his hard length. Brodie groaned, momentarily overtaken by the sensation.

"Moira, lass, ye undo me," he rasped.

Brodie captured Moira's lips in a searing kiss, his ardor raging like wildfire. She returned it fervently, fingers tangling in his hair as she pulled him closer, desperate to feel every inch of him.

His calloused hands roamed her body, mapping every curve and hollow. Moira gasped as his fingers found her most sensitive places, stoking the flames of her desire to new heights. She arched into his touch, silently begging for more.

Brodie needed no further encouragement. With a soft growl, he positioned himself at her entrance. Their eyes locked, speaking volumes without uttering a word—love, trust, commitment, passion. Then with a powerful thrust of his hips, he joined them as one.

Moira cried out, overwhelmed by the exquisite fullness of him inside her. Brodie stilled, allowing her a moment to adjust to his size. He peppered her face with gentle kisses, whispering sweet Gaelic words of love and devotion against her flushed skin.

When Moira's hips began to undulate beneath him, Brodie took it as a sign to move. He withdrew almost completely before surging forward again, starting a rhythm as old as time itself. Moira met him thrust for thrust, her legs wrapping around his waist to pull him impossibly deeper.

Their coupling was as wild and untamed as the Highland moors—a clash of lips, limbs, and heated flesh. Brodie drove into her with powerful strokes, spurred on by her breathy moans and the rake of her nails down his back.

The world fell away until there was nothing but this moment—the slide of sweat-slicked skin, the mingling of gasping breaths, the intensity of their connection. Brodie moved within Moira, pushing them both toward the precipice of ecstasy.

Moira felt the coil of pleasure winding tighter and tighter in her core with each powerful thrust. Her fingers dug into the firm muscles of Brodie's back as she held on, lost in the sensations overtaking her body.

"Brodie, I…something is happening…" she managed to gasp out, her voice hitching.

Brodie's dark eyes locked onto hers, pupils blown wide with passion. "Let go for me, mo gràidh," he urged huskily, his brogue thickened with desire. "I've got you."

His words were her undoing. With a keening cry, Moira shattered, waves of pure bliss crashing over her. Her body clenched around Brodie's as the intense pleasure radiated out to her very fingertips.

Brodie groaned, the feel of her pulsing around him almost too much to bear. With a few more erratic thrusts, he followed her over the edge. A hoarse shout tore from his throat as he emptied himself deep inside her welcoming heat.

They clung to each other as they came down from their high, chests heaving and hearts pounding in sync. Brodie pressed his forehead to Moira's, a sheen of sweat glistening on his skin.

"Mo chridhe, mo bhean," he murmured reverently. "My heart, me wife."

As the moon illuminated the Highlands, Brodie and Moira lay entwined, their hearts synchronized with Scotland's ancient rhythms. The world of clans and conflicts faded, leaving only the united warrior and strategist within the chamber's walls.

Flickering candlelight succumbed to darkness as Brodie and

Moira embraced the night. Their rhythmic breathing intertwined with whispers of wind that danced around the heavy tapestries in their chamber.

Moira nestled closer, her head resting on Brodie's chest, a gentle weight above his heartbeat. Her red hair spilled over him like autumn leaves, carrying the earthy scent of peat smoke. His arm encircled her slender form, wincing when she grazed his bandaged shoulder.

"Forgive me," she whispered.

"Think nothing of it," he reassured, adjusting to ease her concern. The warmth of her skin challenged the chill Highland air seeping through the cracks in their stronghold.

In the silence, Brodie considered seeking out the services of the healer from his own clan but decided that some things were worth waiting for.

"Ye should've let Ailis tend to ye more," Moira said, fingers tracing his uninjured arm.

"Rest," he replied, kissing her head. "Tonight, we have each other—and that is enough."

As they surrendered to sleep, Brodie's last thought was of gratitude for Moira's indomitable spirit.

◆──◆── ❖ ──◆──◆

CHAPTER EIGHT

STEEL CLASHED IN the courtyard as Brodie's precise movements displayed his Highland warrior lineage. From the infirmary window, Moira watched, her fingers idly sorting bandages, captivated by his lethal grace. Ailis's voice drew her back to reality.

"Moira, are ye with us?" Ailis steadied herself as she tended to another warrior.

"Aye, sorry," Moira replied and concentrated on her work but remained aware of Brodie outside the walls.

When the training ended at sunset, Brodie entered the infirmary, his eyes locking onto hers. The unspoken bond between them held strong.

"Shall we walk?" he asked as he offered his calloused hand.

Quickly retrieving her cloak, Moira joined him. They strolled along a forest path, inhaling the crisp scent of pine and earth.

"Today's training was relentless," Brodie broke the silence. "The men are improving."

"In the infirmary, it's been calm—mostly blisters and sprains," Moira added, conveying their shared responsibility.

Reaching the loch at the edge of the forest, Moira hesitated before speaking. "Brodie, I've been thinking…You were right to marry quickly—to forge this bond without delay."

"Why do ye say that now?"

"I wouldn't have wanted to lose ye without knowing what it is to be your wife," she confessed. "Our union provides the strength we both draw from."

As Brodie gently cupped her cheek, a shiver ran down her spine. "We are together. That is the true source of our strength."

She leaned into his palm, savoring the contact. Her eyes reopened with newfound resolve. They turned back toward the keep ready for the trials ahead.

Moira's thoughts lingered on Brodie. The day had been slow, but when night fell, they found solace in their private chamber. The hearth's glow lit the room as Moira reached for Brodie's arm, alarmed by its unnatural heat.

"Brodie, your arm! It's burning up. I should fetch Ailis—"

"Moira, no," he interrupted urgently. "Seek out me great-grandfather instead."

Baffled yet trusting, she raced to find the man among ancient tapestries depicting battles of old. Breathless, she urged him toward their chamber where Brodie lay in pain. The elder McClain approached with confident hands and as he did so, an indescribable power filled the air. Slowly, the redness and heat faded from Brodie's arm until it was unmarred—no scar or trace of injury remaining.

"Wha—how did you...?" Moira's words faltered, her mind reeling.

"Rest now," the elder McClain commanded before leaving them alone.

Brodie met Moira's gaze, his vulnerability evident. "I'll explain later. But for now, we keep this secret."

Moira nodded, still processing what she had seen. As she settled beside Brodie, the warmth between them spoke to a connection deeper than either could understand.

Flickering candlelight played over Brodie's solemn face, while Moira grappled with the miraculous healing she had just witnessed.

"Tell me," she implored, her voice barely a whisper.

"My family carries a legacy, Moira," Brodie began, capturing her hand. "Centuries ago, one of our ancestors married a woman with inexplicable powers. Since then, every seventh son in our line has inherited aspects of her abilities. Before he married her, the seventh son had powerful luck, but it's different now."

"Gifted?" Moira questioned, recalling Granny's tales.

"Aye, gifted," Brodie confirmed, his grip tightening. "But it's a secret that could tear apart our clans if known. Can I trust ye not to reveal what runs through me blood?"

Moira felt honor-bound to protect him. "Ye have me word," she whispered back. She wasn't certain she could explain it if she tried.

"And what of me sisters and me? Will we have seven sons each?" she asked. She wasn't sure she believed it, but glancing at his arm, she knew it had to be true, no matter how improbable it seemed.

"Only the wife of the seventh son bears that fate," he clarified.

Understanding settled within her as their shared secret deepened their connection. She leaned forward and pressed her lips to his. Their hands explored and caressed, their urgency escalating until Moira took command of their union. This time there was only the fierce joy of two people entwined in the ancient dance of love.

SUNLIGHT FILLED THE infirmary as Moira's sisters tended to the wounded. Ailis moved efficiently from one patient to another, her dark hair tied back and green eyes focused. Moira, distracted, sorted through a pile of clean bandages.

"Your mind seems elsewhere," Fiona noted, standing beside Moira.

"Perhaps," Moira admitted, keeping Brodie's secret about his lineage to herself.

In the late afternoon, Moira and Ailis exchanged their healer's aprons for cloaks and quivers, venturing into the Highland forest to hunt.

"Let's find a stag before sunset," Ailis said with determination in her eyes.

As they left the keep, guards trailed discreetly behind them—a comforting yet frustrating necessity. Moira missed the days when she and her sisters could move about freely and not have to constantly be worried about the danger of encroaching armies.

"Aye, always watching," Moira muttered.

Ailis said, "Better our own than Sinclairs."

They navigated the dense underbrush, their senses alert. Soon enough, Ailis spotted a majestic stag grazing in a clearing. Wordlessly, they readied their bows, releasing their arrows with deadly precision. Approaching the fallen animal, Moira felt a mix of pride and reverence for its sacrifice.

"Granny will have her pot ready for this one," Ailis commented as they prepared the stag for transport. "Her venison stew warms the soul."

Moira smiled at the thought of Granny's legendary meal that awaited them. "Agreed—there's no finer way to honor this beast."

Securing the stag, the sisters returned to the keep. Moira's heart warmed with satisfaction, and anticipation of the feast ignited joy in the fading light.

The heather crunched softly beneath their boots as Moira and Ailis walked ahead of the guards who carried the stag back to the keep. Shadows stretched across the rugged Highlands, painting them in amber and gold.

"Freedom's a rare gift these days," Ailis mused, gazing at the landscape. "Despite the war, we can still roam with our bows."

"Aye," Moira replied, her thoughts drifting. "Lucas Gordon warned us of the battle ahead."

"Trust is hard-earned," Ailis agreed. "To stand strong, we must lean on truths."

As McAfee Keep loomed above them, they noticed soldiers

clad in different tartans practicing on the open grounds.

"New allies—Clan MacKenzie and Clan Ross," Ailis observed. "The emissaries are doing their jobs. I pray they'll be able to get more clans to join us soon."

"With strength like this, we might just turn the tide," Moira said, hope swelling in her heart.

Ailis whispered a prayer that more clans would join their cause.

As they entered through the gates, sounds of clashing swords filled the air. United and purposeful, they were ready for what lay ahead.

Shadows flickered on the bedchamber walls as Moira sat, hands clasped tight. Brodie entered, soothing the turmoil that stirred within her from witnessing the clans' armies.

"Ye look troubled, lass," he said softly.

"I've been thinking about Clan MacKenzie and Clan Ross. Have any other lairds answered our call?" Moira asked.

"Only those two. We've yet to hear from the others," Brodie replied, face etched with responsibility.

Her heart sank, but she mustered determination. "And if they dinnae come? Are we enough?"

Brodie sat beside her, his hand finding hers. "We are Highlanders, Moira. We fight fiercely for our own. But alliances take time."

She sighed and squeezed his hand. "Patience was never me strong suit."

"Nor mine," he admitted, half-smiling. "But for our clans—for our future—we will wait and stand ready."

Moira nodded, newfound strength surging through her. With Brodie by her side, they would face the uncertain future together, their bond unyielding as war approached.

◆———— ⚜ ————◆

CHAPTER NINE

THE HIGHLAND AIR bristled with restless energy as Moira McAfee watched from the parapet of McAfee Keep, eyes on the horizon.

"MacGregor… Mackenzie… Campbell…" Moira murmured, counting the emblems waving in the wind, symbols of alliances formed out of necessity. Emissaries had returned from each clan, their arrival marking a reprieve from bloodshed and bolstering their confederation.

Moira was thrilled so many clans had decided to join them in their fight. At first, she'd been surprised that more hadn't shown up, but now that the emissaries had explained to each laird what was happening, and how their lives would change if they didn't stand up for their Highland ways of life, they were coming around.

A cheer erupted as Moira joined her clansfolk in the courtyard where preparations for the evening's ceilidh were underway. Torches flared to life, filling the air with warmth and aromas of roasting venison and barley bread. Musicians tuned fiddles and pipes; melodies rose above conversations within ancient stone walls.

Duncan's voice boomed. "Tonight, we dance not as separate clans but as one." Moira found herself swept into the whirl of kilted men whose faces bore marks of harsh winters and fierce battles.

Feasting followed dancing with platters piled high. Laughter mixed with clinking tankards, and tales of valor and mischief ignited camaraderie amid shared purpose.

Brodie sidled up beside Moira, remarking on the joyous atmosphere despite looming threats. To this, Moira replied, "It is this very joy that reminds us what we're fighting for."

As the ceilidh carried on, a Highland alliance formed not only through oaths but shared laughter and dance—a fleeting peace nestled between inevitable battles on the horizon. Duncan had often told his daughters that alliances were made faster through shared meals than shared battles. The feasts were to help solidify the alliance.

The ceilidh's fervor softened to hushed stories and laughter when Moira noticed Lucas Gordon weaving through the McAfees. His freshly woven plaid attire, clasped by a brooch, mirrored their own.

"Doesn't seem right," grumbled a nearby clansman.

Moira watched as Lucas greeted an elder, receiving only a tentative smile before being left alone. Despite her people's reservations, she couldn't deny his role in their survival thus far.

"Ye ken they're none too pleased with him," Brodie said quietly, joining Moira.

"Have they spoken openly against him?" Moira asked, her gaze still on Lucas.

"Aye. They say a snake cannae change its scales."

"Yet his counsel has steered us clear of Gordon traps and Stewart's ploys," she reasoned. "I would be the first to mistrust the man, but he's proving worthy of our confidence in him."

"But trust is hard-won here," Brodie replied. "Perhaps time will prove his worth."

Moira watched as Lucas tried once more to engage with younger warriors but withdrew under the weight of suspicion.

"Or perhaps time will unveil a truth we dare not face," Brodie added softly, his words slicing the festive air.

Moira felt unease for the man who fought alongside them, yet stood apart. His future and loyalty remained enigmatic. "I dinnae think we can mistrust him at this point. We cannae fully trust him either, though. I suppose we'll all have to learn to trust him and pray that he is worthy."

MOIRA STUDIED THE parchment, her fingers tracing the lines of ink that marked clan allegiances. She noticed the Lindsays were unclaimed by either side and felt a sense of urgency.

She approached her father who was conferring with his advisors in the dimly lit hall. "Father," she said, presenting the parchment, "the Lindsays do not appear. I remember Elsa Lindsay; we shared words and laughter. I believe I could sway her to our cause. We were fast friends when we were younger."

Duncan's hand stroked his silvery beard as he considered her proposal. "It's a perilous time, Moira. The roads are filled with danger."

"I understand the risk, but consider the reward," she pressed. "With Lindsay support, our position strengthens."

"Very well," he sighed. "Brodie will accompany ye along with a couple of guards. Ye will heed his counsel."

"Thank ye, Father," Moira inclined her head slightly.

"Keep yer wits about ye and return swiftly," Duncan instructed.

"Swiftly," she echoed before leaving to find Brodie under a star-speckled sky. The Highland wind whispered through the pines, carrying the scent of impending change. Embracing its chill and challenge, Moira set out to gather her companions for the journey.

DAWN BROKE AS Moira secured her mare, the Highland chill biting at her cheeks. She observed Brodie checking the guards' horses before they mounted and began their journey.

"Keep a keen eye on the terrain," Brodie instructed the guards. "We must not alert the Stewarts, and their allies, as we go through Sinclair land."

The grizzled guard nodded, while the younger one adjusted his sword belt, understanding the gravity of their mission. Moira glanced at the McAfee Keep, feeling pride in her clan's strength. With a nod to Brodie, she led them along the narrow forest track.

Riding in silence, only the rhythmic thud of hooves and raven calls punctuated their travels. The dappled sunlight cast shadows on their path as stray curls escaped Moira's hood, vibrant like embers.

As they traversed from woodland to open moorland, the temperature dropped with the setting sun, and Moira tightened her cloak. Brodie indicated a clearing shielded by rocks for their campsite.

They dismounted and efficiently set up camp without discussion. Huddled around a modest fire later that evening, they ate sparingly and conserved provisions.

"Ye should try to rest," Brodie told Moira, concern evident in his eyes. "We'll need your strength come morning."

"I'll take first watch," Moira said through chattering teeth. "I'm not one to cower from the cold."

"Stubbornness won't keep ye warm," Brodie replied, amused. "But I admire your spirit."

They settled into their watches, the Highland sky stretching above them, stars mocking human frailty. Moira's thoughts turned to the task ahead and the uncertain welcome awaiting them. As she drifted to sleep, with Brodie's arms cradling her against him, dreams of swirling kilts and clashing swords filled her mind.

THE HORSES' HOOVES clattered on cobblestones as they entered Lindsay Keep, a stronghold weathered yet unyielding amidst rolling hills and towering pines.

Moira assessed the courtyard before dismounting gracefully. Her red hair contrasted the muted colors of the keep as Laird Lindsay greeted them with authority and hospitality.

"Thank ye, Laird Lindsay," Moira said, Brodie at her side. "We seek yer support in an urgent matter."

"What stirs conflict between the Stewarts and the McAfees?" Laird Lindsay inquired, ushering them inside. "I have heard many stories of the conflict, yet no one seems to be able to tell me what is at the heart of it."

As Moira recounted their struggle against the Stewarts, Laird Lindsay's resolve deepened. "Ye have me word," he pledged. "The Lindsays will nae let anyone change our ways."

Grateful for his quick commitment, Moira asked after Elsa. A smile graced Laird Lindsay's face as he called to her.

Elsa's arrival brought laughter and hushed secrets between old friends.

Elsa embraced Moira warmly, the years apart melting away in an instant. "It's been far too long, me dear friend," Elsa said, her eyes sparkling with joy. "What brings ye to our keep?"

Moira's expression grew serious. "I'm afraid it's not a social call, Elsa. We need your help."

As Moira explained the Stewarts' plot and the growing alliance against them, Elsa listened intently, her brow furrowed with concern. "The Stewarts have always been ambitious, but this is beyond anything I could have imagined," she said. "Of course, we will stand with ye and the other clans. The Highlands must remain free."

Moira couldn't help but smile at her friend's words. With the Lindsays' support, their cause gained even more strength. "Thank you, Elsa. Your friendship and the support of Clan Lindsay mean more than ye know," Moira said sincerely. "Together, we will show the Stewarts that the Highlands cannot be tamed or conquered."

The two women clasped hands, their bond of sisterhood reforged in the face of shared adversity. Brodie watched the exchange with a glimmer of hope in his eyes. The Lindsays' allegiance brought them one step closer to thwarting the Stewarts' schemes.

As the sun began to set, casting a golden glow across the keep, Laird Lindsay insisted that Moira and her companions stay the night. "You must rest and recover your strength before the journey back," he urged. "And we have much to discuss and plan."

Over a hearty meal of venison stew and fresh bread, the conversation turned to strategy. Laird Lindsay listened intently as Moira and Brodie laid out the growing network of alliances and the Stewarts' latest maneuvers. "We must strike swiftly and decisively," Laird Lindsay declared, his fist thumping the table. "The Stewarts will not expect a coordinated assault from multiple clans. It may be our best chance to catch them off guard."

Moira nodded in agreement. "Aye, and we must ensure that our forces are well-positioned to cut off their supply lines and isolate their strongholds. The Stewarts are cunning, but they are not invincible." And as the allied army grew bigger and stronger, there was no doubt they would have the manpower to do whatever needed to be done. Each clan that joined them brought more strength, and her confidence grew that they would be the victors.

As the evening wore on, talk turned to lighter matters, and laughter echoed through the halls of Lindsay Keep. Elsa regaled them with tales of her own adventures, and Moira found herself grateful for the respite from the constant strain of war.

Elsa told them of her betrothal to one of her father's men, blushing as she mentioned that he was strong and would be a good husband to her.

Moira smiled at her friend's happiness, but a twinge of envy touched her heart. Her own marriage hadn't been celebrated as she would have liked. Her path was one of duty and sacrifice, and she had accepted that long ago. But that didn't mean she couldn't wish for her wedding to be more celebrated than it had been.

Perhaps when it was all over, and the Highlands had returned to their normal way of life, she and Ailis could throw a huge ceilidh to make up for the wedding celebrations that hadn't occurred. She would talk to Ailis about it…after they'd beaten the Stewarts.

As the night grew late, Laird Lindsay showed Moira and Brodie to their quarters. The room was simple but comfortable, with a crackling fire in the hearth and soft furs on the bed. Moira sank onto the mattress, feeling the weight of exhaustion settle upon her.

Brodie hesitated by the door, his expression unreadable in the flickering firelight. "I'll take the first watch," he said quietly. "Ye need yer rest, Moira."

She nodded, too tired to argue. As Brodie slipped out of the room.

As she lay in the darkness, staring up at the rough-hewn beams of the ceiling, a soft knock sounded at the door. She was unsure if Brodie had finally decided to join her, or if someone else was knocking.

"Come in," Moira called, sitting up in bed.

Elsa slipped into the room, a single candle casting a warm glow across her face. "I couldn't sleep," she confessed, perching on the edge of the bed. "I keep thinking about what lies ahead, and I fear for what the future may hold."

Moira reached out and squeezed her friend's hand. "I know, Elsa. The road before us is uncertain and fraught with danger. But we have each other, and we have the strength of our clans behind us. We will face whatever comes, together."

"I cannae wait until ye are at McAfee Keep, and ye can meet me sisters. It's odd that we've been friends for years, and ye've never met the two of them."

Elsa smiled. "Meeting them will be a true pleasure. I dinnae know if Father wants me to join him at yer keep, but I think there's strength in numbers, and I will push him to do so."

"We cannae let years go by when we don't see one another again," Moira said. "Ye will be very welcome in me home."

CHAPTER TEN

BRODIE AND MOIRA led a column of Lindsay soldiers across McAfee land. Brodie observed the familiar landscape, noting new fortifications for the upcoming struggle.

Moira surveyed their united forces. Elsa's presence alongside the Lindsay laird hinted at the fragile coalition they'd formed. Though Moira was pleased that Elsa's clan was joining them, she wasn't certain the other clan fully understood what they were doing. They had to stop a monster from taking over the Highlands and changing them into something else entirely. She wasn't even certain it could be done, but she would do everything she could to make certain no one was hurt.

Entering the keep, sounds of metal clanging and voices filled the air. They dismounted, greeted by respectful nods from nearby clansmen.

"Welcome home," Brodie said as he steadied Moira.

"Home," she replied. "But not to rest."

They approached Alisdair, Fiona's husband, who stood among other lairds. Laird Lindsay strode forward confidently and exchanged greetings with Alisdair.

"We bring strength in numbers and heart," Laird Lindsay affirmed, followed by nods of agreement from those gathered.

Moira observed the conversation as relations began forming between clans. Beside her, Brodie stayed vigilant—aware that their choices would impact generations to come.

The Campbells, who were part of the alliance, had been

longtime-enemies of the Lindsays, and they were all worried there would be some friction.

Steel clashed as Brodie helped with the training of the clans allied with the McAfees in drills, their movements a powerful dance of war. Morning mist covered the Highland grasses while Moira observed from the training field's edge.

"They move as if long-time allies," Fiona commented, joining Moira.

"Aye," Moira agreed. "Old grudges set aside out of necessity."

Ailis nodded, her dark hair catching the light. "Our common cause unites us."

Elsa approached, her skirts rustling against tall grass. "Moira, I've been seeking you."

"I've been watching all the clans train together," Moira replied, introducing Elsa to Ailis and Fiona.

"Yer embroidery is impressive," Ailis remarked, gesturing to the beautiful work on the other woman's blouse.

"Thank ye," Elsa said. "I take pride in me needlework." She seemed genuinely pleased that her handiwork had been noticed.

"Our clan women share yer appreciation for craftsmanship," Fiona added.

"With time," Moira interjected, "we may teach ye about wielding a blade too."

Elsa's eyes widened with apprehension and curiosity. "Oh, I'm not sure if I—"

"Ye'll not be alone," Fiona assured her. "We all start somewhere, Elsa. In these times, standing up for oneself is crucial."

"Aye," Ailis echoed, her tone encouraging. "But let's focus on our shared goals now."

As they spoke, the persistent sounds of training served as a reminder of the harsh realities beyond their conversation. Moira observed the unyielding determination on the faces of the men—Lindsays and Campbells united against a common enemy.

As the tales of bygone feasts and misadventures echoed through the room, one couldn't help but wonder if Ailis'

Highland cow encounter was a result of her trying to challenge the beast to a staring contest.

Elsa's laughter seemed to suggest that maybe the cow won, and now it proudly boasts about it to all the other animals on the farm. And while Fiona and Moira's chuckles filled the air, it was rumored that they had once tried to teach the cows a Scottish jig, much to the amusement of everyone at McAfee Keep. In that moment, it became clear that even Highland cows have a sense of humor!

"Your laughter is refreshing, Elsa," Ailis complimented.

Elsa blushed. "And your spirit, Ailis, is as strong as the Highlands themselves."

"I need help in the infirmary," Ailis said earnestly. "Your needlework suggests you'd be excellent at tending wounds."

"I would love to be of help. Are ye certain I wouldnae be in the way?" Elsa asked, surprised.

"Not at all," Ailis assured her.

"Then I would love to help!" she agreed. "I may not know swordplay, but I can wield a needle precisely."

"You'll be a blessing to those in need," Ailis assured her.

"Unlike me," smirked Moira with playful grace. "I prefer the clangor of steel to stitching thread. I help when I can, but I think Ailis is always pleased when I help in the kitchens instead of the infirmary."

Elsa smiled. "We each have our own battles."

"And together, we stand stronger for it," Moira added, eyes aflame with determination.

IN THE GREAT hall of McAfee Keep, conversations buzzed around. The warm glow from torches illuminated clansmen and guests alike. Moira observed carefully as Lindsay soldiers mingled with her kin, feeling an unusual sense of unity.

"Moira," Elsa whispered, tugging at her sleeve. "I want ye to meet someone."

"Lead on," Moira replied, rising steadily from her seat.

Elsa led Moira, Fiona, and Ailis to a man standing apart from the crowd, his posture betraying a hint of shyness. He met their gaze with a kind expression.

"Meet me betrothed, Bryson," Elsa announced.

His smile was timid as he extended his hand. "'Tis an honor."

Fiona's warm welcome eased the tension while Ailis offered a respectful nod. Bryson murmured his gratitude, blushing. Moira was surprised a soldier could be so shy, but she simply smiled.

Lucas Gordon caught their attention from across the room, dressed in a McAfee plaid. He approached with confidence. "Evening, ladies." His eyes appraised Elsa briefly before Moira interjected.

"This is Elsa's intended, Bryson."

"Congratulations," Lucas said insincerely before excusing himself. Moira almost felt sorry for him as he walked off. They needed Lucas, but he found no joy within their ranks, as he wasn't trusted. The other soldiers didn't find him to be someone to confide in or befriend.

He had been too much a part of the enemies' plans, and they couldn't be certain of his loyalty to them. He'd already switched sides once. Who was to say he wouldn't do it again?

Lucas Gordon assessed Bryson from across the room, his jaw tense but eyes intrigued when they landed on Elsa. Enveloped in a gown that softened her, she laughed easily, contrasting Moira and Ailis's stoic expressions. She was very different from the sisters, and to Lucas's mind, much better, for she was a proper lady.

"Let me show ye the infirmary," Ailis whispered to Elsa. They slipped away, their skirts brushing the stone floor as they headed for the infirmary.

In the dimly lit corridor, the feast's echoes receded. Inside the infirmary, lined with cots and shelves of supplies, Elsa began assisting Ailis in organizing.

"I believe ye'll have a fine hand for healing," Ailis said genuinely but strategically.

Elsa beamed in response. Moira leaned in conspiratorially. "We've dealt with Lucas before. He didn't appreciate our preference for swords over sewing needles."

Ailis smirked as she added, "He made it clear we were out of place when we visited his family's lands for the Highland Games. Of course, he was following orders to keep us away from Lachlan and Brodie. He may have been better mannered if he hadn't had to deal with us hoydens."

"But he's now integral to McAfee land," Elsa observed with admiration.

"We'll stand firm," Ailis affirmed, returning a jar to its shelf. "He has agreed to help us, and we welcome the information he has readily given."

Much later, Moira opened her bed chamber door, revealing a candlelit space where Brodie awaited by the hearth. The calm in his brown eyes extinguished her anxieties as she rushed into his embrace.

"Ye've done well," Brodie said softly. "Bringing the Lindsays to our side is no small feat. I'm proud of ye."

Moira leaned in, her cheek against the rhythm of his heart. "I hope they prove to be able allies. For us and for our future," she whispered, her hair a cascade upon his chest.

Their lips met in a tender kiss that intensified, fueled by their shared struggles and victories. With quiet efficiency, clothes were discarded, laces and buckles undone under the guidance of longing fingers. In the dim candlelight, they reunited, their exhaustion forgotten as every touch and whisper fortified their bond.

As fervor subsided into gentle caresses, they lay entwined beneath woolen blankets. Brodie's hand traced patterns on Moira's back as she focused on his steady breathing. In their chamber's embrace, with the night poised outside the keep's walls, their world condensed to just each other.

The warmth of their connection eased them into sleep, daily burdens dissolving into dreams. They drifted off entwined, ready to confront the future side by side—as one.

◆—◆—✦—◆—◆

CHAPTER ELEVEN

NEW ALLIES ENTERED the Highland Confederation's encampment early the following morning. Alisdair and Laird Fearghas McClain strode purposefully among the warriors, diverse clan banners flitting in the breeze.

"Keep the lines straight!" Alisdair commanded, his voice slicing through shield clangs and eager chatter. "We must become one clan under the same sky. Let naught divide us in our purpose!"

Amidst new arrivals, Brodie spotted Lucas, a restless figure whose gaze strayed to the distant peaks. He approached Lucas on dew-kissed grass.

"Ye seem distant, Lucas," Brodie observed. "Is yer mind with those who've ye left to join us?"

"Aye," Lucas admitted. "I've left behind kin and comrades… but I couldna follow Clyde Stewart's command any longer. His reign…it's harsher than our homeland's windswept crags." Lucas shook his head. "He threatened to kill me in front of me father."

Brodie encouraged him to continue, listening intently as bitterness laced Lucas's words recounting mercilessness and cruelty under Clyde Stewart. As they stood within their growing army, shadows of that dark regime loomed around them.

"Your courage willnae be forgotten," Brodie said, gripping Lucas's shoulder. "Here, we fight as brothers for the freedom of these lands." At least he hoped Lucas would stay true to their alliance and not return to the Stewarts. There was no way of knowing though, and he must keep watch on the other man to keep those he loved safe.

The army slowly began to resemble a single, honed blade. Alisdair and Laird McClain worked among the men while Brodie stood vigilant—uniting and welcoming all.

THE CLASH OF steel echoed in the Highland air as warriors from various clans sparred upon the training field. Lachlan surveyed the melee for signs of discord.

"Mind yer stance, lad!" he called. The young warrior adjusted, and Lachlan nodded before moving on.

Two clansmen collided mid-thrust, their swords locked together. Tempers flared with accusations of dishonorable tactics. Lachlan strode toward them, commanding order. They had enough enemies to deal with without turning on one another.

"Enough!" His authoritative voice silenced the fighters. "We train as brothers-in-arms, not enemies."

The men backed down and rejoined the fray under Lachlan's watchful gaze. As exhaustion set in, a cry of pain disrupted the battlefield. Lachlan rushed to an injured man, blood seeping through his fingers.

"To the infirmary!" he bellowed, applying pressure to stem the bleeding. Another McClain warrior joined him, and together, they carried the wounded toward the infirmary.

"Have care with him," he instructed as they entered the stone-walled sanctum. Ailis directed the healers with calm efficiency.

Lachlan whispered reassurances to the injured clansman and stepped back as they set him down in the infirmary. Ailis would heal the man now. He hated that his grandfather couldn't be called for every single injury, but it wasn't practical to do so. The entire Highlands need not know about the special powers of the

McClains.

He returned to the somber field, reminded of the fragility beneath their hardened exteriors. With unity and resilience, they would face what lay ahead.

AILIS EXAMINED THE gash on the man's weathered skin. "Clean it first," she instructed Elsa, handing her a cloth soaked in herbs. Elsa wiped the wound with steady hands, focused. "I am nervous. I've never stitched a man's skin before."

"Small and close stitches," Ailis advised. Elsa nodded and carefully began her task.

"This is very different than stitching on cloth!" Elsa exclaimed as her needle sank into the man's flesh for the first time.

Moira knelt beside another clansman, his ankle twisted harshly from training. She offered reassuring words as Ailis approached and prepared to realign the bones. Both sisters met each other's gaze, understanding the pain to come.

"One… two…" On Ailis's count, the joint was swiftly set into place, Moira holding the man steady despite his pained gasp.

"Done," Ailis announced, wrapping the injured ankle.

"Rest now," Moira added before rising from her position. She hated assisting with the setting of bones, but it couldn't be done by one woman, and the men were all out training. If it must be her, then she would do her duty without complaint.

Lucas Gordon entered the infirmary. He approached Elsa, absorbed in stitching a wound, and complimented her skill.

Elsa's cheeks flushed, but she remained silent. Lucas teased her about her quietness, leaning closer. He was obviously smitten with the lass, and it wouldn't do. She was to marry another.

Moira noticed from across the room. She grabbed Lucas's arm and led him outside. "Elsa is betrothed," Moira warned. "Leave her be."

Lucas feigned innocence, claiming it was friendly banter. Moira suggested he focus on getting to know some of the displaced Sinclair women instead.

Lucas's silence filled the cold corridor until he finally spoke with a chilled voice. "Fine, I'll seek company at supper with those less…spoken for."

Moira assessed his resolve but didn't coddle his wounded pride. Sometimes it seemed as if Lucas was a completely changed man, and then she'd see him do something like this, and she wondered if he was even capable of change. She shook her head. He was not hers to teach. She turned and strode away, her thoughts shifting to the tasks ahead.

Outside, Moira found Brodie waiting in the crisp Highland air. They headed toward the forest line where deer trails crisscrossed. Their food supply was lower than Granny would like with all the extra soldiers to feed.

As they walked, Moira broached the topic on her mind. "Yer brother Boyd, ye said he had powers?"

Brodie kept his focus on the path. "Aye, Boyd doesn't heal like me great-grandfather, but he can turn into any animal he chooses."

"Is that why Ailis swears she saw him disappear before her eyes?"

He nodded. "He likes to choose a small insect so that it looks as if he is vanishing from sight. We've tried to convince him to be circumspect, but he simply doesn't seem to have it in him to do so."

"Why not bring yer grandfather to aid our infirmary?" she asked.

He slowed his pace before sharing an unsettling truth. "Moira, there are things about me kin not meant for others to ken. Revealing our secrets could bring more harm than good."

"I understand," she conceded, though her heart ached for the sufferings that might have been eased by such gifts.

They moved into the forest silently, determined to bring

Granny deer for them to feast on in the days to come.

The forest enveloped Moira and Brodie as they ventured deeper into the ancient trees standing sentinel over their land. Brodie crouched, examining a set of fresh tracks pressed into the damp earth.

"Deer passed through here not long ago," he whispered, motioning for Moira to follow. They moved with practiced stealth, bows at the ready.

A twig snapped in the underbrush ahead. Brodie froze, signaling Moira to do the same. Through the foliage, a majestic stag emerged, its antlers reaching skyward. Brodie nocked an arrow, drawing the bowstring taut. Moira mirrored his actions, aiming true.

In a breath, they released their arrows. Twin shafts found their mark, and the stag fell, its life given to sustain the clans. They approached their quarry, offering silent thanks for its sacrifice.

As they prepared the stag for transport, a distant cry echoed through the trees. They exchanged a glance, hands instinctively reaching for their weapons. The cry came again, closer this time—a human voice tinged with desperation.

Without hesitation, they abandoned their kill and raced toward the sound, leaping over fallen logs and dodging low-hanging branches. They burst into a small clearing and froze at the sight before them.

A young woman, her dress torn and muddied, cowered against a tree as a group of rough-looking men circled her like wolves eyeing prey. The men turned at Moira and Brodie's sudden appearance, sneering with cruel intent.

"Well, well, what have we here?" the apparent leader drawled, his eyes roving over Moira in a way that made her skin crawl. "Two more lambs stumbling into the wolf's den, eh?"

Moira met the man's gaze unflinchingly, her bow drawn and aimed at his heart. "Step away from the lass if ye value yer miserable lives." The men wore the kilt of the Gordons, and she knew they had come from Sinclair lands to hurt those they could find.

The men laughed, a harsh, grating sound that echoed through the clearing. "Bold words for a wee lass," the leader mocked. "Mayhap we'll have some fun with ye too."

Brodie stepped forward, his own bow at the ready. "Ye'll not lay a finger on either of them, ye filthy curs. Now back away, or I'll put an arrow through yer black hearts."

The men hesitated, eyeing the deadly serious expressions on Moira and Brodie's faces. The leader's hand twitched toward the sword at his hip, but before he could draw it, an arrow from Moira's bow pierced his throat. He fell to the ground, gurgling as blood poured from the wound.

Chaos erupted. The remaining men charged at Moira and Brodie with a roar of fury. Arrows flew, finding their marks in two more attackers. Brodie dropped his bow and drew his sword, engaging the closest assailant in a fierce clash of steel.

Moira rushed to the young woman's side, pulling her to her feet. "Run, lass! Get to safety!" The terrified girl didn't hesitate, fleeing into the trees as the battle raged behind her.

Moira turned back to the fray, drawing her own sword. She and Brodie fought back to back, their blades flashing in deadly arcs. The men were skilled fighters, but they were no match for the Highland warriors' fierce determination.

Moira and Brodie fought with a ferocity born of righteous anger, their blades singing through the air as they cut down their opponents one by one. The remaining men, seeing their comrades fall, began to falter, their resolve crumbling in the face of the Highland warriors' onslaught.

The last man standing, a hulking brute with a scar across his left eye, lunged at Brodie with a roar of fury. Brodie sidestepped the attack, his sword flashing out to slice the man's sword arm. The brute howled in pain, his weapon falling from nerveless fingers.

Moira stepped forward, her blade leveled at the man's throat.

"Yield, ye coward, or meet yer maker."

The man glared at her, hatred burning in his eyes, but he slowly raised his hands in surrender.

Brodie quickly bound the man's hands behind his back, his grip firm and unyielding. "Who are ye, and why were ye attacking that lass?" he demanded, his voice low and dangerous.

The man spat at Brodie's feet, his lip curling in a sneer. "I answer to no McClain dog," he growled. "Ye think ye've won, but there are more of us out there, waiting to strike."

Moira pressed the tip of her blade against the man's throat, drawing a bead of blood. "Speak plainly, or I'll send ye to meet yer fallen friends."

The man's eyes widened, a flicker of fear breaking through his bravado. "We're just doing what we're told," he stammered. "The Stewarts pay us well to sow chaos in the Highlands, to weaken the clans from within."

"The Stewarts," Moira repeated, exchanging a grim look with Brodie. "They seek to divide us, to turn clan against clan."

"Aye," Brodie agreed, his grip tightening on the bound man's arm. "And they use scum like this to do their dirty work."

The captured brute glared at them, defiance still burning in his eyes despite his precarious position. "Ye think ye can stop what's coming?" he sneered. "The Stewarts will rule these lands, and all who oppose them will fall."

Moira's blade pressed harder against the man's throat, silencing his tirade. "We'll see about that," she said coldly. "But first, ye'll tell us everything ye know about the Stewarts' plans."

The man's eyes darted between Moira and Brodie, calculating his odds of escape or rescue. Finding none, he slumped in defeat, his bravado crumbling.

"Fine," he spat. "I'll tell ye what I know, but it won't do ye any good. The Stewarts are too powerful, too cunning. Ye'll never stop them."

Moira and Brodie dragged the man back through the forest to the keep, the stag forgotten in the face of this new threat. As they emerged from the trees, curious eyes turned their way, taking in the bound prisoner and the grim expressions on the warriors' faces.

Alisdair McClain strode forward, his brow furrowed with concern. "What's this? Who is this man?"

"A Stewart lackey," Brodie replied, shoving the man to his knees before Alisdair. "He and his men were attacking a young lass in the forest. We stopped them, but there's more to it than just a random assault."

Alisdair's eyes narrowed as he studied the captive. "Speak then, ye filth. What do the Stewarts plot against us?"

The man glared up at the McClain laird, defiance warring with fear in his expression. "They plan to take these lands, to crush the Highland clans beneath their boot. They've infiltrated yer ranks, turned yer own people against ye. Ye'll never see it coming until it's too late."

A murmur of unease rippled through the gathered crowd. Alisdair raised a hand for silence, his gaze never leaving the prisoner. "And what part did ye play in this scheme?"

"I was just following orders," the man said, a hint of desperation creeping into his voice. "They told us to sow discord, to make the clans mistrust each other. To weaken ye from within so ye'd be easy pickings when the time came."

Alisdair's jaw clenched, his eyes flashing with barely contained fury. "And ye thought ye could attack an innocent lass as part of this plan? Ye're naught but a coward and a fool."

He turned to Moira and Brodie, his expression grim. "Take him to the dungeons. We'll question him further, see what else he knows of the Stewarts' treachery."

As the prisoner was dragged away, Alisdair addressed the gathered crowd. "Let this be a warning to us all. The Stewarts seek to divide us, to turn us against each other. We must stand united, now...more than ever, if we are to weather this storm."

Moira stepped forward, her voice ringing out clear and strong. "Aye, we must stand as one! The Stewarts think they can break us, but they underestimate the strength and spirit of the Highland clans. We've faced threats before and emerged victorious. This time will be no different."

A cheer went up from the assembled crowd, fists raised in solidarity. Moira felt a swell of pride at their resilience and determination. They would not be cowed by the Stewarts' schemes.

As the gathering dispersed, Moira turned to Brodie, her expression somber. "We must be vigilant, Brodie. The Stewarts have eyes and ears everywhere. We cannot trust anyone outside our closest allies."

Brodie nodded. "Shall we go and retrieve our stag, and see if we can get another?"

Moira smiled, nodding. "That sounds like exactly what I want to do."

❦

CHAPTER TWELVE

MOIRA PACED THE chamber, her red hair a dim ember in the darkness. The walls of McAfee Keep loomed with foreboding intensity.

Clyde Stewart's treachery ignited an urgency within her. A single misstep could disrupt the precarious balance of power among Highland clans. Drawing a deep breath, Moira steeled herself for action.

The door creaked open, admitting Brodie. His lean figure exuded steadfast resolve, and his deep brown eyes brought calm to her chaotic thoughts.

"Moira," he greeted solemnly.

"Brodie," she responded, "a serpent lies among us." It was the only thing she'd been able to think about all day.

His expression revealed readiness to confront any threat. "Speak plainly."

"That man claims Clyde Stewart planted spies among our kin. What say ye?"

Brodie considered the claim. "Such tactics are not beyond Clyde's cunning," he acknowledged tensely. "We must consider the possibility."

Brodie paced by the hearth, embers casting a weak glow across the room. "Identifying Clyde's loyalists without alerting them is like trying to catch smoke," he said, facing Moira.

"We must weave our own web, Brodie," Moira replied, stepping closer. "We'll tell a tale as a decoy for traitors."

"Feign weakness in our defenses?" Brodie considered the plan, nodding. "Yes, a controlled falsehood could draw them out. We'll be cunning." He smiled at her. "It is good I married a woman with a devious side."

"And I am happy to marry a man who appreciates me," Moira said with a grin. Then her face grew serious, and he knew she was thinking about their problem again. "We take two men at a time. Feed them each a different lie. Their allegiance will be revealed when word reaches the Stewarts."

"Agreed." Brodie's tone was resolute. "I shall be the one to spread this false intelligence."

"And I will keep watch from above," Moira declared, looking toward the courtyard below.

Their plan was a dance of shadows and subterfuge amid uncertain loyalties. Failure would come at a steep price, but they crafted their scheme tight enough to ensnare even the cleverest of spies.

"Then it's settled," Brodie said, his gaze meeting Moira's. They shared an unspoken oath to protect their clans at any cost—their fates now irrevocably intertwined within this conspiracy.

Brodie navigated the dim corridors of McAfee Keep, with Moira's steps a whisper behind him. They passed tapestries depicting tales of valor and hardship, their colors muted in the scarce light. The McAfees descended from the Picts, and they were a storied and ancient clan.

The library door creaked open to reveal walls lined with weathered tomes and parchment scrolls. Brodie moved directly to a hefty oak table and unfurled a map, its edges worn from countless strategists' touch. It was the very same map the lairds had used as they'd planned their defenses.

"Here," he pointed to several lines on the map. "These are the paths our traitor might take to carry word to the Stewarts."

Moira leaned over the map, studying the routes etched with precision, each line a possible thread of betrayal weaving through their lands. The paths ran like scars across her beloved Highlands—a land tainted by treachery.

Her gaze lifted to meet Brodie's unwavering eyes, seeking his quiet strength. The air between them grew dense with gravity as they shared an unyielding resolve without spoken words.

In Brodie's gaze, Moira found support—a testament to their bond formed by a common cause. Together, they stood on the precipice of danger, their destiny as uncharted as the maps before them.

The musty scent of old leather and ink enveloped the room as they considered each route on the map, aware that their fate hinged upon these ink-stained trails.

Brodie pushed back his chair, the scrape of wood barely audible in the silence that had engulfed them. He stood beside Moira, his hand a gentle weight on her shoulder.

"Ye have me word, Moira," he said with resolve. "We'll guard our clans with everything we possess."

Gratitude laced her voice as she replied, "Thank ye, Brodie. I trust yer word."

They leaned over the map, pointing out potential hiding spots for traitors or secret messages.

"Here and here," Moira murmured. "Anyone lingering without cause would be suspect."

Their voices filled the room with strategy and foresight. Brodie mapped out their chessboard of defenses while Moira breathed life into their plans.

"Perhaps a rumor of weakened walls, or an unguarded post," Brodie suggested.

"Let them believe they have the upper hand," Moira said, determination in her gaze. "We'll set a trap of our own making and watch as they reveal themselves."

He looked up from the map, admiration flickering in his eyes. "Yer courage is what will lead us through this night. Ye are an amazing lass."

"Then let us hope it burns bright enough to blind our enemies," she answered.

Together, they prepared to weave a web of deception—one that would ensnare those who threatened their kin and lands.

Flickering candlelight cast shadows on the chamber walls as Moira paced. "We must gather more insights," she said, stopping before Brodie. "Trusted kin can help us uncover Clyde's pawns."

Brodie nodded, his eyes meeting hers. "We'll need to be subtle. If word spreads, it might spook them into hiding or hasten their plans."

"Discretion will be our ally," Moira agreed, approaching the table where a map lay unfurled. "First, secure McAfee Keep."

Brodie leaned over the map beside her, studying the lines marking forests and glens. "The watchtowers—"

"Double the guard and have our best archers rotate shifts," Moira interjected. "No one approaches unseen."

"Traps along the routes as well," Brodie added, pointing to narrow passes snaking through the terrain.

With determination in their eyes, they fortified not just the stones of their keep but the spirit of their people.

Brodie's fingers traced a river on the map before stopping at a fork. "Clyde is cunning, but predictable," he murmured. "He'll expect us to fortify the main road into the keep, but it's the hidden trails he might use to his advantage."

Moira's brow furrowed as she considered his words. "Then we shall turn his predictability against him," she declared. "We will make him believe our focus lies elsewhere while we secure every possible approach."

"Exactly," Brodie replied, a subtle smile playing at the corners of his mouth. "We'll set false camps along the obvious routes, giving the impression of vulnerability where there is none."

"Let's walk the grounds at dawn," she proposed, "to survey the land and decide where these decoys will be most convincing."

"Agreed," Brodie responded, rising to his feet.

As they stood side by side, a silence settled over them—a shared moment of determination. Theirs was a union forged by mutual respect and an unspoken oath to protect their people.

"Whatever comes," Moira said quietly, her hand brushing against Brodie's, "we face it together."

"Absolutely," he said, his dark eyes reflecting the solemn vow.

Moira studied the map, its intricate lines and symbols foreshadowing their struggle. She looked up at Brodie, the library hearth casting shadows upon his face. "Brodie," she began earnestly, "thank ye for standing with me."

He met her gaze, his eyes conveying deep promises. "No need to thank me, Moira," he replied confidently. "You are the heart of yer clan—fierce, unyielding. Together, we'll weather the storm."

Her lips curved into a small smile as her fears lessened in his presence—a man of quiet strength.

With a nod, she stepped away from the table, smoothing her tartan skirts. "We should set forth then," she declared resolutely.

Brodie tucked the map under his arm and joined her by the door. They shared a meaningful glance before stepping into the dark corridor together. The air buzzed with the Highlands' ancient energy as they ventured into the night.

As they left the warmth of the library behind, Moira and Brodie faced whatever lay ahead—their alliance guiding their clans through impending challenges.

The stone corridors of McAfee Keep echoed with Moira's and Brodie's footsteps. Candles cast a glow on their faces as they entered their private chamber. The door closed, sealing them away from looming threats.

Moira leaned against the oak door, her eyes meeting Brodie's with intensity. Their fingers intertwined, finding comfort in their connection.

"Tomorrow, we set our destiny," she whispered, moving gracefully toward the hearth.

"Aye," Brodie replied, joining her by the fire. "With your sisters and me brothers, we'll trap Clyde Stewart."

Their plan relied on deception and strategy, relying on their siblings' unique skills. Moira mused aloud about the need for precision as she watched shadows play across Brodie's face.

"One misstep could lead to ruin."

Brodie brushed a strand of hair from Moira's cheek. "Precision is our ally, and discretion our shield," he assured her. "We have planned for every contingency."

In the silence that followed, they savored a rare moment of stillness before the storm.

Moira's determination returned. "We should rest," she said, her urgency contradicting the need for sleep. "We will need our strength come morning."

Brodie agreed. "No matter what tomorrow brings, I stand with you."

Her heart swelled, recognizing him as more than an ally but a symbol of courage and hope.

"Let us face the dawn as one," Moira declared.

They prepared for bed in silence, contemplating the upcoming day. Only the hearth's crackling and the wind's whispers accompanied them.

In the darkness, Brodie's hand found Moira's, their silent vow resonating. Together, they drifted into fitful sleep, dreaming of a future won by their clans' unity.

CHAPTER THIRTEEN

AT DAWN, MOIRA'S red hair stood out in the gray morning as she leaned forward, scanning the courtyard below.

"Ye ken what must be done, Lachlan," she said to her brother-in-law. "We cannae let the traitors slip through our grasp."

Lachlan nodded, determination etched on his face. "Aye, I'll watch 'em close." His hand went to the dirk at his belt.

Moira turned away—no time for further assurances.

Brodie spoke with Alisdair, his deep brown eyes intense. "Speak naught of the true purpose," he instructed. "Let them believe ye seek their counsel on mundane matters. We need to see who flinches when the wind shifts."

"Understood," Alisdair responded, calm and steady.

Brodie descended toward the gathering soldiers, calling them aside two at a time. From the parapet, Moira observed the interactions, Fiona beside her.

"Can ye tell anything from up here?" Fiona asked.

"Only that Brodie is skilled at this game," Moira replied. "We must trust in his methods." While she knew her husband was lying as he talked to the men, there were no signs of it. A lesser woman may become worried that he was a skilled liar and could tell her anything. Instead, Moira chose to be proud of her husband's penchant for deception. Why would she worry that he would lie to her, when she knew he was a trustworthy man? He lied for the safety of his clan. Nothing less.

Before Fiona could respond, Ailis called up from lower down

the wall. "Moira! I need yer eyes on this."

"Go," Fiona urged.

With Moira joining Ailis, she glanced back toward Brodie and the men one last time. As they paced alongside each other, her gaze never left the soldiers below, searching for any hint of treachery threatening their clans.

"Anything amiss?" Ailis questioned urgently.

"Naught yet," Moira replied, "but if serpents hide in the heather, we'll find them." Her words were a vow, spoken with a conviction rooted in her clan's survival. No one would hurt any of the allied clans if she could help it.

The Highland breeze whipped Moira's woolen cloak around her as she stood atop the parapet, scanning the stone and scrub below. Behind her, the McAfee Keep cast protective shadows. Among the men below, one figure caught her attention—Lucas Gordon striding toward Sinclair lands. Moira felt shock and betrayal with each step he took. She had been certain he was on their side, and she felt sick to her stomach at the idea he was betraying them.

"Lucas..." she whispered, gripping the cold stone. Time passed—an hour or more—as suspicion and uncertainty consumed her thoughts. Then, Lucas reemerged alongside two men loyal to the Sinclairs—Bearnard and Horas, who had tried to keep the two younger McAfee sisters from marrying the McClain brothers. Not that it had worked. With a muttered curse, Moira descended the turret stairs, each step fueling her resolve against treachery.

At the training field, Brodie stood firm while Lucas and his companions faced him without weapons but full of defiance. Acknowledging Moira with a nod, Brodie listened as she accused Lucas of playing a game.

"Naught but the game of survival," Lucas replied, chin lifted in defiance. "We come to stand with ye against the Stewarts. The men are all losing their loyalty as they see Clyde Stewart hurt others for nothing but the pleasure of it."

Brodie's tone revealed skepticism as he questioned their sudden pledge of loyalty, which Bearnard and Horas tried to defend by citing losses to the Stewart's greed and choosing kin over foes.

Moira's gaze met Brodie's, the men's assurances offering no comfort. Their claims hung heavy, as tenuous as the distant mist-shrouded peaks. Silence fell, a contemplative veil, as they searched for truth in the tangled web of alliances and loyalties.

THE GREAT HALL of McAfee Keep hummed with conversation as Moira entered with her sisters, Ailis and Fiona. They caught the attention of Brodie, Lachlan, and Alisdair by the hearth, while Lucas Gordon and his companions—Bearnard and Horas—awaited.

"Ye've come to pledge yer allegiance away from the Stewarts," Moira said, her voice echoing across the hall.

"Aye," Bearnard replied wearily. "The cost has been too dear. We yearn for peace, not endless bloodshed."

Ailis studied the suitors before responding. "Peace is a noble pursuit, but trust, once broken, is not easily mended."

Fiona observed the men intently, offering support through her silent presence.

Afterward, as the suitors were led away, Brodie pulled Moira into a dimly lit antechamber. The torchlight flickered on his face as he spoke, "Before ye saw Lucas take leave toward Sinclair lands, I hadn't shared our strategy with him."

Moira searched his expression. "Then why would he fetch his comrades before hearing our plans?"

Brodie frowned. "His actions suggest he knew more than he ought or suspected enough to seek reinforcements."

"Or allies," Moira considered. "Either way, it's a dangerous game—a game we must unravel to protect our kin and our future."

"Agreed," Brodie said. "We must tread carefully. The fate of the Highlands may well rest on what we uncover." He shook his head. "I want to trust him, but I dinnae ken why. He made things very difficult when we were on Gordon land."

Moira stepped back into the hall, the responsibility heavy but her posture unbowed. Her eyes held determination as she faced adversity for the safety of her family and the freedom of the Highlands.

THE HIGHLAND BREEZE carried the scent of pine as Moira nocked an arrow, her gaze locked onto a deer. Beside her, Brodie crouched low, weapon ready. Lucas, Bearnard, and Horas hid in the underbrush.

"Steady," Brodie whispered.

She released her breath slowly and let the arrow fly. A clean kill. The forest echoed with twangs of bows and thuds of falling game.

As they collected their bounty, Moira strained to hear whispered conspiracies or plans but heard only admiration for precise shots and discussions about loyalty.

"Choosing the right side is like choosing the right moment for the kill," Lucas said as he dragged a buck by its antlers. "Too soon or too late makes all the difference."

Brodie met Moira's gaze, communicating shared uncertainty without words.

By sunset, they had four deer between them. Granny McAfee greeted them at the gate. "Ah, what a sight! The larder will be full tonight." She gestured for servants to relieve them of their burdens. "I fear we will need to keep hunting, but I worry for those who are doing the hunting. What will happen if the Stewart alliance finds ye?"

"I dinnae believe the Stewarts are watching for hunters,"

Lucas added, nodding respectfully toward them.

Granny praised them but later leaned closer to Moira with a solemn expression. "Be wary, child. Trust must be earned. Watch 'em close."

"I'll not forget," Moira said.

As Granny shuffled away, Moira turned back to Brodie, who was studying their guests with vigilance. "Granny wants us to watch them closely."

"Let us be so," Brodie replied. Together, they would protect their clans and land.

THE FIRE CRACKLED in the great hall as the assembled lairds listened intently. Moira and her sisters stood close to the wall, their breath fogging in the chill air, watching the proceedings.

"Speak yer piece," Duncan McAfee commanded, his voice rumbling.

The men pled their case, speaking of losses and hearts turned sour against ruthless ambitions. Hours passed, whispers flitted among the sisters as the wind howled its lonely song outside the stone walls.

The heavy oak doors groaned open, and Duncan emerged at the forefront, carrying the weight of their decision. The sisters clustered around him, eyes expectant.

"I believe them," he said, his gaze meeting Moira's. "Their tales bear truth, and their desire to stand with us rings clear."

Relief filled Moira; Ailis and Fiona exhaled in unison. "Then we'll welcome them as allies," Moira said with conviction. "Together, we'll face whatever trials may come." But in the back of her mind, she promised herself and the entire alliance that she would still keep an eye on the three men. She wasn't sure she could trust them completely.

Duncan nodded his approval, trust given was a fragile gift

that could forge strong bonds in shared purpose.

HOOFBEATS AND MURMURS carried on the crisp air as Moira stood upon the parapet, her red hair tousled by the breeze. Across the land, she spotted weary figures emerging from Sinclair territory—which had been taken over by the Stewart alliance.

"More have come," Moira called to Brodie in the courtyard below.

"Let us greet our new brothers in arms," he replied.

Together, they descended into the castle heart where Ailis and Fiona joined them, forming a unified trio against their ancestral stronghold. The newcomers halted at the gates, dismounting tensely. Duncan addressed them authoritatively.

"Ye come seeking refuge or purpose?"

"Both, Laird McAfee," the foremost man answered earnestly. "We cannae follow a man like Stewart."

Duncan declared, "Then ye are welcome to join us, as long as we are united against tyranny that threatens our beloved Highlands."

A murmur of shared determination rippled through the crowd. Men began intermingling, exchanging names and tales of disillusionment with Stewart. The sounds of camaraderie mingled with sword clashes as training resumed.

"Looks like our plan is taking root," Ailis said, observing the men band together.

Moira allowed a small smile. "It'll take more than Clyde Stewart to tear it asunder."

MOIRA SURVEYED THE Highlands from McAfee Keep's parapet, her breath visible in the brisk morning air. As dawn banished shadows, figures emerged from Stewart territory—men abandoning the Stewart for a new allegiance.

Her hands gripped the rough stone battlements, resolve steeling within her. Each newcomer symbolized the waning power of the Stewart clan. Not one returned to their former laird. Instead, they joined the McAfees.

"Another group arrives," Fiona said excitedly.

"Aye," Moira replied, a determined smile on her face. "This bodes well for us." She couldn't help the small bit of skepticism she felt toward the men who were joining, but she was determined not to let it show.

Brodie and Lachlan welcomed the arrivals at the gates. After brief exchanges, the newcomers were guided to the great hall where they would learn about joining the McAfee cause.

"Stewart must be gnashing his teeth in frustration," Ailis remarked with satisfaction. "His power wanes while ours grows—with his own soldiers."

"We must remain vigilant," Moira warned. "But our hope strengthens with each warrior who forsakes him."

"Hope is good," Fiona agreed, "but steel wins wars."

"Then it's fortunate we have both."

Descending from the parapet, Moira moved among her allies. They trained and planned, conviction growing that they would thwart Stewart's ambitions.

As twilight transformed into night, Moira stood atop her keep's walls once more, contemplating all who fought within these lands.

"Today, no man crossed back to Stewart," she said softly to herself, her words carried away by the wind. "Tomorrow, we will stand even stronger." Confidence surged within her, mingling with the pride of her clan and the love for her people. In that quiet moment, Moira felt the tides of destiny shifting, and she knew they were ready for whatever challenges lay ahead—as long as the soldiers stayed loyal.

CHAPTER FOURTEEN

I N THE PALE dawn, Duncan stood atop McAfee Keep's parapets, his gaze fixed on the misty Highlands. A messenger was sent at first light with a missive for Clyde Stewart—a call for peace. It was an attempt to stop the violence consuming their lands.

If Stewart could be convinced that his plans were not what was best for the Highlands, perhaps they could end things peacefully. He wasn't willing to lose another soldier from the alliance without at least trying.

Duncan watched as the emissary disappeared into Sinclair lands. This meeting wasn't just about stopping a war. It was about securing his clan's future.

As the sun cast shadows on the keep, distant hooves announced Clyde Stewart's arrival. Duncan descended from the battlements, determined with each step.

Clyde and his entourage rode through the open gates, their eyes watchful beneath gleaming helmets. The Stewart obviously expected this to be a way to separate him from his forces, but Duncan would never betray an alliance.

"Welcome, Clyde Stewart," Duncan said, masking his tension with calm authority. "We gather here for concord."

Clyde dismounted, his presence commanding even in silence. He examined the assembled clansmen before meeting Duncan's gaze.

"Peace is precious, Duncan McAfee," Clyde started, smooth yet dangerous. "If there is deceit or me safety is compromised…"

The unspoken threat lingered.

"The thistle will become a storm of thorns," Clyde finished, his guards subtly reinforcing the warning.

Duncan nodded, recognizing the stakes. "Your safety is assured, as is ours. The Highlands have bled enough. I would never betray an attempt at peace, and neither would any of the other lairds who have joined us."

"Aye," Clyde replied. "Let us speak of peace."

Entering the great hall where their clans' futures would be determined by words instead of swords, Duncan led unwaveringly, bracing for the battle of destinies ahead.

The chamber air, normally rich with peat and pine, was heavy with tension. Clan representatives huddled in clusters, their murmurs echoing off the stone walls. Wariness marked their faces as they pursued the chance for peace.

Moira observed from beneath an ancient tapestry, her fingers tapping impatiently against her thigh. A cautious optimism emerged among the attendees.

The oaken doors groaned open as Clyde Stewart entered. His imposing figure dominated the doorway, the light casting an eerie halo around him. Silence filled the room as he walked in, his guards trailing behind like wolves stalking their alpha.

"Good morrow to ye all," Clyde said, his deep voice cutting through the silence. A smile played on his lips but did not reach his watchful eyes.

"Let us speak frankly," he continued, "for we are all weary of bloodshed." His words hung in the air like a binding spell between the clans.

Moira scrutinized each phrase for hidden motives. Even as Clyde spoke of unity, she detected power struggles beneath the surface. The rumors about his ambitions were well-known, and Moira knew she must keep a careful eye on him.

"Peace is the foundation upon which prosperity is built," Clyde declared, drawing his audience into a vision of the future with himself at its center.

The clan representatives nodded with varying enthusiasm, hoping that this meeting might bring change. Moira remained steadfast, aware that while words could form alliances, only vigilance would maintain them.

A hushed tension filled the negotiation hall, as Moira's unwavering gaze locked onto Clyde Stewart. Without warning, the sound of clashing swords and distant shouts pierced the air.

"Betrayal!" The cry echoed from outside.

Chaos ensued among the representatives. Clyde's fleeting look of satisfaction did not go unnoticed by Moira. Her hand instinctively gripped her sword. Assessing exits and threats, she barked orders to her warriors, who formed a protective ring around their leaders.

As the assault drew nearer, Moira's training took over; her mind focused on defending both her clan and the fragile unity they dared to dream of. Amid betrayal and battle, she stood strong and ready.

Gasping for breath amid the dust and blood, Moira kept her sword steady. Brodie called to her, his presence a beacon in the chaos. Their gazes locked in a silent exchange burdened with doubt. Could she trust him and his clan? The Stewarts' treachery served as a painful reminder of how fragile alliances could be.

Brodie's steady gaze held a resolve mirroring her own, inviting Moira to join him. Their families' destinies were intertwined by shared blood and battles.

The sounds of conflict intensified, bringing her back to the present. A Stewart raider lunged, and she parried instinctively. As she dispatched her opponent with a decisive blow, her hesitation vanished.

Facing Brodie once more, Moira nodded sharply, her fiery hair wild in the chaos. Without needing words, she stepped into the fray at his side. Their swords worked together in deadly harmony against the onslaught.

Together, they fought relentlessly amid discord. Each of Moira's moves was echoed by Brodie's own, their rhythm honed by shared purpose.

Having chosen to fight alongside Brodie in this crucible of battle, it was a decision made for all future possibilities—if they could survive today.

As their blades responded to each lunge from Clan Stewart warriors in a fluid dance of sharp edges and swift parries, the air reeked of iron and earth. "Left flank!" Brodie commanded. Moira pivoted on instinct.

Their adversaries were relentless like a dark wave, yet Moira met each surge with tenacity. Meanwhile, Brodie served as the anchor amid the stormy combat, anticipating enemy moves as if reading currents in Highland lochs.

An unspoken trust between them had been forged through countless skirmishes. Amidst betrayal, that trust was their most potent weapon.

The clamor of battle intensified, warriors' cries merging with the metallic clash of swords. The ground trembled under the brutal force, highlighting the urgency of their situation.

Moira's sword pierced tartan and flesh with precision. Chaos swirled around her, while inner clarity guided her blade. McAfee by birth, she defended her ancestral land fiercely.

Brodie, a lethal shadow, infiltrated enemy lines seamlessly. As a duo, they exemplified Highland wrath and cunning—unrelenting as the mountains sheltering their clans.

In the uproar, Moira sensed the fight's balance shifting like the subtle Highland seasons. With Brodie at her side, each breath fueled their momentum toward an uncertain dawn.

From her clan's stronghold, Moira observed Clyde Stewart directing the chaos below. He moved with certainty, his voice slicing through the noise.

"Forward!" Clyde commanded, and his warriors surged with newfound ferocity.

Below, the McClain and McAfee clans united against the invaders. Lachlan McClain's broadsword swung precisely, his rallying cries driving his kin to stand firm. The ground shook beneath their feet, steel clashes echoing off McAfee Keep's stones.

"Stand fast!" roared Lachlan, his eyes burning with unyielding leadership.

Ailis fought fiercely among her comrades, dark hair a wild tempest as she parried and thrust with determination. Her green eyes glowed defiantly, embodying the untamed spirit of her people.

Bound by unity, the clans pushed back against despair and became an impenetrable wall against each Stewart advance. Their unwavering allegiance fueled their intent: this land was theirs, and together they would defy the Stewart's ambitions.

The air carried the scent of blood and disturbed earth as Moira's blade sliced through the air. She moved gracefully, her red hair whipping around her like a war-banner. In the uneven Highland terrain, she danced to the rhythm of battle.

"Moira!" Brodie called, his face smeared with dirt and determination. As their eyes met, a silent pact was forged.

Together, they stood side by side, synchronizing their movements in combat. Moira dispatched a Stewart attacker with ruthless efficiency, earning cheers from nearby McAfee clansmen.

Brodie warned Moira of an approaching soldier, allowing her to counter and disarm him. "Thank ye," she grunted, acknowledging their seamless synergy built on hours of practice together.

The battle intensified as the sky darkened, foreshadowing an upcoming storm. The Stewarts pressed harder, their ferocity intensifying alongside the impending tempest. Moira sensed the changing tide but remained resolute even when Brodie was thrown to the ground by a surprise attack.

"Stand up, Brodie!" she commanded, fighting her way to his side and pulling him back up.

Their bond reinforced them as they fought off enemies in unison, turning the onslaught into a dance of defiance against overwhelming odds.

"Ye are a force of nature, Moira," Brodie said breathlessly.

"And ye, Brodie, are the rock upon which they break," she

replied with a fierce grin.

Together, they charged back into battle with renewed determination.

Steel clashed around Moira as she parried a thrust, the sound of her blade ringing through the Highland air. Focused and unwavering, she seized an opening in the enemy's defense and struck down her attacker.

"Push them back!" Her voice rang out over the battlefield.

Her call ignited courage in her comrades, their spirits lifted by her presence. The McAfees and McClains—along with all their allied clans—roared and surged forward, Moira at the forefront with lethal grace.

Brodie fought beside her, his keen mind guiding them. Their eyes met before they charged together, cleaving through Stewart lines.

The Stewarts faltered, their ranks crumbling under the united clans' assault. Cries of retreat spread until the attackers withdrew, leaving behind the wounded and fallen.

Exhausted, Moira observed the retreating foes as smoke billowed from the earth. "Survived," she remarked to Brodie. "We held firm for our kin and land."

"At what cost?" he questioned solemnly.

"Too high a price," she conceded. "But we thwarted their ambitions."

Moira whispered a vow to the winds: "Let them remember this day. Let them know the Highlands' heart beats strong within us."

"Indeed," Brodie replied steadily, gripping her hand. "And let us not forget who we are, and what we fight for."

The night enveloped the warriors as they remained steadfast, guardians of a bloodstained legacy.

MOIRA STOOD AMONG the remnants of war, her breath misting in the chill Highland air. The scent of blood mingled with heather and earth—a reminder of freedom's cost.

She released a long breath, watching it dissipate into the evening sky, carrying away some of the day's weight. Her red hair was matted with sweat and grime, framing a face etched with fatigue and contemplation. Gripping her sword, its blade nicked and stained, she could only think of Brodie's words: "We are the shield of our people." Now alone, she reflected on the trust placed in his strategic mind.

"Moira," someone called from behind.

She turned to face Brodie as he approached, his own expression marked by leadership and survival. As their eyes met, she recognized the depth of their connection—allies in arms and keepers of secrets beneath the armor. She wanted to run into his arms, but she stayed where she was. She knew they would both appear stronger that way.

"Today, ye led with courage fierce enough to kindle the spirits of our ancestors," Brodie said softly yet firmly.

Moira nodded wearily. "And ye with ancient wisdom," she replied, respect resonating in her tone.

In the dim light, she studied the man who had proven himself both comrade and confidant, as well as loving husband. Their alliance forged in adversity bound their fates together beyond mere politics—an unyielding pursuit of peace that seemed elusive like the mist over the glens.

A wave of resolve cleansed her doubt. She had chosen to trust Brodie, and that choice remained steadfast despite the unknown dangers ahead.

"Tomorrow, we begin anew," she declared. "For our clans, for the Highlands."

"Indeed," Brodie agreed, extending his hand. "Together, we navigate this storm. Our unity will guide our people through it."

Their fingers intertwined, sealing their shared purpose as symbols of hope for the Highland folk.

Night fell upon the scarred battlefield with Moira and Brodie standing firm, determination burning within them. The challenges of tomorrow awaited, but they would face them together—resilient and united in Highland destiny.

⁂

CHAPTER FIFTEEN

MOIRA WRAPPED A linen bandage around the soldier's arm, her concentration unbroken by the infirmary's activity. The muffled sounds of swords colliding outside called to her, but she remained focused on her role. As much as she wanted to be outside training with the men, she knew it was her duty to take care of the injured.

"Steady now," she said, grounding the young man before her. "This will hold until ye can fight again." Gentleness didn't seem to be in her nature, but she worked hard to make sure the soldiers felt a soft touch as she treated them.

She moved from cot to cot, devoted to those who fought for their lands and people. As she stopped by each cot, she talked softly to the soldier in it, thanking them for all they had done to help the Highlander's cause.

Outside, Brodie McClain observed the sparring warriors with sharp focus. He corrected stances and offered advice, his quiet strength setting the training rhythm. His attention never wavered from each injury, no matter how minor. Each man was as important to him as their cause. He couldn't fathom losing even one of them.

"Off to the infirmary," he ordered one man with an unnoticed cut. "We can't lose ye to infection."

The warrior hesitated, pride battling sense, but Brodie's firm look sent him to seek medical care.

Inside the infirmary, Moira readied herself for more healing.

Stray strands of red hair framed her focused expression as she worked tirelessly for her clan's survival.

Throughout the day, Brodie continued his watchful guidance among his men. As Highlanders born from rugged mountains and strife, they stood strong together, ready for whatever lay ahead.

ELSA STOOD BY Bryson's cot, eyes fixed on the bloodstained bandage around his thigh. She adjusted the cloth on his feverish forehead with trembling hands.

"Stay with me, Bryson," she whispered, her voice blending in with the infirmary's background noise. Her worried expression betrayed her concern for any sign of pain from him.

Throughout long hours, Elsa stayed by his side, tensing at each delirious moan and flinch. Time blurred together as her vigil continued. She cared for him diligently, offering water and comfort as he slowly healed. She wished there was a way to heal him instantly, but she knew better. His life was hanging by a thread, and it was up to her to see to his comfort.

Bryson's breaths became steadier, his moments of clarity more frequent. Color returned to his cheeks as the strength in his handgrip grew. Elsa smiled at his signs of recovery, grateful he was finally getting stronger.

Finally, Bryson's fever subsided, leaving a weakened man alive. As she observed his peaceful slumber, relief washed over Elsa. She silently thanked God for sparing her betrothed, vowing to remain by his side forever. As Bryson healed, Elsa's world regained a sense of stability and she could breathe freely once more.

AMID THE SNOW-CLAD hills, a lone peregrine falcon pursued its prey. Moira's gaze followed its hunt, as Brodie readied his bow nearby. She tolerated her days in the infirmary because she knew her nights beside Brodie were her reward for a job well done.

"We are gatherers of strength for what lies ahead," Brodie said, releasing the arrow. It found its mark as more clansmen crested the ridge, their multi-patterned tartans displaying their clan's identity, but not stopping the men from joining together as one large fighting force.

"Every clan united to save our way of life," Moira observed.

"Indeed, a confederation of wills," Brodie agreed, gathering the hare.

Moira appreciated the respite from the infirmary. "Thank ye, Brodie."

"Ye belong here, among the thistle and oak," he replied, smiling respectfully.

They collected their quarry for the feast that night, where tales of valor and alliances would be shared. Distant bagpipes marked the gathering of clans and the strengthening of their army.

"We need to present a united front to all the clans coming to join us. Perhaps we try introducing the people from different clans today and see if we can get them to start sitting wherever they wish without worrying about what clan they come from," Brodie suggested.

"Tonight, we celebrate not only the catch but a new chapter for our people," Moira agreed. Together, they returned to the keep on a path forged by camaraderie and unwavering belief in the Highlands' resilience.

Brodie's arrow struck the stag in the clearing, and Moira's arrow quickly followed. The successful hunt left several deer lined up as proof of their skill. Thankfully, they hadn't come out to hunt alone, and the men who had joined them would help bring the game back to the keep.

Dressing the kills, Moira's hands moved deftly, but her thoughts lingered on recent events. "The Stewarts' men—Lucas,

Bearnard, and Horas—turned the battle, didn't they?" It was still hard for her to believe the three men who had been her and her sister's constant annoyances were now on the same side as Moira and her clan.

Brodie sheathed his blade. "Aye," he confirmed, his brown eyes intent. "Their courage ignited something fierce in others."

"Others?" Moira asked.

"More men have joined our ranks since then," Brodie explained. "Those three became a symbol—a beacon for the brave or repentant. We have had a steady stream of men leaving the Stewart's rule and coming to our side since."

Moira studied the horizon where long shadows stretched over the Highlands. "Fearlessness breeds followers," she murmured. "I would have thought those three would have been the last to turn."

"Aye," Brodie agreed, picking up one end of a deer. "Let's get these back for tonight's feast."

"Feast?" Moira echoed, lifting the other end.

"To celebrate new swords pledged to our cause and strengthen camaraderie among the clans."

They made their way through the dense woods, carrying more than just their quarry—their hopes and fears for their homeland rested deep within their hearts.

MOIRA ADJUSTED THE shawl on Granny McAfee's shoulders, observing Lucas, Bearnard, and Horas. Their stance revealed newfound allegiance as they conversed with Brodie.

"Those lads have a look of redemption," Granny remarked, following Moira's gaze. "They are truly with us."

"Aye, Granny. And perhaps a chance for new beginnings," Moira agreed, considering introductions to recent widows who deserved companions of equal valor. She knew at least Lucas was looking for a woman after the way he'd been with Elsa.

In the great hall, the McAfee stronghold buzzed with anticipation as clansfolk gathered amid the aromas of roasting venison and peat smoke. Moira mingled with the assembly, her spirit lifting with each shared laughter and greeting. It truly felt as if their battle was already won.

Brodie raised his cup above the crowd, praising the unity of warriors from different clans. The call of "Slàinte mhath!" filled the air as cups clashed in salute.

The feast symbolized their strength and enduring spirit. Moira thought, "Tonight, we are all one clan, united by freedom and fellowship."

As night fell, laughter resonated against stone walls, and fiddle and pipe melodies intertwined. Amid the festivities, Moira sensed the Highlands' future taking shape through alliances, dances, and toasts.

In the feast's lively atmosphere, Moira approached Lucas, Bearnard, and Horas with determination. Her red hair gleamed under torchlight as they turned to face her, both curious and respectful.

"Lucas, Bearnard, Horas," Moira said, confidently gesturing toward a small gathering of women. "Meet Elspeth, Mairi, and Aileen Sinclair."

As introductions were exchanged and tentative smiles shared, Moira observed their interactions. Elspeth relaxed under Lucas' confidence, Mairi laughed with Bearnard amidst the festive noise, and Aileen attentively listened to Horas' passionate words.

A feeling of hope grew within Moira for new beginnings and healing across clan lines. The Sinclair women deserved peace after enduring so much turmoil, many of them losing both sons and husbands.

She wanted to stand near them and make sure the men were considerate and kind to the women, but she was one of the hostesses of the clan, and she needed to be spending time with all she could.

Moira turned her attention back to the gathering, making her way through the lively crowd. She greeted familiar faces and welcomed newcomers, her presence a beacon of strength and unity. As she moved, her thoughts drifted to the challenges that lay ahead—the battles to be fought, the alliances to be forged, and the wounds to be healed.

Among the sea of tartans and glowing faces, Moira caught sight of Brodie. Their eyes met, a silent understanding passing between them. They both knew the importance of this moment, the significance of bringing together clans that had once been divided. With a nod, Brodie raised his cup in her direction, a gesture of respect and shared purpose.

As the night wore on, the festivities continued in full swing. The great hall reverberated with the sounds of laughter, music, and the clinking of cups.

As Moira continued mingling with the clansfolk, she overheard snippets of conversations and laughter that filled the hall. Suddenly, someone familiar called above the din.

"Moira! A moment, if ye please," came a deep voice from behind.

Turning around, Moira spotted Laird MacLeod approaching with a warm smile. "Laird MacLeod, it is a pleasure to see ye here tonight," Moira greeted him with respect.

"The pleasure is mine, Moira. Your hospitality knows no bounds," Laird MacLeod replied graciously. "I must say, this feast is a grand celebration of unity."

Moira nodded in agreement, scanning the hall. "Aye, it warms me heart to see so many clans coming together in harmony."

As they conversed about alliances and future endeavors, a sudden burst of laughter interrupted their discussion. Moira turned to see young Malcolm MacGregor regaling a group with a humorous tale.

"Laird MacLeod, have ye heard the one about the mischievous selkie who stole a fisherman's catch?" Malcolm's voice carried across the hall, drawing chuckles from those around him.

Laird MacLeod chuckled heartily. "Ah, Malcolm always knows how to lighten the mood with his stories."

Just then, Brodie joined their impromptu gathering, raising his cup in greeting. "To unity and friendship among clans," he toasted, capturing the attention of those nearby.

"To unity!" the surrounding voices echoed as cups were raised in unison.

Amid the revelry, Moira felt a surge of pride for her people and their unwavering spirit. She knew that together, they would face whatever challenges lay ahead with courage and determination.

As the night continued to unfold with music and camaraderie filling the air, Moira found herself surrounded by friends old and new. Each shared moment and exchanged smile only reinforced her belief in the power of unity and fellowship among their clans.

As the hour grew late, the festivities began to wind down. Guests bid their farewells, their spirits lifted by the night's camaraderie and the promise of a united future. Moira stood by the great hall's entrance, offering words of gratitude and encouragement to those who departed.

"Moira!" Brodie called, offering his hand for a dance. His eyes sparkled with mirth in tune with the music filling the hall.

Accepting Brodie's hand, Moira felt her exhaustion ease as they danced together. Noticing Lucas, Bearnard, and Horas still conversing with Elspeth, Mairi, and Aileen—laughter blending with the music—made her heart swell.

"Looks like yer plan is working," Brodie commented with a knowing look.

"Perhaps," she replied with a hopeful smile. "Tonight, anything feels possible."

United clans filled the great hall as they danced on into the night.

As the dance ended, Brodie enfolded Moira in his arms, their warmth a soothing embrace amid the surrounding laughter and conversation. Moira observed Lucas, Bearnard, and Horas with their respective partners across the hall, hoping this marked the beginning of lasting happiness for them all.

"Aye, lass," Brodie agreed softly. "If tonight's joy is any sign, they're well on their way."

In their room, cool air whispered through an open window as they undressed each other tenderly. Lying together, they kissed with a mixture of gentleness and passion.

"Everything is looking up," Moira breathed, thinking of Bryson's recovering health.

"Aye, it is," Brodie whispered back as they moved together in unity, two souls entwined in serenity and hope after weathering the storm.

CHAPTER SIXTEEN

DAWN PIERCED THE morning mists as Moira McAfee stood by the narrow window of the keep, her red hair loosely bound. She watched the sentries change shifts along the McAfee stronghold's stone walls.

"Last night's whispers spoke of unrest," she said, steady despite the distant thud of morning drums. "Soldiers weary of the Stewart's promises. We must act swiftly."

Brodie, leaning against a heavy oaken table, absorbed her words with his gaze fixed on her eyes that held strategic clarity.

"Ye suggest we entreat with these men?" he asked, admiration mixed with caution.

"Aye, under cover of darkness. A few could slip past Sinclair's watch and return with allies," Moira replied. She'd thought long and hard about the idea before broaching it with Brodie.

Brodie rubbed his chin thoughtfully. "I like the idea, but I'd not risk our soldiers. Me brothers and I, along with Kevin, will go. We ken the land and the peril."

Moira hesitated before nodding in agreement. "See to it that ye all return by first light. We cannae afford to lose any of ye." She walked into his arms, throwing hers around him. "And I cannae ken me life without ye."

"Ye have me word," Brodie assured her, kissing the top of her head. "I wouldnae leave ye alone to marry some other man."

As they planned, the air thrummed with anticipation. The stakes were high for their clans' future success in this venture.

With a final nod, Brodie left to gather his brothers and Kevin—loyal as Highland bedrock.

Together, they met with three men they'd come to trust who had already joined them after leaving the Stewart's command—Lucas, Bearnard, and Horas.

The three men proved invaluable as they explained the layout of the camp and provided a crude map of how things were. They gave good suggestions that would help keep the men alive.

"I believe we should go with ye, Brodie. Let's leave yer brothers here to lead the army if we cannae return for some reason," Lucas suggested.

Alisdair looked as if he wasn't sure if they could be allowed to go but finally he nodded. "Take no unnecessary risks!"

Brodie smiled. "We will be careful. Ye shouldnae risk yerselves. I agree with Lucas." Words he never thought he would say, but they were true.

Lucas grinned at Brodie. "We will come back alive. I promise ye that."

As the sun began to set, casting long shadows across the rugged Highland terrain, Brodie and his small band of trusted allies prepared to embark on their covert mission. They donned dark cloaks and secured their weapons, their faces set with grim determination.

Moira stood at the gate, her green eyes filled with a mixture of pride and concern as she watched them mount their horses. She knew the risks they were taking, but she also understood the importance of their task. If they could persuade more of the Stewart's men to join their cause, it could turn the tide of the impending conflict.

Brodie rode to her side, his voice low and reassuring. "Dinnae fash yerself, lass. We'll return afore ye ken it, wi' new allies at our backs."

Moira nodded, her hand resting on his arm. "Aye, I ken it. But promise me ye'll take nae unnecessary risks. Our people need ye, Brodie. I need ye."

With a final squeeze of her hand, Brodie turned his horse and led his band of loyal men out through the gates and into the gathering dusk. They rode in silence, the only sounds the muffled thud of hooves on the soft earth and the occasional snort of a horse.

As they neared the Stewart's encampment, they slowed their pace, relying on the shadows to conceal their approach. Lucas, Bearnard, and Horas guided them, pointing out the sentries and the best route to avoid detection.

They dismounted a safe distance away, tethering their horses in a sheltered copse. With a final nod, they crept forward on foot, their cloaks blending seamlessly with the night.

"Remember, nae unnecessary risks," Brodie muttered, his authoritative voice ensuring no challenge went unanswered.

With silent farewells, Brodie led his team into the night. They moved like shadows across the land, marked only by the rustle of heather and the distant hoot of an owl.

Hidden within an ancient copse of trees near the enemy camp, Brodie huddled with Lucas, Bearnard, and Horas. A dim lantern revealed a crude map on the forest floor.

"Here," murmured Lucas, pointing to a circled area. "The main guard post."

"We can skirt 'round the eastern edge. It's less watched," Bearnard added, tracing a route.

"What say ye, Horas?" Brodie asked, turning to him.

"None have joined us on Sinclair land," Horas replied hesitantly. "But they're spread thin—we outman them if we play this right."

Their eyes met in silent understanding: their strategy would be tested on wit and stealth to sway fragile loyalties from Sinclair's promises.

"Let's move out," Brodie commanded confidently. Extinguishing the lantern and tucking away the map, each man readied themselves for the task ahead—unseen predators amid unsuspecting prey, their motives as sharp and dangerous as their concealed blades.

Brodie crept through the dense bracken. Beside him Kevin moved with a predator's grace while Lucas led the way, navigating toward the huddle of tents emerging from the darkness ahead. Bearnard and Horas followed, their expressions focused.

"Remember, no bloodshed unless forced," Brodie whispered as they reached the outskirts of the camp. The sentries were trusting; Kevin and Horas neutralized them without raising alarm.

Watching, Brodie shook his head. Their army and their men were much better prepared for the battle to come than the enemy was if they were all like the sentries.

The group split, weaving between tents. Inside one, Brodie found two men. "Ye serve the Stewarts...but what have they offered ye? Join us, and fight for a cause that values yer lives."

Outside, Lucas convinced a pair of seasoned warriors to join their cause in exchange for honor and protection. As the night wore on, discontent among Stewart soldiers bore fruit.

Before dawn, twenty defectors left the Sinclair encampment behind, following Brodie through the Highland wilderness. The journey was tense but shrouded in mist and shadow.

As they crossed into McAfee land, sunrise touched the horizon. Relief washed over them momentarily before Brodie welcomed them to their new alliance—weary but determined, their breaths joining in unity.

HORSE HOOVES POUNDED the earth as a rider approached the gates of the McAfee stronghold. Alisdair watched from atop the stone parapet as the gatekeeper opened the portcullis.

"Message from the Stewart," announced the rider, urgency in his voice.

Alisdair descended the steps with measured tread, Fearghas

by his side like a shadow, watching the messenger intently.

"Speak," Alisdair commanded, his voice echoing off ancient stones.

The young messenger produced a rolled parchment sealed with the Stewart clan emblem. "Clyde Stewart commands ye heed his warning," he said. "Any McAfee or ally found on Sinclair land will be tortured and killed on sight."

Fearghas's grip tightened around his dirk, but Alisdair remained unwavering. "Thank ye for bringing us this message," he replied, his tone betraying no concern.

The messenger dismounted and laid down his sword. "Please," he implored, his chest heaving. "I dinnae wish to serve under a banner stained with cruelty. Might I join yer cause?"

For a moment, silence hung heavy before Alisdair stepped forward, offering his hand. His eyes locked with those of the former Stewart soldier.

"Ye seek refuge and a chance to fight for honor? Ye shall have it here," Alisdair declared, gripping the young man's shoulder. "Welcome to our alliance."

The other men nodded in silent agreement; their ranks swelled not just in number but in conviction. It seemed that every man who came over from Stewart's army convinced them even more of which side they should be on.

"We do nae bend to threats," Fearghas added, resolve in his voice. "We stand united, stronger with each soul that joins our ranks."

The young man straightened under their acceptance, marked only by the quiet acknowledgment of shared purpose.

"Train him well," Brodie told Lucas, emphasizing the importance of their newest member's integration into the clan.

They returned to the keep, where plans unfolded and a future was forged—one in which everyone could shape their destiny with honor.

Brodie McClain surveyed the group of men who had joined their ranks under the cover of darkness. Each face reflected hardship and strength, much like the landscape that surrounded them. Brodie exhaled slowly, preparing to address his new brethren.

"Listen well," he began, his voice strong and authoritative. "Ye're no longer bound by the Stewarts' treachery. Here, ye'll join the McAfee force, united against a common foe."

The men watched him intently as Brodie outlined their integration into the clan's forces with strategic precision. "Train alongside our seasoned warriors, learn their ways. In battle, guard each other's backs fiercely." He paused. "Even if someone is a former enemy of yers, he is now yer ally, and ye must remember that on the battlefield as well as in yer everyday interactions with each other."

Murmurs of assent passed among the group. Brodie scanned their faces, ensuring they understood not just the words but the commitment required. "Carry the honor of this land—fierce as mountain winds and immovable as ancient stones. Fight for the future of these Highlands we call home."

As morning progressed, the men dispersed to train with others on the field. The respite had been necessary for both newcomers and experienced warriors alike. Wooden swords clashed, grunts and footfalls creating a symphony of preparation as stances and parries were corrected by watchful eyes.

At the edge of the practice field, Brodie stood watchful and guiding. As afternoon wore on, dust from exertion filled the air alongside a growing sense of unity. Each strike honed their readiness while trust blossomed between old and new clansmen.

From his vantage point, Brodie observed their resolve solidifying like iron blades. And as shadows lengthened toward day's end, training ceased not from weariness but with quiet confidence in their united force.

Moira leaned against the stone window frame, observing the men in the training field below. Among them, she spotted Brodie, his swordplay captivating her like an epic saga. Though she longed to join, Moira understood her role as a strategist and organizer for the McAfee clan.

In the infirmary, she shifted from patient to patient with gentle care, fiery hair glinting in the light as her eyes conveyed concern.

Later, she led a small group of women on a hunt, determination resonating through her authoritative voice. As they entered the woods, earthy scents enveloped them, Moira's spirit lifting with each step. This was her land and her fight—and she would protect it fiercely.

The bowstring's twang disrupted the forest's serenity as an arrow narrowly missed its target and grazed Lucas's arm. Chaos erupted, followed by Moira's command to get him to the infirmary.

At McAfee Keep, Elspeth Sinclair quickly tended to Lucas's wound, her calm demeanor easing tensions. She requested Moira to relieve her from kitchen duties so she could focus on healing. Moira agreed despite her reluctance to take Elspeth's place in the busy kitchen. The only thing she hated more than infirmary duty was kitchen duty.

Navigating the clamor of clanging pots and raised voices, Moira tackled vegetable preparation with practiced precision. As she stirred massive pots over open flames, a ladle sailed past her ear—an argument between two cooks. The hectic kitchen was its own battlefield, but conflict wasn't foreign to her.

"More wood for the fire, Moira!" demanded one of the cooks, her muscular arms flexing.

Moira hauled logs, pausing to swipe a stray lock of hair from her eyes. Her muscles protested as she kneaded dough, but she remained resolute in serving her clan.

Glancing out the small window above the preparation table,

she observed the empty training grounds. The distant echo of clashing swords filled her with longing, but she shook it off and whispered, "Focus, Moira." Her strategic mind had won them allies, making every chore worthwhile. She returned to her tasks, ready for whatever awaited her.

— ❧ —

CHAPTER SEVENTEEN

First thing the next day, Moira entered the infirmary, her red hair contrasting the stone walls. The morning chill clung to her skin, but urgency propelled her forward. Inside, its occupants breathed softly.

Lucas lay feverish on a cot, his complexion pale and sweaty. Elspeth Sinclair sat beside him, her hands holding his in a silent plea for healing.

"Elspeth," Moira whispered, resting a hand atop theirs. The older woman looked up with weary eyes.

"Moira," she returned calmly.

"He's strong," Moira insisted. "He'll pull through."

Hope flickered in Elspeth's eyes. Moira's conviction wavered momentarily before she spoke again. "Excuse me for a moment."

With as much as Lucas had helped them, and as wrong as she'd been to doubt his allegiance, she knew she must do whatever she could to make sure the infection that had set into Lucas's wound didn't harm him more than it already had. She knew the only answer was to seek out Brodie's Grandfather Colin who would help her if she asked. At least she hoped he would.

She wouldn't tell anyone what he was doing, and surely that wouldn't break her promise to Brodie not to tell anyone about Colin's healing powers.

With that, Moira left the room, her heart racing like a war-horse charging into battle. She carried the weight of her decision as her ancestors had—with unwavering courage and determina-

119

tion to protect their kin at any cost.

Moira rushed through McAfee Keep's corridors, seeking Brodie's great-grandfather. She found him in the apothecary chamber, his gaze knowing and wise.

"Grandfather Colin," she said firmly, "I need your aid. Lucas is gravely ill. We may lose him without your healing touch."

The old man contemplated her request before agreeing. "For the bond between our clans and the peace it brings, I will do this."

With relief, Moira ensured the infirmary would be cleared for his work. Elspeth and Ailis hesitated but ultimately left to eat. Alone with the patients, Moira sat by Lucas, waiting and hoping that Colin's magic could heal where modern means failed.

The infirmary door creaked as Colin entered. Moira's heart quickened, watching him move from one patient to another with practiced grace. "Just heal them enough to ensure no one will die," Moira said, biting her lip. "We cannae risk yer secret getting out."

Colin approached the sick, hands hovering above them as he focused all his energy on healing them. The air seemed charged with energy, prickling against Moira's skin—a testament to his healing ability.

When Colin reached Lucas, Moira held her breath. His hand settled gently on Lucas's forehead. After a moment of stillness, Lucas stirred and woke. Awake and lucid, he met Moira's eyes.

After a quiet exchange between Moira and Colin, he departed the room with a nod. As the door closed behind him, the other women returned from their reprieve.

"Moira, what sorcery is this?" Ailis asked in disbelief, observing the now improved patients. "Everyone is better than when we left to eat!"

"Ye ken the old stories," Moira replied confidently. "Sometimes spirits of the glen aid us."

"Or perhaps ye are a miracle worker," Ailis said, smiling despite her fatigue. "Whatever magic ye possess, 'tis a blessing."

Moira didn't want to take credit for Colin's work, but she

didn't know how to explain what had happened otherwise. Surely it was better if her sister believed she'd healed them than if she knew the truth. Either way, she wouldn't break her promise to Brodie.

MOIRA PACED THE stone corridor, the air cool and damp with the scent of pine. Her heart threatened to drown her thoughts.

She found Brodie in the courtyard, observing young warriors train. "Brodie!" she called, hiding her turmoil.

His deep brown eyes narrowed as he turned to face her. "Moira," he acknowledged evenly. "What brings ye from the infirmary so hastily? Did we lose Lucas?"

"May we speak in private?" she asked, brushing back her red hair that glinted in sunlight.

Brodie dismissed the young men, and they stood under an ancient oak's shadow. "Speak then," he said once alone.

"I've sought yer Grandfather Colin's aid to heal the wounded," Moira began hesitantly.

Frowning, Brodie replied, "Ye've overstepped. Grandfather doesnae have energy to spare." His words were measured but laced with anger.

"Please understand, I did it for the alliance," Moira implored, recounting Lucas's choice for unity even when trust was lacking between them. "He doesnae deserve to die when he has done naught but help."

The weight of responsibility lay heavy on Brodie as he responded, his voice low and controlled, "Ye've acted boldly, but not every choice can be made alone. We must think of consequences."

She nodded solemnly. "I know I've erred. And I'll do what I must to make amends."

The breeze shifted, and a promise of change lingered. Brodie's expression softened as they faced their crossroads together.

"Go," he said, a hint of reluctant admiration in his voice. "See to Lucas and the others. We'll speak more later."

Moira turned, her resolve unwavering. She would stand by her decisions and face the future with courage and honor—for herself, her clan, and their alliances.

The sound of Brodie's departing footsteps echoed in the stone corridor, a solitary drumbeat that signaled his retreat. Moira stood rooted to the spot, the chill of the Highland air seeping into her bones as she watched the broad shoulders of her husband diminish into the distance. She had hoped for understanding, perhaps even a begrudging respect for her boldness. Instead, she was met with a stern rebuke and the cold turn of his back.

In the silence that followed, Moira's thoughts churned—full of turmoil. She had played her hand, reached out to the old magic held within gnarled fingers, and now the price of her gamble loomed over her like a gathering storm. With no confidante to share her burden, she felt the weight of isolation pressing down upon her, a mantle woven from her own impetuous threads.

The infirmary door creaked open, pulling Moira from her reverie. She stepped inside the dimly lit room, the scent of herbs and the warmth of the hearth wrapping around her. Almost everyone was gone, the majority of pallets empty, save for one where Lucas lay with Elspeth at his side. The young warrior's brow was free of fever's sheen, his chest rising and falling with the steady rhythm of peaceful slumber. Elspeth's dark hair cascaded over her shoulder as she leaned forward, whispering words of comfort only he could hear.

Ailis, the healer, approached with a vial of salve in hand. "'Tis remarkable," she said, her voice tinged with awe. "They've all improved so swiftly."

"Aye," Moira replied, masking her inner turmoil with feigned surprise.

"Lucas is the last," Ailis continued, tending to the bandage on his arm with practiced care. "If the infection does not return by the morn, he'll be free to leave."

Elspeth nodded, her gaze never leaving Lucas's face. There was a resilience in the set of her jaw, a silent strength that spoke of enduring love and steadfast hope.

"Thank ye, Ailis," Moira said, her voice soft but firm. "Ye've done well by them."

"'Twas not me hands alone," Ailis admitted, her eyes meeting Moira's with a knowing look.

Moira felt a pang of guilt. "Aye, we've been blessed by fortune this day."

She lingered a moment longer, watching the gentle rise and fall of Lucas's chest, the delicate interplay of shadow and light across his features. Duty called her away, but her heart bade her stay, to witness this fragile peace before the storm of her actions would surely break. With a final glance at Elspeth's vigilant form, Moira turned and left the infirmary, the echo of her steps mingling with the whispers of healing and the unspoken truths resting heavily on her soul.

PINE AND EARTH scents enveloped Moira as she strode through the forest, bow in hand. The hunt provided a welcome distraction from her recent choices.

An autumn breeze whispered, carrying distant sounds of the keep. Moira scanned the underbrush for signs of movement. She moved silently until a flash of brown caught her attention. In one fluid motion, she drew an arrow, nocking and releasing it. The rabbit fell, and she quickly retrieved it.

As she collected her prize, a twig snapped behind her. Whirling around, bow ready, she found Kevin MacGregor emerging from the thicket.

"Ye shouldnae be following me," she chided.

"Ye know ye cannae leave the keep alone, Moira," Kevin

replied. "I merely perform the task assigned to me by the McClain brothers."

Moira assessed his earnest gaze and nodded once before delving deeper into the forest with him.

Three more arrows found their marks as the afternoon waned. When retrieving the last rabbit, Kevin stepped forward to help carry it.

"Allow me," he said. Moira acknowledged this with a nod of thanks.

Later, returning to the keep, Moira asked about Grandfather Colin. Kevin described him as wise and strong but he was a renowned healer, and he preferred to keep his healing away from the sight of others.

"The entire family works hard to keep certain things private, and the rest of the clan knows naught about what is happening. I've puzzled some things together in the years I've served them, and I feel as if I ken more than most."

"Thank ye, Kevin," Moira said as they made their way back to the keep together, feeling lighter despite her emotional turmoil.

"The McClain brothers are surrounded by tales," Kevin said, as if divulging a secret. "Mystery clings to them like mist on lochs at dawn."

"Do ye trust them?" Moira asked, seeking more than affirmation.

"Every one of them," he replied with an oath-like nod. "I'd lay down me life for any brother without hesitation."

His words stirred both admiration and guilt within Moira, recalling how she disappointed Brodie. As they left the forest's shelter and approached the keep, her thoughts turned to mending the bonds between them.

Right before reaching the gates, Moira asked, "How does one right a wrong done in good faith?"

Kevin's expression softened. "By showing courage to face it," he advised and continued walking.

Determined, Moira whispered to herself, "Forgiveness is

earned." With resolve hardening with each step, she decided to prove her commitment through actions rather than grand gestures or eloquent words.

Once Moira and Brodie were in their chamber for the night, she once again apologized for overstepping and asking his grandfather to heal when it wasn't her place.

Brodie listened intently as Moira apologized, his gaze steady but not unkind. The flickering candlelight cast dancing shadows across his face, softening the angles of his chiseled jaw. When she finished speaking, a heavy silence settled between them, broken only by the crackling of the hearth fire.

"I understand why ye did it," Brodie finally said, his voice low and measured. "Ye have a good heart, Moira. 'Tis one of the things that I admire most about ye."

Moira felt a flicker of hope ignite within her chest. "But I should have consulted with ye first," she admitted, her eyes searching his. "I let me impulsiveness guide me, and in doing so, I betrayed yer trust."

Brodie sighed, running a hand through his dark hair. "Aye, ye should have asked me first, but I cannae blame ye for trying to help another. Please only do so with me permission though."

Moira was relieved he didn't seem angrier. She walked to him and rested her head on his broad shoulder, sighing when his arms came about her. She would do better in the future. For she must.

◆━━━❧━━━◆

CHAPTER EIGHTEEN

Lucas Gordon trudged across the dew-drenched grass of the training field, his breath misting in the chill Highland air. Though his limbs ached from the relentless drills and sparring, he felt invigorated by the purpose that had seeped into his bones since aligning with the enemies of his clan. As the sun crested the craggy peaks of the Highlands, casting long shadows over McAfee Keep, Lucas paused to wipe the sweat from his brow and glance toward the keep's entrance.

There, beneath the archway where ivy clung like ancient guardians, stood Elspeth Sinclair. Her hair caught the morning light, and her gaze held a special something that drew him near, a compass to true north. Lucas made his way to her, each step bringing him closer to the woman he'd come to truly care for.

"Ye are doing well with yer training," Elspeth observed, her voice calm and deep.

"I must. I cannae leave me own clan and fight against them if I don't have a purpose," Lucas replied, his normally assertive tone softened by the genuine admiration he held for this woman whose resilience outshone the steel of any blade.

Their conversation meandered through the intricacies of alliances and strategies, yet always returned to the simple comfort found in shared silences and unspoken understanding. In these moments with Elspeth, Lucas discovered fragments of himself he thought lost—fragments not bound by the chains of legacy or the shadows of doubt.

The unexpected clamor of hooves and the murmur of many voices snapped Lucas and Elspeth from their feelings. They turned as one toward the stirring horizon where a formidable procession crested the hill. Banners fluttered like the wings of predatory birds, and at its head rode a figure of imposing stature, clad in the colors of the Sutherland clan.

"By the saints…The Sutherlands?" Lucas muttered under his breath, disbelief etching lines upon his brow.

"Unannounced and unforeseen," Elspeth added, her own surprise mirroring his.

As the cavalcade approached, the gates of the keep swung open, revealing a throng of onlookers whose whispers swelled into a cacophony of speculation. Lucas felt the electric charge of anticipation; the arrival of the Sutherlands was no trivial matter.

Laird Sutherland dismounted with a grace that contradicted his years, his presence commanding immediate attention. "We've ridden hard from our lands," he declared, his voice cutting through the murmurs like a cleave through bracken. "The McKays have spoken to us of what brews here, and we'll not stand idly by while battles shape the future of the Highlands."

A ripple of astonishment coursed through the gathering people, leaving in its wake a burgeoning sense of fortuity. Lucas exchanged a look with Elspeth, a shared recognition that the tides were indeed turning, perhaps now in their favor.

"Welcome to McAfee Keep, Laird Sutherland," Lucas said, stepping forward. "Your men will find kinship among our ranks."

Elspeth's eyes met his, reflecting the hope that flickered like the first spark of a much-needed fire. Together they watched as the Sutherland soldiers melded with the others, a confluence of destinies entwined by the common thread of honor and the right side of history.

The sun cast a warm, amber glow over the training fields where men clashed in mock combat, their exertions now buoyed by the arrival of the Sutherlands. Brodie glanced toward the horizon, his eyes reflecting the fiery sky and the spark of new possibilities. With a nod to Lachlan and Alisdair, who stood beside him, he murmured, "This changes everything."

Lachlan permitted himself a rare smile, his eyes filled with the promise of victory. "The Sutherland swords are worth tenfold any ordinary blade, and we've a sea of them now," he said, pride resonating in his voice like the distant call of pipes over the loch.

Alisdair, ever the strategist, folded his arms across his chest as he surveyed the swelling ranks. "Aye, and each man brings a heart ready for battle. The Stewarts will not find us easy prey come dawn." His words were a talisman against uncertainty, spoken with the assurance that came from years of leading men into the fray.

As twilight descended upon the keep, the air filled with the scents of roasting meats and freshly baked bread. A feast was underway, its tables groaning beneath the weight of Highland bounty, and torches flared to life, casting dancing shadows that mingled with the growing laughter and camaraderie.

Moira moved through the throng with an ease that spoke of her familiarity with such gatherings. Her red hair, unbound for the occasion, caught the light of the flames and seemed to weave its magic among the men. She greeted each soldier with a touch on the arm or a shared jest, her lively eyes shining with mirth and purpose.

"Welcome, friend," she said to a grizzled Sutherland warrior, offering him a trencher piled high with food. "May your stay here be as hearty as your reputation."

"Ah, lass, ye honor us with your hospitality," the warrior responded, his weathered face softening into a grin. As Moira continued on, the man watched her go, a newfound warmth kindling in his chest—a feeling shared by all who found themselves under the protective gaze of the McAfee lasses.

Throughout the night, the sounds of celebration echoed against the stone walls of the keep, each cheer and burst of song speaking of the unity forged among the clans.

Amid the revelry of the feast, Moira's gaze found Lucas and

Elspeth, inseparable as they had been since the day he rose from his sickbed. His arm encircled her waist with a sense of belonging, while she leaned into him, her eyes aglow with a serenity that softened her usual stoic demeanor. It seemed as though the very air around them shimmered with unspoken vows, until, in a moment that felt both impromptu and inevitable, they stood before the clan priest.

"Let it be known," the priest boomed, voice resonating over the din of celebration, "that this union is forged not only in love but in the fire of our times." His hand swept over their clasped ones, and the crowd hushed to bear witness to the ancient words of commitment. With the binding of hands with the clan tartan, the couple was pronounced wed.

The feast erupted anew, the skirl of bagpipes giving rise to exuberant cheers. Moira watched, her heart lifting with each lively reel and jig, as clan members brandished cups high in salute to the newly married pair. Even under the weight of impending battles, they danced—a testament to life and resilience. There was no reason to fight battles that were stronger than what they were a part of—a ceilidh full of feast and wedded bliss.

As the night deepened, the doors of the great hall swung open once more, admitting four stout men wearing the plaid of the Gordon clan. Their arrival, unexpected yet timely, turned heads as they made their way toward Lucas.

"Yer father sends his regards," one of the newcomers said, his voice carrying the unmistakable burr of the Gordons. "And more than just words, he sends us to stand by your side."

Lucas, his face filled with pride for both his new bride and his family's support, nodded firmly. Raising his goblet, he beckoned the McClain brothers over. "These men have journeyed from Sinclair land on the word of me father, Laird Gordon. Let us ensure their choice is honored among us."

Brodie stepped forward, clapping each Gordon soldier on the back. "Ye've come to a good place, lads. We fight for the same cause," he assured them, his voice carrying the weight of a seasoned warrior ready to embrace new allies.

"Then let us drink to new bonds," Alisdair added, raising his cup in solidarity, while Lachlan's eyes gleamed with strategic satisfaction at the fortuitous turn.

Moira moved among them, her expression one of fierce joy. Each cheer for unity, every handshake between old allies and new, announced over and over that they would be victorious. In the warmth of the great hall, surrounded by the strength of many mighty clans now joined, they celebrated not just a marriage, but the alliance that would bolster them in the trials to come.

THE LAST STRAINS of the fiddle's tune ebbed into the thick stone walls of the hall as Moira McAfee found herself alone with Brodie McClain. The feast had been a whirlwind of laughter and camaraderie, but now it stood quiet, the echoes of merriment lingering like spirits in the rafters. They stood close to the hearth, its embers glowing softly, casting a warm, flickering light on their faces.

"It's a fine thing, the Gordons joining us," Brodie said, his voice a low rumble that seemed to resonate with the dying fire. "Lucas has proven a strong link between our clans."

"Aye," Moira replied, her eyes reflecting the firelight and the fierce determination within. "And the Sutherlands…their arrival was unexpected, like a gale force wind that fills sails when ye least anticipate it."

Brodie nodded, his contemplative gaze meeting hers. "We sent no word, no plea for aid. Yet they came. It's as if the very stones and streams of the Highlands are speaking, urging us to stand together."

"Perhaps they are," Moira mused, her lips curving into a smile that didn't quite mask the astonishment still living in her eyes. "The Sutherlands' reputation precedes them. Their warriors are as strong and loyal as the ancient pines. We could not ask for better support."

"True," Brodie agreed, the corners of his mouth lifting in admiration. "Their presence here tonight has bolstered the men's spirits more than any rousing speech I could have mustered."

"More than that, it has forged a belief in victory that may well turn the tide against those who seek to dominate our lands." Moira's hands clenched at her sides, knuckles whitening—a physical manifestation of her resolve.

"Then let us hold fast to that belief," Brodie said, reaching out to gently uncurl her fingers. "For with unity comes strength, and with strength, we will prevail."

The embers of the dying fire cast a dim glow over the room where Brodie and Moira stood close, their breaths mingling in the cool Highland air. Outside, the stars were veiled by the sweeping clouds that often shrouded the rugged landscape in mystery. Inside, however, no such obscurity existed between the two; everything seemed startlingly clear.

"Look at them, Brodie," Moira whispered, her gaze piercing through the wooden shutters to the courtyard below where silhouettes danced and celebrated late into the night. "Our clans united, our allies steadfast. The very ground upon which we stand feels like it is with us."

"Aye," Brodie replied, his voice a low reverberation that matched the firm resolve in his eyes. "Every move we've made, every preparation—it's all coming together." His hand found hers, fingers intertwining with a grip that spoke volumes of shared purpose and silent promises.

Moira turned to face him, her own hands rising to frame his face, tracing the lines of determination etched there. "You believe then? That we are on the cusp of something great?"

Brodie nodded; his gaze locked with hers. "I do. With our combined might and the heart of the Highlands beating within us, we have forged more than just an alliance. We've kindled hope."

Hope seemed to ignite something more between them, a

fervent warmth that spread from where their bodies touched.

Without another word, they moved together, lips finding lips in a kiss that was both a seal of their unity and a prelude to deeper communion. Brodie's arms wrapped around Moira as if he intended to shield her from the world, yet she needed no protection. She was the embodiment of the fierce McAfee spirit, and in his embrace, she found not shelter but an equal force.

Led by the urgency that thrummed through their veins, they shed their garments piece by piece, each layer falling away like the pretenses of diplomacy and strategy that ruled their days. Here, in this intimate space, they were simply Brodie and Moira—man and woman, warrior and shieldmaiden, bound by desire and the pulse of a cause greater than themselves.

As they joined their bodies, the stone walls of the keep seemed to resonate with their rhythm. The connection between them transcended flesh. It was a melding of wills, a dance of souls that knew no defeat.

And as they reached the crescendo of their union, the world outside—the alliances, the machinations, the impending clash of steel—faded into insignificance. In that moment, as they clung to each other, breathless and sated, only one truth remained: they were indomitable, invincible, as long as they stood side by side.

In the stillness that followed, with only the crackle of the dying embers for company, Moira allowed herself the luxury of believing wholly in their destiny.

The rhythmic cadence of their breaths entwined, Brodie's arm draped over Moira in the protective cocoon of their bed. The glow from the last embers of the fire cast a warm dance of light and shadow across the room, painting their bodies in a soft orange hue. Moira traced the lines of Brodie's hand with her fingertip, feeling the calluses born of swordplay that matched her own.

"Remember when it was just whispers in the dark?" she began, her voice a hushed marvel against the quiet of the night. "A few disgruntled voices against a tyrant's rule?"

Brodie's chest rumbled with a low chuckle, vibrating against her back. "Aye, I do. It was just you, me, and our siblings daring to dream of something greater."

"Look at us now," Moira mused, a sense of awe threading through her words. "An alliance strong enough to challenge the very foundations of his claim."

"More than just numbers, Moira," Brodie added thoughtfully, his fingers absently playing with a lock of her fiery red hair. "We've ignited a flame in the hearts of clansmen and women alike. A shared vision for the future of the Highlands."

"Aye," Moira agreed, turning within his embrace to face him, her eyes seeking his in the dimness. "From a tiny spark to a raging inferno. Our cause has become massive… wonderful even."

"Massive and wonderful," he said, sealing the sentiment with a gentle kiss upon her forehead.

As the silence settled once more, Moira closed her eyes, allowing the weight of their intertwined limbs and shared warmth to ground her. Her thoughts drifted to the unexpected boon of the Sutherlands joining their ranks, the serendipitous twist of fate that had bolstered their forces.

"Did ye ever imagine the Sutherlands would stand with us?" she whispered, almost too faint for even the walls to hear.

"In me wildest dreams, perhaps," Brodie admitted, his voice deep with sincerity. "But reality has outdone me imagination this time."

"An answer to prayer…" she murmured, a smile tugging at the corner of her mouth, her heart swelling with gratitude. "I can hardly believe our fortune."

"Nor can I," he affirmed, tightening his hold on her ever so slightly as if to ensure she was truly there.

Their breathing synchronized once again, each exhale a silent celebration of the day's victories, each inhale a harbinger of triumphs yet to come. As slumber beckoned, Moira let her consciousness drift, buoyed by the realization that they were part of something far greater than themselves.

In the space between wakefulness and dreams, Moira clung to the truth that seemed to resonate through the very stones of McAfee Keep: their unity was their strength, their love and loyalty an unbreakable chainmail woven tight around their cause. With the Sutherlands' arrival, it felt as though the stars had aligned in their favor, carving a path through the uncertainty that once clouded their destiny.

And as sleep claimed her, Moira's last coherent thought shimmered with a profound sense of peace—peace rooted in the conviction that their tiny movement had indeed turned into something massive and wonderful, a force not just to be reckoned with, but one that heralded the dawn of a new era for the Highlands.

CHAPTER NINETEEN

T HE WARRIORS OF the alliance, now bolstered by the formidable Sutherlands, gathered in the shadow of McAfee Keep. A sense of optimism infused the air, a shared sentiment that with this newfound unity, victory was within reach.

Lachlan's eyes were trained on the imposing figure of Laird Sutherland amid the fray. The seasoned warrior moved through the men like a tempest, his broad shoulders flexing as he demonstrated a masterful stroke with his sword, his voice booming over the din of training swords.

"Position and balance," Laird Sutherland commanded, his weathered hands correcting a young soldier's grip. "Anticipate your opponent's next move."

Lachlan mimicked the maneuver, feeling the weight of his sword as an extension of his own will. Around him, the faces of his kinsmen were filled with fervor, their movements growing more assured under Sutherland's tutelage. Lachlan hadn't believed there was much he could still learn about swordplay, but Laird Sutherland had proven him wrong quickly.

Ailis watched from the fringes, her keen eyes assessing each swing and parry. She noted how Laird Sutherland instilled confidence into her clansmen, reinforcing their resolve with his steadfast presence.

"Ye see that, Lachlan?" she called, her vibrant green eyes reflecting the lively scene. "The men are finding their strength!"

"Aye," Lachlan replied, sparing a quick glance in Ailis's direction.

"Again!" Laird Sutherland barked, circling the soldiers who hung on his every word. He paused by a towering brute whose stance was too narrow.

"Plant your feet as if ye mean to uproot the very earth beneath you," he instructed, setting the man's boots firmly apart. The soldier nodded, his eyes gleaming with newfound determination.

Laird Sutherland stepped back, surveying the men with a critical eye. Pride etched into the lines of his face as blade met blade, ringing out like a chorus of hope across the Highlands.

"Remember, lads," he said, his voice carrying on the chill wind, "a sword is only as strong as the arm that wields it, and the heart that guides it. We stand together, or not at all."

And as the sun climbed higher, melting away the remnants of dawn's chill, the warriors of the alliance trained with a zeal that could only come from knowing they were part of something far greater than themselves.

MOIRA'S BOOTS SANK into the mossy earth as she strode through the dense woods, a quiver of arrows slung across her back and a bow gripped firmly in her hand. The crisp air filled her lungs, sharpening her senses as the sounds of clashing swords and grunts of exertion echoed from the distant training field.

She wasn't alone. A band of women from the clan accompanied her, their faces set with determination and their weapons at the ready. Moira knew their strength was not just in combat but in sustaining their people. With the addition of the Sutherlands to their ranks, every mouth was another stomach to fill, and it was her task to ensure none went hungry.

"Keep yer eyes on the thicket," she called, her voice confident but low, blending with the rustle of leaves around them. "The deer are plentiful this season, but they are wily."

Eyes followed her gaze, scanning for any signs of movement within the greenery. The women, each one capable and alert, mirrored Moira's readiness. They understood the importance of their hunt, not just for provision but for morale. A well-fed army was an army with spirits high enough to face the coming challenge.

"Remember, aim true and be mindful of where you shoot," Moira reminded them, her fiery red hair glinting like molten copper beneath the dappled sunlight that filtered through the canopy. "We'll have no accidents today. We cannae afford injuries, not now."

She led by example, moving with stealth toward a clearing where the brush gave way to a grassy expanse. Here, the targets would be clearer, and the risk of stray arrows endangering their kin would be markedly reduced. She paused, gestured to the others to fan out, and signaled them to ready their bows.

With a sharp intake of breath, Moira drew an arrow and nocked it. Her piercing gaze darted to a bush where a shadow stirred, and with the grace of a predator, she drew the string taut against the resistance. The world seemed to hold its breath, the wind momentarily stilling as if in anticipation.

"Steady," she whispered, more to herself than to the others. Her fingers released the arrow, sending it hurtling toward its mark with a whispering hiss. The sound of impact was followed by a communal release of held breaths, and Moira allowed herself a small smile of satisfaction as the others followed suit, their arrows flying true and clear, well away from the sounds of swordsmanship that resounded in the distance.

"Good," she praised as they collected their quarry. "This will keep the fires burning and the stew pots full."

THE GREAT HALL of McAfee Keep buzzed with activity as Moira ushered her band of hunters through its heavy wooden doors. Women from the clan, aprons tied firmly around their waists, welcomed the party, their hands eager to relieve them of their burdens.

"Here, let me take that," one woman said, reaching for a brace of rabbits dangling from Moira's grasp.

"Careful with these," Moira instructed, passing over the game. "They're to be smoked, every last bit of it." Her voice carried the authority of one who knew the importance of meticulous preparation in times of need. She watched as the women set to work, laying out the fresh catch alongside the day's earlier bounty. There was an urgency in their movements—a shared understanding that each task completed brought them one step closer to readiness.

Moira rolled up the sleeves of her blouse and joined in, her skilled fingers making quick work of dressing the game. Her red hair, plaited tightly to keep it from her face while hunting, seemed to catch fire in the glow of the hearth. She moved among the kitchen stations, ensuring that every piece of meat found its way into the careful hands of those tending the curing racks and smoking pits.

"Ye've a steady hand, Moira," one of the elder women re-marked as she watched the younger lass deftly truss a pheasant for smoking.

"Steady hands make for full bellies," Moira replied with a smile, tying off the twine with a practiced knot. "And full bellies make for strong warriors." As much as Moira hated kitchen work, she was adept at it, and she would do whatever was needed to help their cause.

As the room filled with the comforting sounds of productivi-ty—the chopping of vegetables for the stew pots, the clinking of ladles, the murmur of conversation—Moira's thoughts drifted to the men outside, their swords clashing as they drilled under Laird Sutherland's watchful eye. She could almost hear the rhythmic cadence of their training calls, a warrior's litany that pulsed in time with her own heart.

The alliance had brought more than just numbers. The hope of the soldiers and clansmen alike had risen sharply. They now felt as if they had the chance to actually end this war without too many more lives being lost. As Moira surveyed the bustling kitchen, the evidence of this newfound vigor was palpable. Even the women in the kitchen were more hopeful.

There was no room for doubt in Moira's mind, no space for uncertainty. Clyde Stewart would soon realize the futility of his ambition when faced with the united strength of the McAfees and McClains, as well as all the other clans in their alliance.

"Moira," one of the younger girls addressed her, breaking her reverie, "where should I put these?"

"Over there by the east wall," Moira directed, pointing to the designated area for smoked goods. "Make sure they're well-spaced. We'll need every strip preserved for the days ahead."

"Of course, Moira," the girl nodded, her eyes reflecting a mixture of respect and determination that mirrored Moira's own.

"Mind the fire, lasses," Granny called, her voice cutting through the din. "We cannae afford to waste a single morsel."

Moira turned, ready to tackle the next task, when a gentle but firm hand clasped her elbow. Granny McAfee's eyes, bright and knowing, peered into hers from a face lined with the wisdom of many Highland moons.

"Moira, my dear," Granny's voice was a soft yet commanding whisper, intended only for her ears amidst the hubbub. "There's a fine line betwixt confidence and cockiness."

Granny led her a few steps away from the hustle, close enough to still feel the kitchen's warmth on their faces. "Ye've got the heart of a lioness, but even the mightiest beast cannae see all the dangers that lurk in the heather."

Moira stood tall, though she had to tilt her head to look up at her grandmother's sage gaze. "Granny, I ken yer concern, but the Sutherlands' swords are sharp. The Stewarts will be scattered like leaves come autumn."

"Perhaps," Granny conceded, her eyes narrowing slightly, "but never underestimate an enemy cornered. We know not if other clans have cast their lot with the Stewarts."

Moira listened, her jaw set firmly, the muscles tensing ever so slightly. Respect for her grandmother's experience wove through her thoughts, yet her belief in their victory remained unshaken.

"Thank ye for the counsel, Granny," Moira replied, her tone carrying the undercurrent of a river rushing against the rocks. "I'll heed yer words, but the spirits of the glen are with us. We'll stand victorious."

Granny McAfee patted Moira's hand, a knowing smile flickering at the corners of her mouth. "Just remember, the wind can change its course without warning. Keep yer eyes open, child."

BRODIE MCCLAIN PUSHED open the heavy wooden door, his muscles aching from the grueling swordplay. As he scanned the room for Moira, the warm glow of the fire caught strands of her red hair, igniting them like the dying embers of the day's sunset. She moved among the tables with a grace that belied the strength in her step, ladling stew into bowls and exchanging jests with the men.

Brodie leaned against the stone archway, observing as one Sutherland warrior reached out, playfully tugging at a curl that dangled near Moira's shoulder. Her laughter rang clear, and she swatted the man's hand away with mock severity before turning to share a conspiratorial grin with another clansman. The sight knotted Brodie's insides.

Throughout the meal, Brodie's thoughts churned like a stormy loch, his usual calm demeanor overshadowed by the sharp pangs of jealousy. He ate little, his gaze returning time and again to Moira, who was now refilling ale.

"Moira," Brodie finally called.

She turned to him. "Aye, Brodie? Will ye be wanting more to eat?"

"Nay," he replied, the word curt as he rose from his seat. "We'll speak later."

The evening waned, and the hall emptied as warriors sought their rest. In the quiet of their chamber, Brodie closed the door with a soft click that seemed to echo louder than intended. Moira, who had been unpinning her hair, turned to face him, her expression one of open curiosity.

"Ye've not spoken much this eve," she observed, tilting her head slightly.

"Have I not?" Brodie's tone carried an edge, his composure fraying. "It seems ye've talked enough to not notice."

Moira's brow furrowed. "What's stirred ye, Brodie?"

"It's just… ye've been giving much attention to the men. Some could take it the wrong way."

"Take it the wrong way?" Moira's voice rose, incredulous. "I'm making our guests feel welcome, nothing more."

"Is that what ye call it?" Brodie stepped closer, unable to mask the tension in his jaw. "Flirting and jesting as ye go about?"

"Flirting?" Moira asked, every inch the Highland lass who knew her own mind. "I donnae know where ye get such notions."

"Moira, I saw ye," Brodie insisted, though his voice betrayed a hint of uncertainty.

"Then ye saw wrong," she shot back, her green eyes fierce. "I'm a McAfee, and we show hospitality. 'Tis all." She clenched her fists at her sides, more frustrated with Brodie than she ever remembered being. She felt as if he was accusing her of cheating, something she would never do.

Brodie's eyes narrowed as he studied her face, searching for any sign of deceit. But Moira met his gaze unflinchingly, her expression a mixture of hurt and defiance.

"Ye truly believe that?" he asked, his voice low and tight. "That yer behavior is naught but hospitality?"

"Aye, I do," Moira replied firmly. "And if ye cannae see that, then perhaps ye donnae know me as well as ye think."

Brodie flinched as if she'd struck him. For a moment, he looked lost, unsure how to respond. Then his shoulders slumped, and he let out a heavy sigh.

"Moira, I…" He trailed off, shaking his head. "I didnae mean to accuse ye of anything. I just… I worry, is all."

Moira's expression softened slightly at his admission. "Worry? About what, Brodie?"

He hesitated, as if struggling to find the right words. "I worry that one of these men might try to steal ye away from me. That they'll see yer kindness and mistake it for something more."

Moira stepped closer, reaching out to lay a hand on his arm. "Brodie, ye great fool. Donnae ye know by now that there's only one man for me?"

His eyes met hers, a flicker of hope sparking in their depths. "Truly?"

"Aye, truly." She smiled up at him, her fingers tightening on his sleeve. "I chose ye, Brodie McAfee. And I'll keep choosing ye, every day, for as long as ye'll have me."

"Then why flirt with others?" he asked, trying to comprehend her reasoning.

"I wasnae flirting!" Moira felt as if they were talking in circles, and she was done with their discussion.

Their words hung suspended in the cool night air, a silent witness to the gulf that had formed between them. Brodie's eyes searched hers for a moment longer, seeking the fiery spirit he admired even in the midst of his disquiet. Finally, he sighed, the sound carrying with it the weight of unspoken fears and the shadow of doubt that crept into even the steadiest of hearts.

Moira picked up the tartan shawl from the chest at the foot of their bed, wrapping it around her shoulders with a brisk tug. The woolen fabric clung to her like a shield as she turned to face Brodie.

"Ye must ken I have no heart for flirtation," Moira stated

firmly, her words slicing through the heavy silence. "I was ensuring the men felt welcomed, nothing more. My sisters are doing just the same."

"Making them feel welcome does not necessitate such…familiarity," Brodie countered.

"Ye think I cannae discern between courtesy and flirting?" Moira's voice rose, a spark of indignation igniting within her. "I know what is at stake, Brodie. I know the importance of unity in our alliance. Do ye honestly believe I would jeopardize that with idle dalliance?"

"'Tis not what I believe that troubles me," Brodie admitted, pinching the bridge of his nose in an attempt to quell his frustration. "'Tis what others might perceive. I cannae risk men seeing me as a rival for yer affections."

"Then let them perceive strength in our hospitality!" Moira shot back, her fiery hair seeming to catch the very essence of her fervor. "Let them see the McAfees stand firm in both battle and brotherhood."

The room grew cold around them. They stood divided, two wills forged in the fires of clan loyalty and Highland pride.

With a curt nod, Moira turned away, letting the shawl fall from her shoulders onto the bed—a banner of defiance in the face of Brodie's disapproval. She lay down without another word, facing the wall.

Brodie watched her for a long moment, the moonlight tracing the contours of her silhouette. He knew attempting further argument was as futile as trying to calm a storm over the lochs with mere whispers. With a heavy sigh, he extinguished the last candle, surrendering the chamber to darkness and unspoken discontent.

As sleep eluded them both, the air filled with the silence of unresolved tension.

✦

CHAPTER TWENTY

D AWN BARELY GRACED the Highlands when the distant clamor of battle stirred McAfee Keep. Moira rose from the infirmary bench, heart pounding. Outside, the Stewarts and their allies appeared through the mist.

Moira's skin prickled with cold sweat as she thought of her husband, Brodie. Their argument from the night before played on a loop in her mind.

"Moira?" asked Ailis, concern etched on her face.

Without responding, Moira hurried toward the door. Stepping out, she scanned the battlefield for Brodie. Her fiery red hair seemed to blaze with urgency as she spotted him fighting skillfully but surrounded by enemies.

Fear and resolve surged within her; she couldn't stand idly by while he risked his life. Their last bitter words now seemed trivial compared to death's indifferent gaze.

"Please," she whispered into the wind, appealing to God or anyone who would listen. "Keep him safe."

Her plea dissipated amid the chaos, yet it cemented her determination. Brodie's memory emboldened Moira as she braced for the inevitable. With life and death hanging in the balance, there was no time for uncertainty.

Hoisting her gown, Moira dashed from the infirmary and onto the parapet. The Highland air bit into her cheeks as she surveyed the battleground below.

The odds were against Brodie—three men circled him like

hungry wolves.

"I need to help," Moira muttered, gripping the stone balustrade. "Brodie's in peril!"

Fiona arrived beside her, arrow nocked. Twang! One enemy fell. Twang! Another collapsed.

"Nay," Fiona replied when asked if she could reach the third. "He's shielded by Brodie."

"I must go to him," Moira declared.

Fiona reached out a hand. "It's not safe. You cannae go there!"

Fingers steady, she strapped on her sword belt; each buckle a silent vow.

"I will go, sister. My place is by his side."

Fiona gestured to a band of clansmen. They nodded to Moira.

"We'll cut a path straight to my husband. We cannae let him die. I need all of ye to fight off anyone on the way to him, and I will handle his opponent."

The men nodded without question, each of them grabbing weapons. They moved through hidden passages, emerging into the courtyard where battle enveloped them. The sights and sounds ignited something primal within Moira.

"Protect Brodie!" she cried, charging across with her sword drawn, ready for vengeance or victory—whichever fate granted her that day.

The Highland air carried the scent of iron and earth as Moira raced across the bloodied ground. Her red hair streamed like a war banner, contrasting with the keep's grey stone. Amid the fray, Brodie fought gracefully until a sword pierced his thigh, causing his legs to buckle.

"No!" The cry tore from Moira's throat, raw and fierce. Time seemed to slow as she watched her husband collapse. Her heart clenched, but her resolve hardened like the steel in her grip. She would avenge her husband.

She reached him in a breathless moment, just as his attacker raised his sword for a final blow. With a warrior's cry, Moira intercepted, her own blade meeting his with a resounding clang. The man was skilled, but fury lent her strength, and her next strike was true. The soldier fell lifeless before her.

"Take Brodie to the infirmary, now!" She commanded the men at her back, who hurriedly obeyed, lifting Brodie's limp form with care born of loyalty and desperation.

Her green eyes stayed locked on his face, searching for any sign of consciousness, any flicker of pain or recognition. But he was still, too still, and she felt the icy fingers of dread creep into her heart.

"Moira! Come quickly!" It was Ailis's voice, steeped in urgency.

With a final glance at the fallen enemy, Moira sprinted back to the keep, her chest heaving. In the infirmary, the grim chorus of groans and prayers echoed off the stone walls.

Brodie lay upon one of the makeshift beds, his face pale, his dark eyes closed against the world. Ailis and Fiona hovered over him, their expressions etched with concern that mirrored the tumult in Moira's soul.

"His leg..." Fiona's voice trailed off, her hands hovering above the wound as if afraid to touch it.

"We need to take it off," Ailis said, her tone clinical yet tinged with fear. "The damage... I've not seen many walk away from such an injury. I'll need my bone saw."

"Ye will not take his leg," Moira stated, her voice leaving no room for debate. She knelt beside Brodie, taking his hand in hers, feeling the faint pulse of his warrior's heart. "We wait."

"Moira, if we wait—" Ailis started, the healer in her battling with the sister.

"Wait," Moira repeated firmly. Her gaze didn't waver from Brodie's ashen face. The healers exchanged a silent conversation, one laden with the weight of decisions that could mean life or death.

"Very well," Ailis conceded after a tense moment. "Ye must clean the wound as well as ye can."

Moira's fingers deftly worked to clean and bind the wound with the skill of one who had tended to countless others before.

"Thank ye," Moira whispered, pressing a kiss to Brodie's forehead. The battle outside might have ceased, but within the stone walls of the McAfee Keep, a different kind of fight was just beginning—one for the life of Brodie.

Moira's heart raced, watching over Brodie's unconscious form on the cot. The infirmary air hung heavy with blood and pain-filled moans. Her gaze lingered on his bandaged thigh, the fabric stained red. "Ye will not take his leg," she repeated, words anchoring her against consuming fear.

"Moira," Fiona implored, her bow and arrows now forgotten in a corner, "he may never walk again if—"

"Then he'll live without walking." Moira's voice cracked like a whip, silencing any further objections. Brodie had made her promise not to ask his grandfather to use his mysterious healing abilities without consent. Her word was her bond, stronger than the mightiest stronghold walls. She couldn't break it, not even for this.

"Moira, we must consider—" Ailis began, only to be cut off by the steadfast gleam in Moira's gaze.

"Wait. Just wait," she insisted, her hand tightening around Brodie's. She could feel the throb of life within him, the silent plea for patience.

Outside the keep, the clamor of war had dulled to an eerie quiet. Moira rose and moved to the narrow window, peering out onto the battlefield. The once-vibrant grass was marred with the scars of combat, bodies strewn about like rag dolls discarded by petulant children. The banners of the Stewarts, which had boldly proclaimed their intent at dawn, were now nowhere in sight, carried away on the wings of defeat. Their allies, too, seemed like specters melted into the mist that now rolled in from the glens.

"Is it…" Fiona joined Moira at the window.

"Aye," Moira confirmed, a bitter taste of victory on her tongue. "They've scattered. The Stewart will find no more clans willing to bleed for his cause."

"Then it's done," Fiona breathed, relief laced with sorrow. "For now."

"Until the next time the Stewart finds men desperate enough to die for him," Moira added, her voice hollow.

Returning to Brodie's side, Moira brushed a strand of hair from his forehead. The battle had ended, but the war…the war was fought here now, in the quiet determination of waiting, in the silent prayers to God, and in the strength of her love that refused to yield before the shadow of despair.

"Come back to me, me husband," she whispered, pressing another kiss to his brow. "Ye must come back."

The infirmary hummed with groans and whispered comforts while Moira attended the wounded. She briefly pressed a cool cloth to Brodie's fevered forehead, her heart tightening at his pale face as the infirmary door burst open.

"Moira!" Alisdair's voice, authoritative yet laced with a tremor of urgency, cut through the din.

She turned, her gaze locking onto the two brothers striding toward her. Alisdair, with his handsome features set in a frown of concern. Lachlan, his blue eyes stormy and jaw clenched with barely contained emotion.

"We must speak with ye," Lachlan said, gripping her arm and drawing her aside with a gentleness that belied his desperate grip.

"What is it?" Moira asked, her heart hammering in her chest, dreading more ill news.

"Moira, we need ye to clear the infirmary," Alisdair implored, his eyes flickering toward the unconscious form of their brother. "We need to bring our grandfather here."

"Ye know I cannae do that." Moira's voice was firm, even as her insides quaked. "I promised Brodie—And there are so many other men in need of healing. I cannae force them to leave!"

"Moira, please," Lachlan interjected, his voice dropping to a whisper that only she could hear. "Ye ken what he can do. Ye ken what this might cost us if we donnae act."

Their gazes met, a silent conversation passing between them, heavy with the weight of unspoken fears and the sacred trust of family bonds. Moira's resolve wavered, but her promise to Brodie held her firm.

"Without Brodie's leave, I cannot. And he cannot give it," she said, pain and determination warring in her tone.

A moment stretched between them, fraught with the enormity of their plight. Then, without another word, Lachlan turned and strode from the room, his purpose etched in every line of his body.

Moira watched him go, her throat tight. She returned to Brodie's side, her fingers tracing the lines of his face, willing him to awaken and grant the permission she could not give.

Time passed—an eternity in minutes—until the door opened once more, admitting a hush into the chaotic space. The old man, Colin, entered, his presence commanding attention despite his aged frame. Women moved aside, their hands ceasing their work as if by some unspoken command, their eyes filled with reverence and perhaps a hint of fear.

With solemn steps, Colin approached Brodie's bedside. Without a word, he sat, his wrinkled hand hovering over Brodie's chest. A stillness fell upon the room, the air itself holding its breath.

And then, Colin's hand descended, touching the fabric of Brodie's tunic gently. A faint glow emanated from beneath his palm, subtle enough that one might think it a trick of the light. Moira felt a warmth spread through the air, a sense of something ancient and powerful unfolding. She said a silent prayer that the others in the room would not sense the same thing. They could not let the world know about the powers of the McClain clan.

It lasted but a heartbeat before Colin withdrew his hand, the glow dissipating. He did not speak, nor did anyone dare to break the silence that followed. But in his wake, a new energy seemed to pulse through Brodie—a slight easing of his furrowed brow, a deeper rhythm to his breath.

Colin rose, his gaze meeting Moira's, imparting a silent assurance before he turned and left the infirmary as quietly as he had come.

AILIS LEANED OVER Brodie's prone form, her expert hands carefully unwrapping the bandages that had been hastily applied in the chaos. The infirmary was still thick with the scent of blood and herbal poultices, the moans of the wounded carrying the heavy weight of war through the stone walls. Moira stood beside her sister, her red hair a vivid flame in the dim light, eyes fixed on Ailis's every move.

"Ye've done well here, Moira," Ailis said, her voice tinged with surprise as she peeled back the last layer of linen to inspect the wound on Brodie's thigh. In the flickering torchlight, the cut, though deep and threatening, appeared cleaner than one might expect from such a savage blow. "I could swear it looked far worse when they carried him in."

Moira's gaze softened, relief mingling with concern as she watched Ailis probe the edges of the injury. "I just did what needed to be done," she replied, her voice betraying none of the emotions that surged within her at the sight of Brodie's pallid face.

"Ye didn't just clean it," Ailis observed, her green eyes reflecting a knowing spark as she met Moira's gaze. "Ye've cared for him with the hands of a healer. This could have festered by now, but it's on the mend." Her compliment, simple and heartfelt, held an underlying current of pride for her sister's actions.

Moira nodded silently, her thoughts entwined with memories of the old man's touch upon Brodie's chest, the subtle glow that had seemed like a trick of the light yet promised something beyond their understanding. She dared not speak of it, though. Colin's silent assurance was etched into her mind. He had told her without words that Brodie would walk again, and she'd clung to that hope.

"Let's get this dressed properly," Ailis said, breaking the quiet contemplation as she reached for fresh linen. Together, the sisters worked in harmonious silence, tending to Brodie with a meticulous care that spoke volumes of their shared strength in the face of uncertainty.

CHAPTER TWENTY-ONE

THE INFIRMARY WAS filled with activity as Moira sat beside Brodie's cot, studying his wound. Fresh bandages contrasted with his tanned skin. The healers had done their part. Now Brodie needed to stand and test his strength.

Moira watched him, her red hair a fiery cascade over her shoulders, a silent sentinel in the dim light. She remembered the weight of her sword in her hand as she fought beside him, and guilt knotted in her stomach for the argument that had divided their focus before the ambush. Her heart ached with the need to mend things between them, but Brodie's gaze when it met hers was as cold as the winds sweeping across the Highland moors.

"Ye need to try, Brodie," she implored softly, her voice laced with earnestness. "The longer ye wait to start walking again, the harder it will be."

"I ken what I must do," he replied tersely, his deep brown eyes avoiding hers. His voice did not betray his pain, but Moira saw the tightness in his jaw, the slight pallor beneath his usual ruddiness.

"Forgive me for my part in our quarrel," she said again. "I'd take it back if I could."

"Your apologies won't make me walk any sooner, Moira," Brodie snapped, more harshly than she'd ever heard him speak. His anger seemed rooted deeper than his injury, an infection of the spirit that no poultice could draw out. For a moment, she wondered if his grandfather could heal his mind, but she didn't dare ask.

Moira leaned closer, her fierce demeanor softening. "Brodie, please. Yer anger doesnae help ye heal."

He looked at her then, really looked at her, and she saw something shift behind his gaze—a storm brewing, perhaps, or maybe just the reflection of her own worry. "I'm nae angry at ye for wanting to protect me, but your apology is a balm for neither my leg nor my pride."

"Then let me help ye rise," Moira urged, desperation edging into her voice.

"Later," he muttered, turning his head away from her, dismissing her offer and her concern in a single gesture.

Her hands clenched into fists atop her tartan skirt, unable to fathom the distance that had grown between them. As night descended upon the Highlands and the infirmary grew quiet save for the occasional groan of the wounded, Moira remained by Brodie's side, her presence an unwavering constant like the ancient stones of McAfee Keep. Yet as the hours passed, his refusal to meet her gaze stung more sharply than the bite of a Stewart blade.

THE MORNING LIGHT filtered through the narrow window of the infirmary, casting a golden glow over Brodie's somber expression. Moira exchanged a determined glance with Ailis, who nodded subtly. It was time.

"Let's get ye to sit up, Brodie," Moira said, her voice laced with dread, even as she tried to be cheerful. She had no desire to see him in more pain than he already was.

With gentle hands, they eased him upright, propping pillows behind his back for support. Ailis stood on one side of the bed, her athletic frame poised with a healer's grace, while Moira took her place on the other, ready to assist her sister. Together, they guided Brodie's injured leg off the edge of the bed, positioning it carefully to avoid any unnecessary strain.

"Ye can do this," Ailis encouraged, her melodic lilt soothing yet firm. "We'll move yer leg slowly to build strength."

Taking the lead from Ailis, Moira grasped Brodie's ankle and lifted his leg with a controlled motion. His jaw tightened, and she wished she could take his pain away from him. As she flexed his knee, helping him bend and straighten the limb, the whisper of pain found its way onto his face despite his stoic efforts.

"Enough," he gasped after several repetitions, his breath coming in short bursts.

"Ye need to push through, Brodie," Ailis pressed, even as her emerald eyes shimmered with empathy. "I know 'tis not comfortable, but the longer ye wait to stand, the harder it will be. Ye lose some of yer strength every day."

"Can ye stand?" Moira asked, her piercing gaze meeting his, willing him to find the strength he needed.

"Nay," he replied, the exhaustion evident in his voice. "I've not the strength to try walking or even standing now."

"Brother, 'tis better to attempt while yer muscles are warm," Ailis reasoned, her dark hair spilling over her shoulders as she leaned closer.

Brodie merely shook his head and turned away, closing his eyes against their entreaties. Moira felt the weight of his refusal settle between them, an invisible barrier she could neither scale nor dismantle. She bit her lip, the taste of iron sharp on her tongue, knowing that his reluctance was more than physical weariness—it was a sign of a spirit burdened by unspoken fears and unresolved anger.

As the sun cast a golden hue on the infirmary's stone walls, Alisdair and Lachlan walked in, drawing the eyes of everyone inside. They whispered encouragement to the wounded men but continued to the room's end where Brodie lay.

"Ye look stronger today," Alisdair announced with a voice that rumbled like distant thunder, his gaze locking onto Brodie's.

"Strength is of little use when one's legs refuse to bear him," Brodie retorted, his eyes flicking toward his brothers' unwounded limbs with a mix of resentment and resignation. "Do ye expect me to be carried into battle and fight while in a chair?"

"Will ye let us summon Grandfather Colin once more?" offered Lachlan, his suggestion breaking through the veil of pride that surrounded Brodie. "His healing could—"

"Enough," Brodie snapped, cutting off Lachlan mid-sentence. "I will not be the reason others find out about his powers. I need no further aid."

The two elder brothers exchanged a glance, a silent conversation passing between them before they nodded to Brodie and retreated, leaving a heavy silence in their wake.

Moira remained seated beside Brodie, her hands folded neatly in her lap, the fiery strands of her hair catching the fading light. She watched as Brodie's chest rose and fell with each labored breath, his frustration etched deep into the lines of his face. She knew he must blame her for Lachlan going to fetch his grandfather, but she was not to blame! Lachlan had done that on his own despite her protests. Hopefully, Brodie would see reason when she explained it to him.

"Did ye send for him then?" Brodie's voice cut sharply through the stillness, his brown eyes narrowing as he turned to fix Moira with an accusatory stare. "Did ye defy me and call upon me grandfather to mend what I've not given leave to heal?"

"Naught of the sort," Moira replied calmly, meeting his intense gaze without wavering. "I gave ye my word, Brodie, and I am not one to break a vow lightly. 'Twas Lachlan who sought out the healer, despite my protest."

"Ye did not protest loudly enough," he countered, bitterness lacing his words. "Ye could have stopped him if ye truly wished it."

"Stopping Lachlan would be akin to halting the wind itself," she said, holding her ground. "Yer brother acts according to his own heart, same as any stubborn McClain man."

Brodie's jaw clenched, his anger simmering just below the surface, and Moira knew her words provided little comfort against his sense of helplessness. She held his gaze, wishing she could ease the burden of pride and pain that anchored him to that bed, knowing that only Brodie himself could grant the forgiveness he sought from others.

Moira's hand, callused from the hilt of her sword, hovered over Brodie's clenched fist. The infirmary was quiet save for the crackle of the hearth and the occasional groan from a wounded soldier. She searched his face for some sign of solace or gratitude but found none.

"Brodie, I—" she started, only to be cut off by his sharp gaze.

"Ye killed him," he said, voice hoarse but laced with an undercurrent of disdain. "The man who did this to me. Dead by your hand."

His words were as cold as the winds that swept through the glens outside. Moira stiffened, feeling a strange blend of pride and confusion. "Aye, I did. And why wouldn't I? He had wounded ye, and with all the blood, I wasna sure ye'd survive it."

Brodie turned away, his jaw setting as if carved from the very stone of McAfee Keep itself. "Fiona, too. She took care of the others. Do you nae see? I dinnae need ye—or any woman—to fight my battles."

Her heart constricted at his rebuke. Moira had been raised on tales of valor, where the line between life and death often rested on the edge of a blade. She couldn't fathom why her actions, meant to protect, had kindled such anger in him.

"I dinnae understand, Brodie. What have I done that's so wrong?" Moira pleaded, seeking the warmth of connection that once existed between them. "I sought only to save yer life."

"Save it?" Brodie scoffed, his glare unwavering. "Or control it?

Ye think because I'm laid up here that I'm helpless? That I need rescue?"

"Never helpless," she countered, the fire in her belly stoking her words. "But even the mightiest oak needs shelter from the storm."

"Then let the storm come!" he shot back. "I would rather face it on my own than have tales told of Brodie McClain, the warrior who owed his life to a woman's blade."

In that moment, the chasm between them felt as wide as the lochs dotting the Highlands. Moira's hands trembled with a mix of fury and sorrow. She'd been certain that when the conflicts between their alliance and Clyde Stewart had ended she would be happy. Now, looking at her husband, she wondered if she would ever be happy again.

"Perhaps you're right," Moira whispered, her voice barely above the murmur of the dying fire. "Perhaps I was wrong to assume you'd want to live to fight another day."

Turning her back to him, Moira walked toward the door. She didn't dare look back, fearing her resolve would crumble under the weight of his silent scorn. She knew not what the morrow would bring, but tonight, she felt as though she had lost more than just Brodie's favor—she had lost a part of herself in the battle for his life.

THE INFIRMARY DOOR creaked open, cutting a sliver of daylight across the dim room. Moira's head snapped up as Lachlan and Alisdair strode in, knowing they needed to explain to Brodie what had truly happened the day he was injured. She rose to her feet, her gaze flicking between the two brothers and Brodie's sullen form on the bed.

"Ye need to explain what happened to bring yer grandfather to the infirmary to help Brodie. I've told him but he doesnae believe me," she said, her voice steady despite the turmoil raging within.

Lachlan looked at his brother, appearing so pitiful in the cot. His broad shoulders squared as if bracing against an unseen adversary. "Aye, Brodie," he said in that articulate, commanding tone he reserved for matters of clan importance. "It was me doing. I fetched him while she protested. Ye needed tending, and there was no time to waste. Ailis thought she would need to take yer leg!"

Moira shook her head. "Do ye see, Brodie? I didn't ask yer grandfather to come."

Brodie stared at his brother passionlessly. The only person he was angry with was Moira, and he couldn't possibly explain why. "She shouldn't have let ye." In the back of his mind, he knew Moira was right, and there was no way she could have stopped Lachlan once he set his mind to doing something.

Lachlan stood watching his brother for a moment, his expression unreadable, then turned to leave with Alisdair in tow, leaving no room for further argument. At the door, he stopped and said, "Ye need to make peace with yer wife, Brodie."

Moira pulled a stool to his bedside and sat down, her hands folded in her lap. The silence stretched between them, punctuated only by the soft whistle of wind outside.

She reached out tentatively, her fingers brushing the back of his hand. Brodie lay still, his jaw set, eyes fixed on some distant point beyond the walls of the infirmary. He seemed a statue carved from the very stone of the Highlands—cold and unyielding.

"Please, Brodie," she whispered into the darkness. "Look at me."

But he didn't. Not once through the long hours of the night did he acknowledge her presence. She could feel the chasm between them widening with each passing moment, filled with misunderstandings and unspoken pain.

The tentative chirping of birds signaled morning's arrival in the Highlands, but within the stone walls of the infirmary, the atmosphere remained tense and heavy. Ailis approached Brodie's bedside with a determined glint in her eyes, her dark hair pulled back to reveal a face set with purpose.

"Ye must try to stand, Brodie," she said firmly, her hands on her hips and determination filling her voice. "We cannae ken what ye're capable of unless ye make the attempt."

Brodie turned his head slowly to meet Ailis's gaze, his deep brown eyes clouded with doubt. "There's no use," he murmured, his voice carrying the weight of resignation. "A man knows when part of him is lost. I feel it in my bones that this leg will never bear me again."

"Brodie, ye mustn't speak such things," Ailis chided gently, reaching for his hand. "The body is a remarkable vessel—stronger than we oftentimes give credit." Her touch was warm and encouraging, but Brodie recoiled from her grasp as if her optimism burned him.

"Enough, Ailis," Brodie snapped, the calmness in his voice giving way to frustration. "I'll not be pitied nor coddled like some bairn."

Moira, who had lingered in the shadows by the window, stepped forward at her sister's side. Her red hair seemed like a fiery halo in the dawn light, her stance poised and ready for battle. Yet, there was softness in her eyes, a plea for understanding that belied her usual fierceness.

"Ye needn't go through this alone, Brodie," Moira said, her voice betraying none of the hurt from his cold shoulder the night before. "We are here for ye."

"Is that so?" Brodie's retort was sharp, his gaze cutting to where Moira stood. "Or are ye just here to make yerself feel better? To ease yer own guilt?"

"Guilty? For saving yer life?" Moira's tone rose, her hands clenching into fists. "I have naught to repent for in that regard."

"Ye think because ye wield a sword and shed blood that ye've saved me? I didnae ask ye to fight me battles, Moira!" His voice was a low growl now, anger seeping through his controlled exterior.

"Ye think I did it for glory?" Moira's own anger flared, her cheeks reddening to match the hue of her hair. "I fought because I couldn't bear the thought of losing ye, stubborn ass that ye are!"

"Enough," Ailis interjected, placing herself between them, her athletic build a barrier to their mounting fury. "This bickering serves no purpose. We are family, bound by blood and loyalty."

"Blood and loyalty," Brodie echoed hollowly, turning away from them both. His gaze fixed upon the distant mountains visible through the narrow window, as if seeking solace in the wildness of the land. "Leave me be, I have no need for either now."

Silence descended once more, save for the plaintive call of the wind against the keep's sturdy walls. Ailis's shoulders slumped ever so slightly, her resolve bending under the weight of Brodie's despair. Moira stood motionless, her eyes shimmering with unshed tears, as if she too were seeing something far beyond the confines of the infirmary—a hope for reconciliation that seemed as distant as the horizon.

The door creaked as Moira pushed it open, the cold night air rushing in to meet her. She stepped outside, her breath forming small clouds in the darkness.

She walked aimlessly, her mind a tumult of emotions. How had it come to this? When had the man she loved become a stranger to her? Tears streamed down her face, hot and bitter. She made no attempt to wipe them away.

In the distance, a wolf howled, its mournful cry echoing across the land. Moira felt a kinship with the lonely creature. She, too, felt lost and alone, adrift in a sea of uncertainty.

As she walked, memories of happier times flooded her mind. The day she first met Brodie, his eyes sparkling with mischief. The way he'd sweep her into his arms and kiss her until she was breathless. The nights they'd spend talking and laughing by the fire until the wee hours of the morning.

But those days seemed like a distant dream now, a fading memory of a life that no longer existed. The man she loved had turned his back on her. She understood he was suffering, but he wouldn't allow her to help him.

Moira wandered deeper into the moors, the tall grass brushing against her skirts. She had no destination in mind, no plan for where she would go. All she knew was that she couldn't bear to be near Brodie right now, not when the gulf between them felt so vast and insurmountable.

Suddenly, a twig snapped behind her, startling Moira from her thoughts. She whirled around, her heart pounding in her chest. Through the misty darkness, a figure emerged, tall and broad-shouldered.

But as the figure drew closer, Moira realized it was a stranger, and not someone who should be there. The stranger's face was obscured by shadows, but she could see the glint of a sword at his side. Fear gripped her, icy tendrils snaking down her spine. She only had her dagger. After spending all day in the infirmary, it hadn't even occurred to her to fetch her sword.

"Who goes there?" she called, her voice trembling despite her efforts to sound brave.

The man stepped into a patch of moonlight, revealing a face scarred by battles past. His eyes, cold and calculating, fixed upon her with an intensity that made Moira's blood run cold. She took an involuntary step back, her hand instinctively reaching for the dirk she kept hidden in the folds of her skirt.

"Ye shouldnae be out here alone, lass," the man said, his voice low and menacing. "There be dangers lurkin' in these moors that ye cannae even imagine."

Moira lifted her chin, refusing to show fear. "I can take care o' meself," she said, her fingers closing around the hilt of her dirk. "Now, I'll ask ye again—who are ye and what do ye want?"

You think you can outsmart me, little girl?" he growled, his cold eyes glinting with malice. "You have no idea who you're dealing with."

Moira stood her ground, refusing to let her fear show. She met his gaze steadily, her chin lifted in defiance. "I know ye are trying to frighten me," she retorted, her voice surprisingly calm despite the hammering of her heart. "And I'm not afraid of ye."

The man's lips curled into a sneer. He took a step closer, looming over her like a predator ready to pounce. "Is that so?" he mused, his tone dripping with condescension. "Well, perhaps it's time for a little lesson in respect."

In a flash, the man's hand shot out, gripping Moira's wrist in a vice-like hold. She gasped in pain, the dirk clattering to the ground. He yanked her closer, his fetid breath hot against her face.

"Ye McAfees think ye're so high and mighty," he snarled, his eyes blazing with hatred. "But I remember a time when yer clan was nothin' more than a pack o' mangy dogs, scroungin' for scraps at the feet o' the Sinclairs."

Moira's eyes widened in recognition as she ignored the first part of his statement. The McAfees had been the strongest clan in their area for a long while, over a century. "Ye…ye were an advisor to Laird Sinclair," she breathed, the pieces falling into place.

The man's grip tightened, his nails digging into her flesh. "Aye, I was," he spat. "Until yer husband and his kin warred against us, leaving the few remaining Sinclairs to rot."

"The McAfees didnae betray yer clan," she argued, struggling against his grip. "Yer laird was a tyrant, oppressin' his own people. The McAfees simply fought for what was right. And both of my sisters were taken by the Sinclairs against their will at different times! Yer leader was in the wrong for what he did, and me clan and the McClains took care of him."

The man's face contorted with rage. "Lies!" he roared, spittle flying from his lips. "The Sinclairs were a great clan, and we will rise again!"

Kevin stepped out from behind a tree, sword in hand. "Run back to the keep, Moira!" he shouted as the stranger struck his sword with his own.

Moira couldn't move. She felt as if her legs were tangled into roots in the ground. As she watched, Kevin made short work of the man, and within moments, Sinclair was on his knees before Kevin. "Just kill me!" the man shouted.

Kevin shook his head. "Nay, I'll put ye in the dungeon with yer laird and his son. Ye can rot for all I care!" While Kevin held his sword to the man's throat, Moira hurried forward and bound his hands behind his back with her shawl.

Moira followed the two men back to the keep, reminding herself once again, it wasn't safe to be out alone—especially after dark.

CHAPTER TWENTY-TWO

MOIRA ENTERED THE dimly lit infirmary, where the scent of herbs mingled with the moans of recovering men. She paused, scanning the rows of cots until her eyes settled on one figure in particular.

There he was—Brodie, cloaked in blankets that did little to hide his pallor. He was half-raised, propping himself up with a grimace that spoke volumes of the pain he concealed beneath his stoic facade. Moira's heart contracted sharply.

Moira advanced with purposeful strides, her boots whispering against the stone floor. Each step brought into focus the stubborn set of Brodie's jaw, the way his brown eyes, usually so observant and keen, now flickered away from hers.

"Good morn to ye, Brodie," she greeted, her voice carrying the same authority she wielded when commanding her family's warriors. "How fare ye this day?"

"Fair enough, considering," Brodie muttered, shifting uneasily as if even speaking caused discomfort. His glance skittered off to the side, avoiding the piercing scrutiny of Moira's gaze—an evasion that didn't sit well with the McAfee lass, accustomed to confronting issues with the directness of a charging bull.

"Ye dinnae sound convinced of yer own words," Moira observed, folding her arms across her chest as she studied him with an intensity that left no room for pretense. Her stance was as unyielding as the mountains from which she hailed, her presence an unwavering force in the sterile gloom of the healing quarters.

"Nor do I feel it," Brodie finally conceded, his voice a rumble of contained frustration that echoed against the stone walls, resonating with the subdued tension that hung between them like a Highland fog.

The infirmary door creaked as Ailis slipped in, her presence weaving through the murmurs of the wounded. Her dark hair contrasted with the cold stone walls as it swayed gracefully, reflecting years spent navigating rough terrain.

"Ye look as though ye could use some respite, brother," she said to Brodie. Her vibrant green eyes met his in a gaze that held none of Moira's fiery challenge but offered solace instead.

Brodie's scowl lessened almost imperceptibly at the sight of Ailis, her mere presence coaxing the rigid lines of his body to soften. She offered him a smile, its warmth cutting through the chill of his despondence. "A wee bit of effort each day, and ye'll be running again."

Moira watched the exchange, her own resolve reinforcing as she observed the calming effect Ailis had on Brodie. It was Moira who broke the silence, her words carrying the weight of their unspoken agreement. "Let us help ye stand, Brodie. 'Tis time to face this day's challenge."

Brodie's gaze wavered, caught between resignation and the spark of pride that flared within him. The wariness in his eyes wrestled with the innate resolve of a Highland warrior, and after a moment's hesitation, his nod granted them permission to proceed. It was a concession born not of defeat but the kind of bravery that acknowledged the need for allies in battle—even battles fought within the confines of healing walls.

Moira felt the coarse fabric of Brodie's sleeve under her fingers as she and Ailis positioned themselves on either side of his weakened form. They both leaned in, ready to bear his weight, their faces mirrors of determination reflecting back at him.

"Ready?" Moira asked, even as her pulse quickened with anticipation.

Brodie nodded, his jaw clenching—a silent warrior preparing

for an unseen foe. With each of them taking an arm, they hoisted gently, urging him upward. His body tensed, each muscle coiled like a spring, before he pushed against the cot with what strength he could muster.

His face contorted with the struggle, a deep furrow etching itself between his brows as his arms shook. It was a battle against his own flesh, a rebellion against the betrayal of limbs that had once carried him through the wilds of the Highlands with ease.

"Ye can do this, Brodie," Ailis murmured, her voice a soft hum that danced around the effort-filled silence.

As Brodie came to stand, his legs trembled beneath him, as unsteady as saplings in a fierce wind. The growl that escaped him was both of frustration and exertion, a primal sound that echoed off the stone walls of the infirmary.

"Focus on us," Moira said, her grip tightening, her knuckles whitening with the effort to steady him. "We've got ye. Just breathe."

She willed her own stability into him, sharing the very essence of her resolve as she held him upright.

Brodie stood, wavering between Moira and Ailis. The room blurred at the edges, his focus narrowing to the piercing ache in his limbs, an unwelcome reminder of his frailty.

"Ye need not treat me like a bairn," Brodie's voice sliced through the tense quietude, roughened by disuse and spiked with ire. "I am no invalid to be coddled, Moira."

Moira's fiery eyes met his outburst with an equal force of will. Her lips pressed into a thin line; her jaw set with determination. She swallowed the retort that lingered on her tongue, letting silence carry the weight of her unspoken resolve. He was in pain, and she needed to remain calm to help him through it.

"Och, Brodie," Ailis chimed in, her voice carrying the lightness of a summer breeze over heather fields, "ye've got more fight in ye than the wildcats o' the Highlands."

The corners of Brodie's mouth twitched, reluctantly conceding to the humor in Ailis's words. His deep brown eyes, usually sharp with contemplation, softened slightly, allowing for a pained yet genuine smile to break through the storm of his frustration.

"Aye," he responded, the growl in his voice now tempered by the flicker of amusement. "And that determination should help me now."

"Ye must draw on it," Moira said softly, pleased to see a smile whether it was for her or her sister.

The moment balanced between triumph and defeat as Brodie's legs struggled to support him. His stoic determination shifted to uncertainty, and his strength vanished like mist over the moors. He groaned, echoing off the infirmary's stone walls, and crumpled, his body betraying him again.

Moira, still at his side, put an arm around him, her movements synchronized with Ailis's as they caught him in practiced arms. Together, they eased him back onto the cot, their efficiency a dance they had mastered over countless days of tending to the wounded warriors of Clan McAfee.

"Easy now, Brodie," Moira said, her voice a stark contrast to the commanding tone she used when dealing with matters of the clan. She knelt beside him, folding her hands neatly atop the rough wool blanket that covered his legs.

"Setbacks are but part of the journey to mend," she murmured, her piercing eyes softening with empathy. "Ye mustn't let them daunt yer spirit."

Brodie's jaw clenched, and he turned his head away, fixating on the narrow window that showed just a bit of the Highland landscape. In the silence that hung between them, his pride and vulnerability waged a silent war. The steady rise and fall of his chest betrayed the depth of his internal struggle, and for a fleeting moment, he seemed smaller, contained by the confines of his own battered body.

Moira watched him, the lines of worry etched into her brow. She reached out, her hand hovering just above his arm before it fell back to her side, her touch withheld.

"Tomorrow," she promised, "we'll try again."

Ailis stepped forward. She placed a comforting hand on Brodie's tense shoulder, her touch as steady as the ancient pines that surrounded the keep. Her emerald eyes held a glimmer of solace as she leaned in, allowing her presence to envelop him like the Highland mists.

"Ye've the heart of the Highlands within ye, Brodie McClain," she said, her voice carrying the melodic lilt of their shared heritage. "The strength ye've shown is impressive." A small smile graced her lips, not one of mirth but of earnest assurance. "Patience, like the deep lochs, holds its own power. Give yerself time to heal."

Her words seemed to seep into the room, settling among the lingering scents of herbs and woodsmoke, a balm to the prickling tension that had gripped the space. For a moment, it was as if her unwavering belief could will his body to mend, her spirit to bolster his.

Moira rose from her kneel, the determination in her stance as unyielding as the stone walls that had safeguarded their people for generations. Her fiery locks swayed with her movement.

"Tomorrow, we rise anew," she vowed, her gaze locking onto his averted face. "We dinnae yield today, nor shall we on the morrow. Together, we'll face each dawn until ye stand proud upon this land once more."

It was more than a promise to Brodie—it was a declaration to the very essence of their lives, an oath to endure, to persevere, to reclaim the strength that the Highlands demanded of its children.

Moira stood, going to the door of the infirmary. She wasn't needed—or wanted—by Brodie, so she would make herself useful hunting or even helping in the kitchen.

"Moira…"

The voice halted her escape, a whisper threading through the stillness, taut with a raw edge she recognized all too well. She turned, her gaze sweeping past Ailis's soothing presence to settle on Brodie, a shadow of the once indomitable warrior she had come to know and love.

His brown eyes, hooded with fatigue yet filled with an unspoken plea, met hers. "I fear…I may ne'er be the man I was before." Brodie's words trembled in the air, a confession so stark it seemed to echo off the walls, rebounding inside Moira's chest.

She watched as the ghost of his usual confidence wavered. This was Brodie laid bare, stripped of bravado and the comforting mantle of strength they both wore like armor against life's cruelties. Her throat tightened at the sight—at the vulnerability he rarely showed, the very one that bound her to him more fiercely than any clannish rite ever could.

"Ye are not alone in this, Brodie," Moira said, her voice a clear, steady beacon as she took a step back toward him. The room blurred at the edges, the world narrowing to the space between them. "I'll be by your side, and we will face whatever may come."

Brodie's gaze held hers, searching, as if trying to draw courage from the depths of her promise. There was a silent communion then, a melding of fears and hopes that transcended the spoken word. "Ye willna leave me?" His voice sounded like that of a defeated man, and she rushed to his side.

She leaned down to press a soft kiss against his lips, a promise between them that needed no words.

Moira turned once more, leaving Brodie for a while, but taking with her the weight of his confession and the fierce determination to see him restored.

Silence wrapped around Moira and Ailis like the Highland mists as they stepped into the chill of the stone corridor, the heavy door of the infirmary closing behind them with a soft thud. Their footsteps echoed off the walls, a stark reminder of the emptiness that filled the spaces where laughter and chatter once lived.

Ailis's gaze lingered on her sister for a moment, reading the storm of emotions in Moira's eyes. Without a word, she placed a reassuring hand on Moira's arm, her touch grounding, as if imparting the strength of the ancient pines that withstood the relentless winds outside McAfee Keep.

Moira's thoughts raced ahead, weaving through the myriad challenges that lay before them—the weight of Brodie's fears, the whispers of conspiracy that threatened to unravel the fabric of Highland unity, the Sinclair betrayal that cast long shadows over their clan's future. Each step they took was a silent vow, a commitment to not just heal Brodie's wounds, but to fortify the spirit of the clans against the looming threat of the Stewarts' ambition.

With a final glance back at the door that held more than just a wounded warrior, Moira turned away, squaring her shoulders against the tasks that awaited them. She felt Ailis's presence beside her.

They hadn't walked more than a few steps before they ran into Alisdair and Lachlan. "Are ye all right, lass?" Alisdair asked, studying Moira.

Moira nodded. "Thanks to Kevin, I am all right. And I willna be going to the forest alone at night again, especially without me sword." She paused for a moment, biting her lip. "But I do not think we should tell Brodie about my encounter in the forest. He needs to focus on healing and not worry about me."

Lachlan and Alisdair exchanged a look. "If ye think that's best, we will keep yer secret."

"Thank ye," Moira said. As she and Ailis kept walking, she quickly explained about running into a Sinclair in the forest.

"Ye must be more careful!" Ailis chided.

"I will do me best," Moira agreed, though they both knew Moira found danger.

"Just promise to carry yer sword!" Ailis said.

"That, I will do."

━━◆━━ ❦ ━━◆━━

CHAPTER TWENTY-THREE

MOIRA MCAFEE STOOD in the great hall, stone walls echoing with preparations. Her clan bustled around her, hanging tartan banners and arranging wooden tables for the evening's ceilidh. Moira remained still, scanning the room to be certain all was at the ready. Anticipation weighed upon her, contrasting with the festive atmosphere and tightening responsibilities within her.

Young lads hoisted barrels of ale, laughter mixing with the noise of kitchen maids carrying trays of bannocks and smoked fish. Moira's thoughts wandered to Brodie—the man whose quiet strength intertwined with her own unyielding spirit—his recovery tugging at the edges of their shared loyalties.

Taking a deep breath, Moira stepped into chaos. She navigated the hall, offering decisive guidance to her kinsmen's questions.

"Moira, where d'ye want the fiddlers to set up?" asked a burly clansman.

"By the hearth, Hamish," she directed. "The warmth will keep their fingers nimble for the reels."

As she assisted with arrangements, Moira's confident facade hid an internal struggle between duty and Brodie's struggles.

"Moira, is it too much garland?" A timid voice drew her attention to a young girl holding fragrant pine and holly.

"Never too much," Moira reassured firmly but kindly. "The greenery reminds us of life thriving even in winter. We celebrate not just our might, but our endurance."

The girl returned to her task, encouraged by Moira's approval. Observing her, Moira longed to join Brodie and see how her husband was doing that day, but she had other duties that must be seen to first.

"Ye seem lost in thought," Beathan remarked, appearing beside her. "Troubles?"

"Only the usual concerns," Moira answered with a fleeting grin.

Beathan gently reminded her that even the strongest needed a break. Grateful for his wisdom, Moira focused on getting the great hall ready for the ceilidh they had planned.

During the ceilidh, she sought a balance between duty and longing, her heart intertwined with Brodie's.

Ailis approached quietly, her presence barely noticeable. Moira turned to see her sister's eyes gleaming with resolve and a touch of apprehension.

"Moira," Ailis said, "the ceilidh is more than just a celebration tonight. It's necessary for maintaining our alliances."

Moira understood the unspoken worries between them. "We'll use it to remind everyone that our kinship is stronger than any outside threat."

"And what about Clyde Stewart?" Ailis asked, concern in her voice.

"We'll keep our allies close and make sure they know where we stand," Moira responded firmly. "If Stewart raises another army, I'm certain we'll hear about it long before he approaches."

Ailis smiled at her sister's determination. Moira then stepped outside into the courtyard, needing fresh air. There she saw Brodie sitting amidst wild thistles, a mix of pride and concern filling her.

"How did ye get out here?" Moira whispered, reaching out to brush his arm.

Brodie met her gaze, replying with a hint of a smile, "Me brothers told me I would rot if I stayed in the infirmary for another minute, and they carried me out here. I must admit that it's doing me good to be in the fresh air."

"Just dinnae overdo it. Ye've been in a bed for a week now, and ye've lost much of yer strength."

Moira's arm wrapped around Brodie's waist. She studied his face, noting each wince he tried to hide.

"Talk to me, Brodie," Moira urged. "Tell me what ye need."

He leaned on his cane, searching her determined eyes. "I fear I'll never be the man you need me to be."

"Ye forget, my love," she said, touching his cheek. "I chose ye because ye always walked with me."

A fleeting smile crossed Brodie's lips. "Aye, but now…with Clyde Stewart's threat…"

"Ye are not a hindrance, Brodie McClain. Together, we are stronger than any looming threat." She rested her head on his shoulder for just a moment.

Her words kindled a spark in his eyes—a glimpse of their shared passion.

"Your faith gives me strength," Brodie admitted softly.

"Do ye want to try to make an appearance at the ceilidh tonight?" she asked. "Ye aren't strong enough to stay long, but a short time would be nice, I think. The infirmary sucks all the happiness from ye."

Brodie considered Moira's suggestion, a glimmer of determination in his eyes. "Aye, I'll make an appearance. Everyone needs to see that I'm healing, even if I cannae stay long. I ken the McClain soldiers will be happy to see I can move a bit."

Moira squeezed his hand, pride swelling in her chest. "I'll be by your side, mo chridhe. We'll show them our strength." She rested her head on his shoulder for just a moment. It was good to have her husband back.

As the sun began to set, casting a golden glow over the courtyard, Moira went for Brodie's brothers to take him back to the infirmary where he could rest before the ceilidh. Once she found Alisdair and Lachlan, they carried him back to the infirmary, and he slept.

THE GREAT HALL was alive with the spirit of the Highlands. Fiddlers played lively reels while clansmen and women danced, their feet pounding the stone floor in intricate patterns. The aroma of roasted meats and fresh bread filled the air, mingling with the scent of pine and smoke from the hearth.

Moira moved through the crowd, her vibrant hair catching the firelight as she greeted allies and kin alike. Then she scanned the room, noting the placement of each clan and the subtle shifts in power dynamics. She understood that this gathering's importance extended far beyond mere celebration.

As she passed a group of men who had joined them from the Stewart's army, their hushed conversations faltered. Moira met their guarded looks with a cool smile, refusing to let their presence unsettle her.

Moira approached the men, her voice carrying over the music. "I trust ye are enjoying the hospitality of the McAfees this eve."

The men exchanged glances before one spoke up, his tone carefully neutral. "Aye. 'Tis a grand ceilidh."

Moira held his gaze, her words measured. "And I trust ye will remember this kindness, should the tides turn."

The implication hung heavy in the air. The man inclined his head, a flicker of understanding passing between them. "Aye, we'll not forget."

Satisfied, Moira moved on, her message delivered. As she wove through the throng, she caught sight of Ailis deep in conversation with her husband, Lachlan. Their heads were bent close, expressions serious despite the merriment surrounding them.

She walked straight to them. "Lachlan, would you find Alisdair and bring Brodie for the ceilidh. He wants to at least be part of it, though he cannae stay for long."

Lachlan nodded solemnly, his piercing blue eyes meeting Moira's. "Aye, I'll fetch Brodie. He's been eager to join the festivities."

As Lachlan strode off to find his brothers, Moira turned to Ailis, concern etched on her features. "What troubles ye, sister? I saw the intensity of yer conversation."

Ailis sighed, her green eyes reflecting the flickering torchlight. "Lachlan and I were discussing the men who came to us from the Stewarts and Sinclairs. There are whispers that they're plotting something, but we cannae discern their true intentions."

Moira's brow furrowed. "We must remain vigilant. The Sinclairs have always been a slippery bunch, and with Clyde Stewart's ambitions..." She trailed off, the unspoken threat hanging between them.

Ailis nodded grimly. "Aye, we cannae let our guard down. Not even for a moment."

Just then, a hush fell over the great hall as Brodie entered, supported by his brothers Alisdair and Lachlan. Despite the pallor of his skin and the slight tremor in his hands, Brodie held his head high, his brown eyes gleaming with determination.

Moira's heart swelled with pride and love as she watched her husband make his way through the parted crowd. She stepped forward to meet him, taking his arm and guiding him to a seat of honor near the hearth. "Ye're doing so well!"

The smile on Brodie's face told her that he was proud of himself for making it there. She knew his brothers had carried him to the entry to the great hall, and then had set him on his feet, but just a few steps felt like everything to her.

Moira surveyed the great hall of McAfee Keep, taking in the tartan-draped tables, flickering candles, and vibrant wall hangings. Each detail represented her clan's strength and unity.

"Ye look ready to take on the devil himself," Brodie said with affectionate humor.

"Perhaps I am," Moira replied, approaching him.

She observed his subtle wince as he moved to meet her halfway. Though it pained her, she admired his relentless spirit.

"Ye shouldnae strain yerself, Brodie," she chided gently, grasping his hand.

"Ye know, but I'm done wallowing in my own fears. I'm still alive, and I will make my life the best it can be," he said, gripping firmly despite evident pain.

"It's no' just the clan that needs yer strength. I need ye too, more than ever."

"Then ye'll have me, Moira," Brodie vowed, words enveloping her like a warm plaid.

"Always," she whispered back, sealing their promise with a tender kiss.

Moira sensed a lighter burden on her shoulders. With Brodie by her side, they were an unbreakable force capable of facing any threat together.

He was only able to stay at the ceilidh for an hour, and she spent every moment of it at his side before returning to her duties as one of the three hostesses. It was nice to just sit and observe the dancers. She enjoyed anything with Brodie at her side.

After making a quick pass through the hall and ensuring people were enjoying themselves, she stopped to watch the dancing for a moment again. Everyone looked happy.

The rhythmic stomping and clapping filled the hall, faces filled with happiness. Moira stood at the edge, and a smile tugged at her mouth. She joined the circle as a burly clansman waved her over.

Moira's laughter cut through the music as she danced gracefully. Dancers moved in time to the drumbeat, hands weaving and feet tapping in an intricate pattern passed down generations—a testament to Highland heritage.

"Ye've not lost yer touch," Ailis praised, spinning past Moira.

"Nor will I ever," Moira retorted, eyes sparkling with joy as she spun.

Torches cast a warm glow, and musicians struck up lively tunes that made everyone tap their feet. Laughter mingled harmoniously with fiddles and pipes.

As soon as the last guest had retired for the night, Moira headed back to the infirmary and her Brodie.

"I had a fine time this evening at the ceilidh," Brodie said softly, smiling at Moira. "It's more than merriment they share—it is hope." He covered a yawn.

"Aye," she agreed, pride evident in her voice. "The men have truly learned to fight and live as one large clan. I never thought I would see so many come together against a single threat." She smiled mischievously. "Other than the English, of course."

He chuckled softly, enjoying her humor. "Thank ye for making certain I was able to be there for part of it."

"I dinnae think I could have made it through the night without ye." Moira clasped his hand. "Ye ken, we will weather any storm that comes," Moira murmured amidst the celebration.

"Like the mighty oaks outside these walls," Brodie replied with a nod, his voice steady as the ancient trees.

"Whatever comes, Brodie, I stand ready, with ye at my side." Her voice carried the weight of commitment, bound by love and sealed by their ancestors' blood.

"And I with ye, Moira."

"Then let us face the morrow with heads held high," she said, her voice bright with conviction.

"Until the end of our days," Brodie promised.

She rested her head on his shoulder for a moment. It was good to have her husband back. They would have to start the difficult part of getting him walking on his own soon, but for tonight, she felt as if they were united once again.

CHAPTER TWENTY-FOUR

FIRST THING THE following morning, Moira walked to the infirmary. She and Ailis planned for this to be the day Brodie would start walking without help again.

Moira reached for linen bandages, eyes darting to locate salves and tinctures, while Ailis collected fresh water and clean cloths. They approached Brodie McClain's bed in an unspoken dance of readiness.

Brodie lay under woolen blankets, caught between sleep and wakefulness. The sisters' rustling roused him, his deep brown eyes flickering open before a mask of resolve settled on his features. He swung his legs over the side of the bed with a controlled grimace.

His lean frame masked the strength within his muscles, every movement revealing the internal battle inside him. Brodie clenched his jaw as he pushed against the mattress, propping himself up on trembling arms. His gaze remained forward, focused on the difficult path of recovery ahead. He knew the days ahead would be filled with pain, but he was determined to walk again. His fears about losing Moira would allow him to do nothing else.

Inhaling deeply, Brodie allowed them to hoist him upward. His feet met the cold stone floor, and he focused intently on each step forward. The initial steps were a sheer test of determination, but he persisted, feeling the burn in his muscles with every movement. Moira and Ailis matched his pace, as they did their best to support him and not allow him to fall.

Sweat trickled down Brodie's forehead as he clenched his jaw, refusing to be defeated by his body. Moira and Ailis provided unwavering support, holding onto him with unyielding steadiness. The distance between the bed and wooden beam across the room shrank with each step, the women's hushed encouragement fueling his determination.

"Tha thu làidir, Brodie. You are strong," Moira whispered.

"Each step is a victory," Ailis added softly.

Brodie reached the beam, his fingers brushing against the rough wood. He allowed himself to lean against it briefly, a small triumph within the infirmary's stone confines.

His brothers arrived and carried him into the courtyard. The vibrant green grass contrasted with the muted tones he'd grown used to. The sky was a vast blue canvas streaked with white clouds. Mountains surrounded them, their snow-capped peaks guarding valleys and lochs below.

He inhaled deeply, smelling pine and earth—the essence of home. When he'd sat in the courtyard the previous day, he'd realized he had too much to live for to give up, which had been his first inclination.

With Moira's shoulder for support and Ailis gripping his other side, Brodie moved toward a rough-hewn bench in the courtyard heart. Sitting down, his legs trembled like aspen leaves around them. His brothers' distant voices encouraged him.

"Stand tall, brother!" Alisdair called.

Lachlan yelled, "We're with ye every step!"

Brodie surveyed the wildflowers as Ailis readied herself.

"Ready," he said, breathing in the earthy scent.

With Moira's support and Ailis's guidance, Brodie stood on unsteady legs atop uneven cobblestones.

"Focus on the horizon," Moira advised as they moved forward. "Let it guide you."

"Watch the stones, feel the earth," Ailis encouraged.

Their voices propelled him onward as each step tested his

balance. Fixating on distant mountains, Brodie found his rhythm amid the resolute Highland terrain, his own story interwoven among its challenges and triumphs.

THEY WERE BACK in the courtyard the following day, giving Brodie a new goal for how far he needed to walk. Yesterday's goal had been difficult, but today's looked near impossible.

Brodie steadied himself on the cobblestone path, gripping Moira's and Ailis's arms with each step. "Each step is a victory," Moira encouraged.

Ailis smiled. "Yesterday's mark is behind you now." True enough, the small pile of stones they used to measure progress lay in the distance. Brodie's muscles quivered with fatigue, but he pressed on.

"Rest now," Ailis suggested.

"Nay, while I've daylight left, I'll use it," Brodie replied.

Moira nodded. "Then we walk with ye."

The afternoon sun cast long shadows upon the stone walls of McAfee Keep as Brodie continued walking. His breathing grew more labored, limbs trembling, yet his eyes fixated on the path ahead.

"Lean on us," Ailis murmured when Brodie faltered.

"Ye are never alone," Moira added firmly. Their unwavering presence gave him strength to press on.

"Another step, then another," Brodie whispered, determination driving him forward.

As Brodie's endurance waned, love for his clan and companions pushed him forward. When he finally stopped, he knew today's exhaustion would be tomorrow's strength—a strength forged from the very stones beneath his feet and the unyielding spirit of those who stood with him.

BRODIE WAS SORE and in no mood to work the following day, but Moira and Ailis pushed him to at least try.

"Enough!" Brodie's word ricocheted off the courtyard walls. He glared at his trembling legs. "I'm no use to anyone like this—"

"Ye are more than the strength of yer legs, Brodie McClain," Moira interrupted. She touched his arm reassuringly. "Rest now."

Brodie nodded, accepting Moira's wisdom and acknowledging the strength in others.

"Forgive me," he whispered coarsely. "I seem to always get angry with the two of ye when ye are doing nothing but trying to help me." Brodie shook his head. "I dinnae mean to be rude."

"Nothing to forgive," Ailis replied, offering her shoulder. "It's the fire in yer spirit that'll see ye through this."

As evening invaded, twilight shadows danced on the courtyard floor. Seated between Moira and Ailis, Brodie relished the fleeting warmth. The sun dipped lower, etching the skyline with its parting hues.

"Look at that sky," Ailis murmured in awe. Captivated by the colorful display, Brodie pledged, "Tomorrow, I'll walk further."

Moira nodded, her red hair blazing like embers, pride shining in her eyes. "Aye, we'll be with ye every step." She pressed a kiss to his shoulder. "We'll not give up on ye. No matter what." Though she hurt every time he became angry with her, she knew things would soon be better as he improved. And she had promised to be with him in sickness and in health. What was this, if not sickness?

The camaraderie fortified Brodie's resolve and their unwavering commitment to one another. Gratitude swelled within him for the day's small victories.

"Thank ye," he said softly. He knew he didn't deserve their compassion, but that seemed to be all they showed him.

As stars emerged to guard the night sky, despair retreated,

leaving only hope and unyielding determination for whatever lay ahead.

Moira and Ailis approached Brodie, their silhouettes contrasting against the sky. In sync, they supported him as he rose from the bench.

"Ready?" Moira's steady voice accompanied her firm grip on Brodie's arm.

"Let's go," Ailis added with an encouraging tone.

Brodie nodded, gathering his strength for the journey back to the infirmary. Moira's fiery hair seemed to capture the waning light, guiding them through the dim courtyard. Ailis's presence provided unwavering support on his other side—her athletic form reassuring him of steady progress.

Their feet carried them to the infirmary where Brodie settled onto the bed with a sigh of relief. He observed as Moira stowed away medical supplies and Ailis ensured his comfort.

"If ye keep improving, in another seven days, I think ye could move back into yer own room with Moira." Ailis smiled at Brodie. "I think that would make ye improve even more quickly."

A determined exchange passed between them—a silent commitment to continue healing until Brodie could stand unaided once more. But they all knew he would need to be able to climb stairs to move back to his room with Moira. And that would be a difficult undertaking.

Brodie nodded in surprise. "Ye are smart, giving me something to work toward. Thank ye."

As Ailis dimmed the oil lamps, Brodie knew another day of trials awaited. But within the infirmary, supported by Moira and Ailis, he believed in a stronger tomorrow.

Stars peeked through the narrow window while Brodie lay on his pillow, body aching from exertion—an ode to that day's success amid the muted atmosphere of the infirmary. There were no other patients in there now, as they had all been sent home with their clans. It was just him.

He closed his eyes, letting his breath guide him inward. The journey had pushed him to his limits, but Moira's fiery courage and Ailis's steadiness became his pillars.

As they pressed on, their hands and voices provided unwavering support, fueling his spirit. "Ye've come far, Brodie McClain," he whispered, echoing their words.

In the gloom, Brodie imagined the path ahead—untrodden trails and challenges waiting. But with Moira and Ailis beside him, the unknown seemed less daunting—the thought of tomorrow ignited a fire in his chest that even night's chill couldn't extinguish.

Their progress was a testament not only to his tenacity but also to their unwavering partnership. Together, they forged an unbreakable bond.

Brodie succumbed to sleep, dreams filled with impending challenges and an insurmountable peak that they would climb one step at a time. Under Moira's fierce resolve and Ailis's quiet strength, anticipation for the next day outshone any lingering doubt.

"Rest now," he told himself, surrendering to the night. "For on the morrow, we rise again."

CHAPTER TWENTY-FIVE

D AWN BROKE OVER the rugged Highlands as Moira and Ailis slipped their hands beneath Brodie McClain's shoulders. Their coordination was a silent dance of care.

"Ready?" Moira asked with quiet strength.

Brodie nodded, defiance etched on his determined face. Together, Moira and Ailis helped him into a seated position. Moira was happy to learn about any healing methods from Ailis, now that an injury had touched her life so completely. She'd thought it was a waste of a warrior before, but now… Now she understood.

"Ye can do this, Brodie," Moira encouraged.

His hands clenched into fists, muscles coiling in preparation. Leaning forward, he pushed through the pain that threatened to overwhelm him. "Up we go," Ailis prompted softly but firmly, her vibrant green eyes focused on Brodie.

He rose shakily. Despite his anger at his own weakness and the treachery that had brought him low, his confidence remained unyielding.

"Step now," Moira instructed while steadying him. Each faltering step was a trial for them all.

"Yer strong, Brodie. Stronger than the oak," Ailis added calmly.

Brodie stepped forward and slowly straightened up. As hard as simple tasks had become for him, he cherished the small accomplishments…like standing without his legs buckling under him.

Brodie's knees trembled, muscles protesting with each step across the stone floor.

Moira steadied him with her grip. Ailis, her sister's quiet counterpart, mirrored Moira's support on his other side. Years of shared trials allowed them to communicate through subtle nods and glances.

"Ye can do this," Moira murmured against their collective breath. She celebrated each one of his victories. He was becoming himself again before her eyes.

Exertion painted Brodie's face with sweat, jaw tense as he fought pain with each stride. "Just a bit further," Ailis coaxed, her lilt softening the room's tension like a tribute to the land's spirit.

Reaching the heavy oaken table, they paused for Brodie to rest. Ailis dabbed his forehead with a cloth while Moira breathed deeply nearby.

"Have ye heard?" Moira whispered to Ailis. "Clyde Stewart is trying to rally the last of the Clan Sinclair warriors?"

"Aye," Ailis replied grimly, her green eyes darkening. "The whispers grow louder with each passing day. Clyde's ambition knows no bounds."

Moira's grip tightened on the edge of the table, her knuckles whitening. "He seeks to unite the clans under his rule, no matter the cost. The very thought turns me stomach."

Brodie, his breath evening out, fixed his gaze on the sisters. "We cannae let that happen. The Highlands must remain free, each clan master of its own fate. We serve only the queen."

Ailis nodded, her dark hair catching the light filtering through the narrow windows. "The Stewarts' treachery runs deep, like a poisoned well. We must be vigilant."

"And prepared," Moira added, her voice hardening with resolve. "Clyde will stop at nothing to achieve his twisted vision. We must be ready to meet him on the field of battle if necessary."

Brodie pushed himself upright, his lean frame still unsteady but determination etched in every line. "I will not let my clan, my family, fall victim to Clyde's machinations. I may be wounded, but my spirit remains unbroken."

Ailis placed a gentle hand on his shoulder. "We stand with you, Brodie. Together, we will weather this storm and emerge stronger."

Moira's fierce gaze swept over them both. "Aye, we will. And when the time comes, we'll show Clyde Stewart and his Sinclair lackeys what it means to face the wrath of the Highlands." But in the back of her mind, she worried about the type of men who were still loyal to the Sinclairs. Was it possible that Stewart would gather an army full of murderers and Brigands? And if so, what would they be willing to do to serve Clyde Stewart?

A knock at the door interrupted their conversation. Moira strode over and opened it, revealing a clansman with a grave expression. "Urgent news from the border," he said, his breath coming in short gasps. "Clyde Stewart's forces have been spotted, and they're heading this way."

Moira's eyes narrowed. "How many?"

"At least a hundred strong. They'll be upon us by nightfall."

Ailis and Brodie exchanged a worried glance. They were in no condition to fight, not with Brodie still recovering from his wounds.

Moira turned back to them, her expression resolute. "We have no choice. We must prepare for battle."

Ailis nodded grimly. "I'll gather the women and children, make sure they're safe."

"And I'll rally the men," Moira said as she helped Brodie back to his cot. "We'll not let Clyde Stewart take what's ours without a fight."

"Can we trust the source?" Ailis replied softly.

"Trust is scarce these days." Moira frowned. "But if it's true, we're all at risk."

"Let's hope not," Ailis said, glancing at Brodie.

"Hope is a luxury," Moira countered quietly. "We must prevail."

HOOVES CLATTERED ON stone. A royal emissary had arrived.

Moira approached the entrance. The messenger dismounted hastily, panting and extending a sealed parchment toward her.

As Moira grasped the letter, she noted the unbroken seal of Mary de Guise—Queen Dowager of Scotland. She thanked the messenger, her tone steady despite inner turmoil.

Returning to Brodie's side, Moira announced, "From Mary de Guise," before breaking the seal and reading aloud: "'Clyde Stewart has blatantly disregarded Scottish law by taking lands not his own, spilling blood without honor…'"

Moira continued, detailing accusations that deepened the gravity of their situation. Brodie's fists clenched—a silent vow to protect what was theirs.

"Stewart's ambition will be his undoing," he declared.

"Or ours if we don't act quickly," Moira added. "We must plan and meet this threat head-on."

Ailis nodded, her expression solemn but resolute, beside her sister.

The silence hung heavily in McAfee Keep after Moira finished reading the letter. Brodie and his kin shifted uncomfortably, their anxiety palpable. Ailis stepped forward, her green eyes glowing with determination. "We cannot let fear dictate our path," she declared, suggesting envoys be sent to allied clans to inform them they were needed yet again. It felt like the armies had barely left, and they needed them back again. She hoped the other clans would take the threat as seriously as they were.

As agreement spread through the room, Brodie's thoughts turned to strategy. But first, he needed to face his own battle: regaining strength in his limbs. With Moira and Ailis beside him, Brodie focused on the task of rehabilitation.

"Steady," Moira encouraged as he pushed himself up from the chair, legs trembling.

"Focus," Ailis added gently.

Brodie took a breath and willed his body to obey. Each shaky step was more than just physical progress.

BRODIE TENSED AS he pushed himself up from the oak chair, his knuckles white. With each attempt to stand, his body protested, but the determination in his eyes remained. Moira stood close, her red hair reflecting her passion, ready to lend support.

"Ye can do this, Brodie," she said firmly. "One step at a time."

Nodding, Brodie slowly rose to his feet, legs trembling and unsteady. The room seemed to hold its breath, filled with anticipation and the faint scent of peat from the hearth.

Gritting his jaw, Brodie took two halting steps forward. Moira's hand hovered near his elbow, promising steadiness should he falter.

When he stumbled, Moira's hands guided him back to security. Her touch was a lifeline.

"Look at me, Brodie," she urged gently.

Their eyes met, and something wordless passed between them—an understanding that weakened pride and pain. He saw not just his own reflection in her gaze but also their shared loyalty.

"Thank ye, Moira," he breathed softly.

"Ye need not thank me," she replied earnestly. "We face this together."

A rare smile graced his lips as they continued their painstaking rehabilitation process. Their bond had grown deeper than either anticipated.

In the secluded stone chamber, Moira's hands moved over the parchment, her red hair cascading like a warrior's banner. The intensity in her eyes grew as she read Mary de Guise's letter once again.

"Can ye believe this?" she hissed to her sisters and brothers-in-law, Alisdair and Lachlan, gripping the letter tightly. "Clyde Stewart endangers not just our kin but all the Highlands."

Ailis, standing by the window, turned to face Moira. Stormy concern filled her usually peaceful green eyes. "I ken," she replied evenly. "But we must tread carefully to avoid provoking a war we can't win."

"Carefully?" Moira scoffed. "While they plot like wolves? Nay, Ailis, 'tis time for action!"

"Action, aye," Ailis agreed, stepping closer with a calming presence. "But it must be precise. We should call a clan meeting and gather more allies who share our cause."

Moira's rigid posture softened at Ailis's words—a strategic spark ignited within her. "Allies..." she murmured. "We have envoys going to the clans who just left with their armies, asking them to come back. Thankfully, there are still McClain soldiers here, and when you add in the McAfees, and the people who joined us after leaving Clyde, we can definitely handle them."

"Exactly." Ailis nodded, the plan taking form in her mind. "We'll need support from Highland Clans bound by honor and tradition—not fear or coercion."

"It's settled," Moira declared, determined despite looming uncertainty. "As Highlanders, we stand together. We'll protect our family, lands, and way of life—no matter what comes."

Their gazes locked, solidifying a silent pact to fiercely defend their clan. Together, they would navigate treacherous politics and weather the gathering storm.

As night fell and there was no army, Moira went to Brodie. "I do believe Clyde took his army to Sinclair Keep. He'll continue using it as his base of operation, I fear."

Brodie nodded. "It would make sense for him to do so. Tomorrow morning will bring battle, most likely, and Alisdair and Lachlan are most likely hurrying to make preparations. Thank God you and the ladies have kept the hunting going, and we can feed whomever we need to feed."

"And we'll keep at it. There's no reason for anyone to go hungry."

CHAPTER TWENTY-SIX

MOIRA'S EYES LINGERED on the gathering of tartan and steel below the infirmary window. Beside her, Ailis focused her intent gaze upon their clansmen—McAfee and McClain united for the coming battle. The courtyard emanated tension as if from a taut bowstring. As Moira met her sister's eyes, an unspoken vow passed between them—a pledge to their kin and their sacred Highlands.

The morning sun cast long shadows over the warriors, each breath visible in the cold air. Duncan McAfee moved among them, instilling strength. His grizzled hair caught glints of light, and even from this distance, the girls could see his reassuring nod as he inspected a young warrior's armor.

"Stay close to Lachlan," Alisdair commanded. "Remember what I've taught ye, and fight not just with yer sword, but with yer mind."

Nods rippled through the ranks as they prepared for battle; blades drawn, backs straightened. Alisdair rallied them: "Today, we stand for our lands, for our families! We are brothers bound by blood and honor. Fight bravely, fight wisely, and may our ancestors guide us to victory!"

A roar of unity followed, seeming to shake the very stones of McAfee Keep.

From the infirmary window, pride swelled within Moira. She watched as the men formed up—the anticipation palpable. Alisdair led the army a short distance from the castle to defend their beloved Highlands.

"May the wind be at their backs," Ailis whispered.

"Aye, and our prayers with them," Moira replied, heavy with emotion. They remained at the window, two sentinels watching until the last warrior disappeared from view—an emptiness filling the courtyard like a silent promise of return. This time they were ready.

The clamor of metal and cries of men filled the air as McAfee and McClain forces clashed with Clyde Stewart's army.

Alisdair, at the forefront, led his men with seasoned precision, their movements synchronized like a deadly dance. In contrast, Stewart's disarrayed forces stumbled over uneven ground, their attacks out of sync. None of the men seemed to be warriors, and that was good for their enemy.

Within the infirmary's stone walls, Brodie strained to discern the battle's tide through the racket outside. Moira stood beside him, recounting events relayed by runners. "Our men hold fast," she said, "Alisdair leads them well. The Stewarts falter under our charge."

Ailis added with determination and concern in her voice, "The McClains fight with honor, Brodie."

"Keep faith," Brodie murmured. "Our cause is just, and our arms are strong."

In the distance, the sounds of battle continued to rage.

The clash of steel echoed through the highlands, an urgent call to the heavens. Below the infirmary window, battle lines shifted, the McAfee and McClain warriors advancing in fluid precision like a serpent through grass.

"Look at them," Moira whispered, eyes tracking their clansmen's swift maneuvers.

Ailis stood close, her hand gripping the windowsill tightly. "They move together, perfectly synchronized," she said with a smile. "Alisdair, Lachlan, and Brodie have trained them all well."

Their forces cut through Stewart lines, disarray spreading like wildfire among the enemy. Clyde Stewart's men retreated before the onslaught, pushed back by claymore and targe.

Moira tensed as the adversaries fled; victory rang from below but tension remained on her face. Ailis touched Moira's shoulder—a steady support—and their eyes met with unspoken understanding. Together they'd weathered the storm of war, still unbroken.

In shared silence, they acknowledged not just victory but its accompanying cost and sacrifices. The fight never truly over, future conflict loomed—but today, they stood united.

The clamor of victory subsided as Alisdair surveyed the scene. Around him, Clan McAfee and their McClain allies moved with purpose under the guidance of their lairds. Alisdair stood beside Duncan, instructing warriors to check for any enemies attempting a final stand.

"Ensure none are left to threaten our backs," Alisdair commanded with unwavering resolve.

The warriors acted swiftly, their loyalty evident in their efficient execution of orders. The lairds' presence served as an embodiment of pride and strength on the battlefield.

In the infirmary, Brodie McClain lay propped up on a cot, his body injured but his mind eager for news. Moira stood at his bedside, recounting the tale of the battle's conclusion.

"Lachlan and Alisdair—they were unshakeable," she said, admiration coloring her voice. "Their strategy was flawless, each move essential. Father is too old to fight, but he was there before the battle, and I ken he watched from a window like we did."

Brodie listened intently as Moira described the battle. Her words painted vivid images that danced across his imagination. As she spoke of the battle's end, a smile reached his deep brown eyes.

"Stewart's men scattered like leaves before the gale," Moira continued. "They fled into the embrace of the glen."

"Then it is done," Brodie exhaled with relief, picturing their lands now safe from immediate threat. Yet beneath his calm demeanor, he acknowledged the precarious balance between peace and peril in the Highlands.

"Done for today," Moira stated, gripping Brodie's hand. "But we remain vigilant."

Brodie felt the truth of her words, and their bond eased the weight of his injury.

The clamor of battle faded to distant echoes across the heath, where remnants of morning mist clung to the hollows. Alisdair surveyed his warriors with discerning eyes. Beside him stood Lachlan and Fearghas McClain. The three of them were enough to scare off most enemies.

"Secure the perimeter! Leave no stone unturned!" Alisdair commanded as his men responded with focused determination. The threat of lingering enemies remained present.

Lachlan added, "We protect our lands and kin! Let no enemy find refuge within these hills!" His call rallied the clansmen, their unity immovable.

Together, the brothers moved among their men, binding those few adversaries who yet breathed, awaiting Highland justice.

Alisdair marched purposefully through the remnants of battle, his stride never breaking. In the distance, he spotted a figure crouching behind a fallen tree, a flash of Stewart tartan catching his eye. With a knowing glance toward Lachlan, Alisdair altered his path.

As they approached, the figure sprang up, revealing the cowering form of Clyde Stewart. His eyes, usually filled with cunning, now darted wildly in search of escape. Sweat glistened on his brow, mixing with the dirt and blood of battle.

"Leaving so soon, Clyde?" Alisdair called. "I thought ye'd stay to face the consequences of yer treachery. Ye disappoint me yet again."

Clyde's face contorted into a sneer, but fear lingered in his eyes. "Ye think ye've won, McClain? This is but a minor setback. The Stewarts will rise again, stronger than ever, and yer precious Highlands will be ours!"

"The Stewarts already rule the Scots. Ye are not one of the rulers." Alisdair's eyes narrowed, his hand tightening on the hilt of his sword. "Bold words for a man who hides behind fallen trees. Face me like a true Highlander, if ye have the courage."

But Clyde had no intention of engaging in a fair fight. With a desperate lunge, he bolted from his hiding spot, his tartan cloak billowing behind him as he fled through the dense foliage. Alisdair wasted no time, reaching for his bow and nocking an arrow with fluid precision.

The bowstring thrummed as Alisdair loosed the arrow, its fletching carving a path through the crisp Highland air. With unerring accuracy, the arrow found its mark, embedding itself deep within Clyde Stewart's right buttock. A cry of agony tore from Clyde's throat as he stumbled, his flight abruptly halted by the searing pain that radiated through his body.

Alisdair and Lachlan swiftly closed the distance, their strides purposeful and authoritative. They approached the fallen Stewart, who now lay writhing on the damp earth, his hands clutching at his wounded posterior. The once proud and arrogant laird was reduced to a pitiful sight, his face contorted in a mixture of pain and humiliation.

"Ye'll not escape justice so easily, Clyde," Alisdair declared, his voice carrying the weight of the Highlands. "Yer treachery ends here."

Clyde's eyes blazed with defiance, even as he struggled to rise. "Ye think ye've bested me, McClain?" he spat, his words laced with venom. "I'll see ye and yer kin destroyed, even if it takes my last breath!"

Alisdair's grip tightened on his sword. It was all he could do not to laugh at the once proud man laid so low. He towered over Clyde, his presence commanding. "Yer fate lies not in my hands, but in those of the dowager queen. Ye'll answer for yer crimes before her, and may the gods have mercy on yer blackened soul."

With a nod to Lachlan, Alisdair motioned for the soldiers to secure Clyde. They bound his hands tightly, the rough hemp digging into his wrists. Clyde's face twisted in a mixture of rage, pain, and desperation as he was hauled to his feet, the arrow still protruding from his buttock, a testament to his cowardice and defeat.

As the soldiers led Clyde away, Alisdair turned his attention to the other prisoners. He went into the dungeon to see who else needed to be sent to the regent for sentencing. Among them, he spotted the proud figure of Arran Sinclair, the laird of Clan Sinclair, who had been in the McAfee dungeons for months. Beside him stood his son, Callum, his youthful face marred by the grime of the dungeon.

Alisdair approached them, his steps measured and deliberate. The Sinclairs had long been allies of the Stewarts, their ambitions intertwined in a web of deceit and treachery. Now, with Clyde's defeat, the Sinclairs found themselves at the mercy of the victors.

"Arran Sinclair," Alisdair addressed the laird, his voice carrying the weight of authority. "Ye stand accused of conspiring against the McAfees and all of the Highlands. Ye will accompany Clyde Stewart to Edinburgh, where you can stand before the dowager queen, and she will decide yer fate."

THE CLASH OF steel succumbed to labored breaths as weary men returned to the stronghold. McAfee and McClain warriors tended to the wounded, their movements both methodical and gentle. Calls for herbs and water mingled with murmurs of comfort offered to comrades in pain. If the injury was bad enough, they were taken to the infirmary.

Exhaustion marked every face, but a swell of pride united them. The day's resolve had turned the tide against Stewart's chaos, forging their camaraderie tighter. Moira observed the makeshift triage in the courtyard, heart swelling at her people's fierce care for one another. Lachlan's voice guided efforts to secure everyone's safety.

"Come, Ailis," Moira urged. "Our hands are needed outside."

Ailis nodded, dark hair shimmering against the stone fortress backdrop. The sisters moved from the infirmary, steps echoing on cobblestone—a testament to Highland women's strength. They passed men who nodded respectfully, eyes filled with gratitude and reverence.

Victory swirled in the courtyard, warriors laughing and recounting tales of bravery. Moira McAfee stood amidst the celebration, feeling the exhilaration that came from the conquering soldiers.

"Farlan broke through their flank!" one of the warriors said, mimicking the moment with broad gestures.

"And young Gilmore felled two men with a single swing!" another added, admiration in his tone.

Moira's heart swelled with pride, but a shadow of foreboding lingered. They had won today, but more challenges awaited like hidden crags in the mist.

Her father, Duncan, touched her shoulder. His eyes held a lifetime of battles but softened as they met hers.

"Let us remember this day!" Duncan called. "For we've shown what it means to be of Clan McAfee!"

"And Clan McClain!" Lachlan called to laughter.

Cheers erupted again, lifting into the cool Highland air, carrying triumph and whispers of an enduring legacy.

Moira and Ailis retreated to the alcove, the noise of victory muted by stone walls. Clasping hands, they shared a meaningful silence before speaking.

"Today we've created legends," Ailis said, her healer's heart aching. "But at what cost? For every cheer, there's a mother who weeps or a child who'll know only tales of their father."

"War is cruel," Moira replied somberly. "Our kin fought treachery, but uncertainty remains." Her grip on Ailis's hand tightened as she felt the weight of responsibility.

"True," Ailis murmured, "loyalty binds us to family and hard choices that protect our clan. Remember, it's not just the sword that keeps us safe, but bonds forged in peace."

"Peace… That's the dream I'll fight for," Moira vowed.

"Let's hope today brought us closer to that dream," Ailis said, releasing Moira's hand. Their eyes mirrored unspoken fears and hopes.

◄——◆——►

CHAPTER TWENTY-SEVEN

THE WOODEN DOOR of the great hall opened to a lively celebration as Moira and Brodie stepped inside. This time, Brodie needed nothing more than Moira's help to get into the great hall and take his seat beside the fire. Torchlight flickered across the room, casting warmth over the lively crowd dancing to the music of fiddles and bagpipes.

Moira inhaled the rich aroma of roasting meats and fresh-baked bread. The scent felt comforting after the damp battle-ground. Brodie's gaze swept across the room, watching as colorful tartans moved with life-affirming energy.

Together, they absorbed the joyful expressions on their kin-folk's faces. Silver brooches gleamed in the firelight. The hearth's warmth thawed the uncertainty that lingered within them.

Amid the twirling dancers and clinking glasses in the McAfee stronghold, Moira and Brodie were enveloped by a vibrant tapestry of Highland mirth.

The ceilidh's energy enveloped Brodie as he sat beside the fire, Moira's hand in his. The stomping boots and fiddle tunes mixed with hearty greetings from his brothers and clansmen.

"Ah, Brodie! Back on yer feet like a true warrior," boomed Fearghas, his father, grinning widely.

"Ye've mended well, lad," Alisdair agreed, broad shoulders draped in Clan McAfee's tartan. Respectful nods and murmurs of admiration for Brodie's strength surrounded them.

Brodie inclined his head with a humble smile, thanking his

brethren.

As Brodie conversed with his wife and kin, Moira felt a gentle tug on her elbow. Ailis stood beside her, brunette locks shimmering against the firelight, green eyes filled with sisterly affection.

"Moira!" Ailis exclaimed. "Ye've been missed. Come, tell us everything!"

A circle of women gathered around Moira, all of their faces familiar to her. They shared stories laced with laughter and victory unique to Highland life.

"Ye should've seen it, Fiona. The Stewarts never stood a chance," Moira recounted proudly.

Their laughter blended seamlessly with the bagpipes' melodies. In her sisters' eyes, Moira glimpsed reflections of her own fiery spirit.

Here, amid the clannish rites and joyous abandon, Moira McAfee stood surrounded by the traditions of her people—feeling the pulse of the Highlands which reverberated with camaraderie, strength, and an unbreakable sense of belonging.

Brodie spotted Moira laughing among the women at the ceilidh. He silently moved through the crowd, his recent injury obvious with his limp. As he approached her, determination filled his eyes.

"May I?" he asked, a challenging tone in his voice.

Surprised, Moira placed her hand in his. They stepped onto the dance floor and moved gracefully together. Moira understood that he needed to appear strong, and she was more than willing to help. "Lean on me if ye need to."

Moira's pride swelled as she watched Brodie dance, claiming his place among his kin. She was very proud of his recovery, and he would be moving back to their room the following day.

Their presence drew attention. Meanwhile, former Stewart soldiers who had joined their alliance cautiously mingled with the McClains and McAfees on the gathering's fringes. Tentative smiles were met with nods, and as they shared drinks, divisions blurred. The men relaxed as they integrated into their new clan.

A jest from one newcomer elicited cheers from the McClain warriors, further breaking down distrust. The firelight cast away old allegiances and lit up a path toward camaraderie instead of conflict. In the back of Moira's mind, an idea was forming. They needed to find a way to keep their alliance strong, and perhaps the way to do that was to hold Highland Games there each year, inviting all of the clans who had joined them in battle.

As melodies and laughter filled the air, Brodie and Moira clung to one another. Neither wanted this ceilidh, the last with his brethren there, to end.

The ceilidh resonated with the rhythm of fiddles and bag-pipes, setting the hall abuzz. Lachlan McClain stood by the firelight, raising his mug high. The room hushed, awaiting his words.

"Clansmen and kin," Lachlan began, "We gather for a single purpose. Let this cup be a toast to unity and peace!" He nodded to Ailis before continuing, "To a shared future!"

"Slàinte mhath!" Voices chorused in harmony as mugs clinked and ale splashed, celebrating the newfound union.

Moira and Brodie slipped away under the open sky, fingers interlaced. The cool night air caressed their flushed cheeks as they stopped at the edge of the light.

Stars peppered the velvet expanse above them, witnesses to tales of strife and reconciliation.

"Even the heavens seem to be celebrating with us," Moira whispered.

"Aye," Brodie agreed. "It's a new start for us all."

"I find meself believing again—in peace, in us," she replied.

Their glance held the weight of battles fought and won. The memory of swords and sorrow gave way to a future written in starlight.

"Let's carry this night within us," Brodie said, squeezing her hand. "As a reminder of what we're fighting for—days filled with moments like these."

"And nights where we can simply be," Moira added softly,

leaning against him.

In the distance, the ceilidh's melody beckoned. Yet, they stayed outside, entwined under the star-filled sky.

Drawn by the slow, intimate fiddle tune, Moira and Brodie rejoined the ceilidh. They entered the circle of dancers, moving in sync to the steady rhythm.

Brodie's steps were smooth, but Moira could see the sheen of sweat and grimaces on his face. Their eyes met, exchanging silent understanding. His hand on her waist guided their movements together.

"Ye've come a long way since the injury," Moira said softly, her voice rising above the quiet bagpipes. "But I think ye may need to sit for the rest of the night. This is too much for ye."

Brodie chuckled. "It was yer stubborn will that kept me on my feet," he replied.

"Och, it's yer own determination that deserves credit," she countered with a smile.

"Perhaps," he conceded, humor lighting up his deep brown eyes. "But without ye, I'd be fighting shadows." His grip tightened around her as they moved—a silent pledge.

"And without ye, I'd be a flame without a hearth to call home," she replied, affection softening her gaze. They knew the significance of those words.

Moira led him to his chair beside the fire and planted herself in the seat beside his. She wasn't willing to let him fall, no matter what he was thinking.

"Whatever comes," Brodie said firmly, "we'll face it together."

"Aye," Moira agreed.

The music swelled into a lively jig, stirring the hall's festive atmosphere. Moira and Brodie watched the dance floor, hands intertwined as tartan-clad clansmen and women leapt and twirled around them.

"Look at them," Moira whispered, motioning to the dancing couple nearby. "They dance as if the earth beneath them is alive."

For this moment, worries of conflict and strife were forgotten. The ceilidh burned with life's promise.

As the night wore on, Alisdair called for the McClain clan to prepare for departure. "We leave at first light!"

"Time we join the others," Brodie said, gazing at the remaining dancers.

"The night is still young in our hearts," Moira replied playfully. "Besides, yer not ready for travel just yet. We'll stay here with the McAfees for a while."

Lachlan and Ailis approached them, deep in conversation. Lachlan's hand rested gently on Ailis' back—a silent vow of return.

"Brothers," Brodie called softly, gaining Lachlan and Alisdair's attention.

Lachlan met their eyes with a leader's resolve. "Aye, let us make ready. This night has been a blessing, but the morrow comes with the sun."

"We will let the McClain soldiers leave as one," he commanded, rallying the clansmen into action. "We must stay behind."

Farewells were heartfelt among allies and former Stewart soldiers alike—shared trials forging bonds stronger than steel.

The McClain men all retired for the night, so they would be ready to leave first thing in the morning. They had been far from their home for too long, and now that Clyde Stewart was on his way to the dowager queen, they knew it was time to return to their homes and families.

THE PIPER'S MELODY disappeared into the Highland night as Brodie and Moira left the lively gathering in the great hall. The celebration behind them became a distant echo, contrasting with the quiet darkness outside. The glowing embers of a bonfire softly illuminated their surroundings.

Moira squeezed Brodie's hand, a comforting touch conveying gratitude and love. They stood at the edge of the firelight, feeling the world around them hushed and expectant.

Together they walked to the infirmary, where Brodie would spend his last night, and there would be more rehabilitation the following day. Then the long walk up the stairs to the room they would share. It sounded like a dream to have the ability to share a room again and live like a normal married couple.

"Tomorrow is ours to shape," Moira said confidently.

Feeling her words' truth, Brodie nodded. They turned away from past memories and faced the dawning future together.

CHAPTER TWENTY-EIGHT

B RODIE LEANED AGAINST the cool stone frame of the doorway, breathing in the scent of peat and heather that wafted from the open window. His feet felt grounded on the wooden floorboards, mirroring the stability of his return to life.

The door creaked behind him as Moira McAfee entered. Her gaze connected with Brodie's as she observed him standing unaided by the hearth. Shadows danced across her face, revealing her emotions.

Relief ignited in her eyes, followed by a joy that colored her cheeks. Brodie watched silently as her posture softened. He recognized this tender side of her, despite the fierceness she usually wielded.

"Ye're on yer feet," Moira stated, wonder woven into her voice.

"Aye," Brodie replied firmly, "I am."

In their shared room, once filled with worry and healing, a new promising beginning emerged—one where they'd face any storm together.

Brodie extended his arms, and Moira stepped into his embrace, her head resting against his chest.

"Moira," he whispered, "we've outlasted the storm."

"Aye, we have," she replied, tightening her grip around him.

They parted reluctantly and Brodie glanced toward the open window where the forest called to him. It was time to reacquaint himself with the world beyond these walls.

"Shall we?" he asked, offering his hand.

Her fingers interlaced with his as they walked outside. Each step Brodie took was measured, a testament to his determination to regain not just his strength but his role beside Moira. The forest floor whispered tales of renewal beneath their boots.

Together, they ventured deeper, Moira matching Brodie's cautious pace. The canopy above dappled their path with light and shadow, dancing to the tune of Highland winds.

"Feels good to be walking again," Brodie remarked, growing more assured with each moment.

"Ye look like yerself again, Brodie McClain," Moira said proudly. "The forest has missed ye."

Sunlight filtered through the trees, casting patterns on the forest floor where Brodie and Moira walked. The air hummed with the sounds of nature: rustling leaves, distant bird calls, and the quiet chatter of woodland creatures.

"I've missed this tranquility," Moira said, her gaze following the beams of light across the ground.

"Tranquility and freedom," Brodie replied, inhaling the scent of pine. "This is vibrant...alive."

As they continued, Brodie's steps grew firmer, his body remembering the rhythm of the wild. Suddenly, he stopped. A grayish-brown rabbit ventured into a clearing nearby.

"Look there," he whispered to Moira.

She watched as he picked up his bow and nocked an arrow. "Take your time," she encouraged softly.

Brodie released the arrow, cutting through the dappled sunlight. The rabbit bolted but couldn't escape his aim. He turned to Moira, sharing in their silent victory.

"Ye've not lost yer touch, Brodie," she said with admiration and affection.

"Thanks to ye, Moira," he replied warmly.

Brodie approached the felled rabbit, its fur still warm. He crouched beside it, offering a silent gesture of gratitude. Unsheathing his knife, he began to work with skilled hands.

"Ye always had a way with the blade," Moira observed, her gaze fixed on the horizon where their home awaited.

"Ye've kept me sharp," Brodie replied, glancing up at her through focused eyes.

"Let us make haste," she suggested. "The hearth calls." Though he'd been walking more freely for the past week, she was a little concerned about him being on his feet as long as he had.

Together, they gathered what they needed and made their way back through the trees. By the time they emerged from the woods, twilight painted the sky in beautiful pinks and oranges.

As night descended upon McAfee Keep, anticipation hung in the air. In their chamber, Brodie and Moira moved around each other with the ease born of intimacy. The soft clink of Brodie's belt buckle, the rustle of bedcovers—all blended into the symphony of the evening.

Brodie watched as Moira braided her fiery hair in the reflection of a small looking glass. She caught his eye and offered him a heartwarming smile.

"Come," she said softly. "The warmth of the bed awaits."

They joined beneath the covers, their bodies pressed close and legs entwined. Here, in their room bathed in amber firelight, they found solace in each other's presence—the past hardships fading away, leaving them wrapped in promises yet to come.

In the stillness, Brodie felt Moira's heart synchronize with his. As sleep approached, they nestled together, knowing each trial faced solidified their united future.

Fingers traced the landscape of scars, mapping a history on skin. Brodie's calloused hand softly explored Moira's arm. She inhaled deeply as his touch ventured across her collarbone.

"Ye ken," Brodie whispered, his voice barely audible over the hearth, "I've dreamt of this… touching ye, feeling yer strength."

"And I, of ye," Moira replied, her hands grazing along his jawline. They moved deliberately, relearning each other's bodies, finding comfort and solace.

As they faded off to sleep after making love, Moira knew she was where she belonged—beside the man she loved.

As DAWN'S LIGHT spilled into the room, Moira carefully slipped out of bed without waking Brodie. Her feet met the cool stone floor, and she stretched. She grabbed her sword, its hilt fitting perfectly in her palm.

The blade caught the morning light as she stepped into the crisp courtyard air. Each swing was a vow to protect what was hers. The sword sliced through the chill, and Moira's mind sharpened alongside it, ready for whatever challenges lay ahead.

Sunlight crested McAfee Keep's stone walls, casting shadows across the dewy courtyard where Moira practiced her swordplay. Her breath visible in the crisp air, she lunged and pivoted with a warrior's grace, her blade sweeping through the cool air.

Beneath a gnarled oak, Brodie observed Moira's fiery hair shimmering like copper as she executed precise strikes. He admired not only her technique but also the spirited determination behind each motion, recognizing their shared independence.

Moira's disciplined training was evident in the strength of her arms and certainty of her stance. Brodie felt pride in both her abilities and their partnership.

As Moira thrust her sword skyward, concluding her routine against the backdrop of the awakening Highlands, Brodie acknowledged they would face any future trials side by side.

Finally, Moira lowered her sword, turning to find Brodie approaching. His confident stride matched her own resolve. His limp was barely discernible, and she watched him walk to her.

"Ye've not lost a step," he remarked, sitting beside her on the weathered bench.

Moira chuckled. "And ye seem to be finding yers again."

They talked about the battles that had been fought in the short months they'd known one another. It had been one battle after another, ever since the McAfees had held the Highland Games.

"I thought ye were the most infuriating man I had ever met," Moira admitted with a laugh. "But I learned quickly ye were so much more than that."

"Yet, 'twas yer fire that guided us through that dark time," Brodie countered, his arm resting protectively around her shoulders.

"Fire and shadow, we were," Moira said affectionately. "Each of us strong alone, but together… unstoppable."

"Unstoppable," he agreed, his thumb brushing lightly against her sleeve.

As late afternoon light played upon Moira's hair and Brodie's contemplative eyes, he said with certainty, "Whatever may come, we will face it as we have since we first met."

"Together," Moira whispered, meeting his gaze.

Their hands interlocked as evening approached—a silent vow passed between them in the growing peace.

As the sun dipped, casting pink and orange strokes across the sky, the world hushed around Brodie and Moira in the courtyard of the ancient McAfee keep. They found sanctuary in each other's steadfast presence. As stars emerged in the twilight sky, possibilities and enduring hope for the Highlands filled the unfolding future.

❖

CHAPTER TWENTY-NINE

MOIRA'S LAUGHTER INTERTWINED with Brodie's. The Scottish Highlands stretched out around them, green hills rolling beneath an expansive sky. They rode side by side, unrestrained as they leaned into their gallops.

As they crested a hill, the breathtaking view of their homeland unfolded before them. They slowed their horses and dismounted, Moira's boots touching dew-drenched grass while Brodie gestured toward a sunlit clearing among tall pines.

"Shall we?" Brodie teased.

"Let's see if you can keep up," Moira retorted, excitement in her eyes.

They faced off with swords drawn against the forest shadows. Their blades clashed in friendly combat, steel ringing amidst leafy whispers. Moira attacked with an elegant ferocity, while Brodie parried using calculated skill and strategy.

Their dance was an ancient rhythm—thrust and parry, feint and dodge. Moira's passion ignited each swing. Brodie remained composed, his focus evident in every controlled strike and step.

With each move, their deep camaraderie was revealed—a connection born from shared battles. As the mock duel concluded, they exchanged a final flurry of blows before stepping back to catch their breaths, smiles wide and genuine.

"Nicely done, Moira," Brodie praised.

"Likewise, Brodie," she acknowledged. "Your defense is as impenetrable as the Highlands themselves."

Laughter echoed again as they sheathed their swords and gazed upon the land that defined them.

Leaning against an ancient oak, Brodie caught his breath while Moira plucked wildflowers beside him.

"The seventh sons of the McClain family are born with gifts far beyond ordinary men," Brodie said, his voice carrying generations of oral traditions.

"Gifts? Like healing the sick or moving objects without touching them?" Moira asked.

Brodie nodded, twirling a twig in thought. "The tales are woven into our heritage. Take Gavin McClain—he healed a whole village struck with fever during the harshest winter."

"Conveniently, none around to confirm such claims," Moira teased. "Maybe they could control the weather too?"

"Mayhap. In fact there are rumors of a woman of power who married one of me ancestors. She could control the weather according to family lore. I cannae promise it's true, because I didn't see it for meself," he acknowledged, still serious. "But the power was always for the good of the clan."

"Having seen it for meself, I cannae deny yer family is…special."

"That we are." He grinned at her. "Now just be happy that ye married me and not the seventh son."

MOIRA AND BRODIE moved like shadows among the towering pines. Their quarry, a regal stag, had led them on a chase through the forest. The thrill of the hunt pulsed through Moira, connecting her to Brodie and the ancient land they traversed. Their teamwork was wordless yet seamless as they flanked their prey, surrounded by the scent of moss and earth.

"Imagine," he whispered, "the ability to mend broken bones or stop blood without potions or stitches. To think thoughts and have the world bend to your will." Moira found herself captivated by these possibilities.

The stag sensed this deepening connection and broke cover. In an instant, Brodie and Moira sprang into action, their earlier conversation forgotten amid the resumed chase.

AT THE BROOK, Brodie and Moira paused. Moira crouched by the water, dipping her fingers into the stream and watching ripples distort her reflection.

"Moira," Brodie interrupted, "did I ever tell ye about the tradition of the seventh son marrying well and bearing another seven sons?"

She laughed, relieved. "Thank the saints, I'm not wed to a seventh son then. Can you imagine the chaos of seven children, especially if one had fantastical powers?"

"But think of the strength in numbers," Brodie jested back, eyes full of humor.

"Strength, or a grand headache," Moira teased back, smiling. "I'll leave such curses to braver women than I."

Brodie chuckled, their laughter easing the weight of clan politics and dark conspiracies for a moment.

MOIRA CROUCHED BESIDE the brook, her fingertips skimming the water's surface. The stream's gentle burble accompanied her tumultuous thoughts as she contemplated Brodie's stories of Highland lore and McClain pride. She ran her fingers through the water, feeling them freeze almost instantly. The first snows of winter were certain to come soon.

"Colin," she murmured, recalling twisted ankles healed and fevered brows cooled with a touch. Though skeptical, the memory of Colin's glowing hand easing pain tempted her certainty. Even having seen it with her own eyes, Moira had a difficult time comprehending that what Brodie said was true. Surely, only his grandfather had powers, and the rest he was making up. Though Boyd had disappeared in front of Ailis.

Moira considered herself grounded in reality—not in whispers and shadows. But this was difficult to wrap her mind around, as she'd seen it with her own two eyes.

Frowning, she struggled with the duality of her nature: rooted in the tangible earth but stirred by the inexplicable. Each story about Colin now felt like pieces of an incomplete puzzle. Did belief alone grant substance to legend?

Her gaze lifted to the rustling leaves above. If Colin had power, what did it mean for their lives and strategies against rival clans? The water flowed past her, indifferent to human turmoil and secrets.

"Come on then," she called to Brodie, determination in her voice. "Let's see what else this forest has to reveal."

A SOFT HUSH settled over the highland glen as Brodie and Moira rested side by side on a bed of heather. The distant call of a buzzard broke the silence.

Moira caught Brodie's eye, and a subtle smile played across her lips. His gaze held hers. It seemed as if the boundless skies and enduring mountains were etched into the lines of his face. In those moments, they acknowledged a kinship deeper than clan ties—a bond forged by their highland souls.

As the sun descended toward the horizon, casting shadows on the hills, they rose together, wordlessly agreeing to return to the keep. They approached their horses and mounted them with practiced ease, their breaths creating plumes in the cooling air.

The ride back was serene, a gentle amble through the forest

and back across the glen. The fading sunlight transformed the highlands into fiery golds and deepening purples. Moira felt profound tranquility as the castle's silhouette appeared against the twilight sky.

She glanced at Brodie, riding at her side, knowing that whatever lay ahead, be it trials of faith or clashing steel, they would face it as one. In the Highlands, where whispers of legend drifted on the wind and bonds were as steadfast as ancient stones, Brodie and Moira had found each other.

Moira couldn't stop thinking about the things she and Brodie had discussed that day...and their laughter. Hearing him laugh again meant everything in the world to her.

She replayed their conversations about McClain heroes and mystic powers. The stories seemed more believable beneath the lengthening shadows, making her question the truth behind old clan tales. Moira was a woman of action, but she found herself considering an extraordinary path.

As they reached the towering gates, Brodie glanced over, his eyes reflecting the last embers of sunset—an acknowledgment of their shared secrets. Dismounting gracefully, Moira felt grounded as her boots met the earth. Brodie offered his hand not out of necessity, but as an unspoken vow of partnership.

They walked toward the stone fortress, laughter softening the hush of evening. The breeze teased strands of Moira's hair free from its braid. Each step held a promise—not just for peace, but for understanding their land and legends. As the gates closed behind them with a resonant thud, their bond solidified.

Their smiles were private oaths to the future as they moved through twilight into the castle's warm embrace. Moira's heart acknowledged something profound. Perhaps the extraordinary was already threading through her life, waiting for only her acceptance to reveal itself.

CHAPTER THIRTY

MOIRA STOOD BY the window, fingers tracing the cool stone ledge as dawn illuminated the rugged peaks of the Highlands. A secret not yet shared was stirring within her—a connection to Brodie beyond measure.

"This changes everything," she whispered, voice barely audible. The weight of her news was different from that of the sword she wielded skillfully; it was a delicate yet potent bond of love. How would Brodie react? Would his brown eyes soften with joy, or would his strategic mind weigh implications and consequences?

She brushed a curl behind her ear, resolve firming. "He must know. He must see the hope I see." Their future depended on the love they fought for amidst conflicts surrounding their clans.

Resolute, Moira descended to the courtyard where McAfee Keep's morning bustle had begun.

"Moira!" Keir called, approaching with an unruly mop of hair and a broad grin—remnants of simpler days before alliances and betrayals dictated life.

"Keir!" Embracing warmly, their worries were momentarily forgotten. Laughter bubbled between them, easy and free.

As they recalled races through forests and outsmarting other children, Moira said, "We're older, perhaps wiser, but the fire of those days never truly fades."

"Never," Keir agreed. "It burns within us, guiding through dark times and reminding us who we are—children of these lands, fierce and unyielding."

Their exchange was filled with their shared history, their childhoods, and the love they had for their childhood friends. Even as leaders and warriors they had become, the essence of their youth remained, indelible and pure.

Brodie stood in the shadow of an oak, his gaze fixed on Moira and Keir below. Laughter reached him on the breeze that whispered through the leaves. He observed their intimacy, suspicion blooming within him. And then he remembered the night before he'd been injured, when she had flirted with many different men right in front of him, and his anger grew.

Keir leaned against the stone wall, relaxed and unguarded. Brodie's eyes narrowed as he searched for evidence of a deeper connection. His heart echoed a silent plea for his suspicions to be unfounded.

Subconsciously, Brodie's hand rested upon the hilt of his dirk—ready to defeat any opponent for the love of his wife. The laughter below struck a dissonant chord within him.

Moira playfully swatted at Keir's shoulder as they reminisced about their youthful adventures. They shared laughter that spoke of innocence and an unblemished bond from a time before betrayal's shadow loomed over the Highlands.

Brodie hid, watching the pair stand in sunlight. His heart twisted with jealousy and doubt, despite his attempts to trust the woman he loved. The scene below remained tainted.

Keir's silhouette disappeared against the heather and pine while Moira stood by McAfee Keep. She placed her hands on her midriff, feeling a secret flutter of new life.

"Fiona and Alisdair's baby will have a cousin soon," she whispered before turning back toward the keep, fiery hair glowing in the late afternoon sun.

After supper, she stood with her sisters, whispering her news. "I have yet to tell Brodie, but I'll do that tonight. Ye may share with yer husbands, but no one else." She was smiling ear to ear, excited to see the look on Brodie's face when she told him he would be a father.

As evening fell, Moira entered their chamber where Brodie stood by the hearth in contemplation.

"Evening, love," she greeted, anticipation causing her hands to tremble. Imagining his reaction to her news, she asked, "Are ye well, Brodie?" Her voice wove through the silence as she prepared to share their future with him.

Moira reached out, her fingertips brushing Brodie's sleeve. "Brodie, there is something I must—"

"Where were ye this afternoon?" he interrupted, his voice sharp. He stepped back, tension filling the space between them.

Moira hesitated, her face paling. "I was outside, in the courtyard. Why?"

"Ah, with Keir." Brodie's eyes narrowed, his posture rigid. "Seemed quite the joyful reunion."

Her heart sank at his cold demeanor. "He's an old friend, Brodie. We climbed trees together and would watch the soldiers training, both of us determined to be just like them."

"An old friend," he repeated skeptically.

"Ye doubt my fidelity?" Her anger surged. "I have given ye no cause for such distrust!"

"Moira, 'tis not about trust—" he started, but she interrupted.

"Is it not?" she retorted, her voice rising. "Then what is it about?"

She stood defiantly, unwilling to let her honor be tarnished by jealousy or misjudgment.

"Ye look upon me as if I've betrayed the very clans we both hold dear," Moira spat, anger radiating from her body. Her posture was unwavering, mirroring the fortress walls that withstood countless assaults.

Brodie's jaw clenched, his voice low and strained. "It is no simple matter when a wife finds comfort in the company of another man."

"Comfort? Aye, comfort in shared memories, naught more!" The tension between them intensified, an invisible barrier difficult to break through. She was growing angrier and angrier as the minutes passed. She'd come to tell him about the bairn she carried, and instead, she was having a confrontation about her own faithfulness…or lack thereof.

"Moira, ye ken well the times are treacherous. Appearances cannae be ignored," he reasoned, but his words felt heavy and obstructive.

"Then let them watch!" Her defiance surged. "I will not live shackled by fear or suspicion." She folded her arms across her chest, determined not to tell him about the babe until he apologized for the way he was mistrusting her.

"Is it so unreasonable to ask for caution?" Brodie's stance softened fractionally as though trying to reach her.

"I have been nothing but loyal to ye, to us," Moira insisted, eyes locked onto his unflinchingly. "If ye cannot trust in that, then what do we have?"

"We—"

"No," she cut him off, her tone steady despite her emotions. "Ye will not undermine my character based on your own unfounded fears."

In the dim light of their chamber, they stood—two forces of nature clashing but bound by something stronger than their disagreement.

Brodie's jaw clenched, his heart racing. Moira stood before him, her hair a fiery halo, her eyes demanding he see past his doubts.

"Can ye not see the truth in my eyes?" she implored, her voice cutting through his turmoil.

He wanted to believe her, but trust was hard-won after what he'd seen. "Moira," he began, only to be interrupted by her resolute expression.

"Enough," she said firmly. "If ye cannot hold faith in me, find solace elsewhere."

Her ultimatum settled heavily in the room. She stood unwavering, a testament to conviction. Brodie watched her turn away, feeling their divide widen with each step. Left alone with only shadows and doubt for company, he realized that the true battle was within himself—to trust in their bond or let fear sever what they had built together.

Moira's hand rested on the icy door handle, her breath steadying as she leaned against the chamber door separating her from Brodie. The silence enveloped her like a Highland mist, suffocating and isolating. Her heartbeat decelerated, synchronizing with the distant murmur of waves lapping at the loch's shore.

Moira moved to the window, observing the moonlit glen extending beyond McAfee Keep. The untamed beauty reflected her inner turmoil—a realm where loyalty and survival collided.

"Independence," she murmured into the night, reaffirming a vow taken by generations before.

Her hands settled protectively over her unborn child, a joy held secret in her chamber. The altercation with Brodie and its ensuing consequences could not darken this hidden sanctuary of hope.

"Ye ken nothing of what resides within me," she spoke softly, blending with the heather rustle outside. "But I'll prove me truth to ye, Brodie McClain. With the resolute beat of me own heart."

The hearth's embers disrupted the quietness, their dance reflecting Moira's indomitable spirit no man could smother—not even one she cherished. In her eyes lingered a myriad of emotions: hurt from unfounded accusations, anger toward injustice, but beneath it all, an unwavering thread of hope for love's triumph.

"Ye must see the honor in me actions, Brodie," she said to emptiness as if he was there confronting his demons. "For I cannot chain me soul to doubt or let suspicion cast shadows on our bairn."

Determined, Moira turned from the window. She would withstand this storm as she had others—with unyielding courage and faith that tomorrow would clear even the cloudiest heart.

"Trust is the bridge between us," she whispered, a tear rolling down her cheek, "and I won't let it fall."

In the stillness of her chamber, Moira clung to her independence, weaving it into threads of hope that by dawn, understanding would awaken within Brodie and they'd start healing their rift.

CHAPTER THIRTY-ONE

BRODIE MCCLAIN SLIPPED away from the great hall, his mind trapped by Moira McAfee's eyes meeting those of a lad from her past. The brief exchange was charged with an emotion Brodie couldn't place.

He moved through the crowd, feeling disconnected from the happy people within. He was filled with a sense of longing as he entered the castle's stone corridors to escape the noise. Navigating familiar passages, he retreated deeper into his thoughts.

Being surrounded by happy people had brought a feeling of restlessness to him. Had he just ruined his chance for happiness with Moira? He thought to apologize, but he still felt hurt by the look he had seen on her face when she'd spoken with Keir.

In a dimly lit room, empty except for a solitary candle casting shadows, Brodie's façade of composure crumbled. He paced before a dying hearth, questioning the implications of that moment for Moira, their clans' alliance, and a future he had only begun to consider.

Leaning against a rough table, Brodie exhaled slowly. Alone, he confronted emotions he had long analyzed but rarely indulged. Even with his strategic prowess, matters of the heart bewildered him—playing by rules he was only beginning to understand.

As DAWN GRACED the Highland peaks, Brodie joined the others in the great hall for breakfast. The room bustled with the sounds of meals and conversations. He sat at the long oak table, his thoughts preoccupied with Moira's lingering effect on him.

"Brodie!" Lachlan McClain greeted him heartily, clapping him on the back. His dark hair framed a face that spoke to both battle and kinship. "I've been looking for ye," he said.

"Good morning, Lachlan," Brodie replied, observing the excitement in Lachlan's manner—an anticipation humming beneath his words.

"Ye've no idea how happy I am for ye, lad," Lachlan continued genuinely. "Times ahead promise prosperity for us all."

Brodie nodded politely, not one to bask in praise or attention. He sensed Lachlan's enthusiasm went beyond formality—stemming from a deep-rooted pride as a Highland laird whose legacy was intertwined with the land itself.

"Prosperity, ye say?" Brodie asked, his confusion evident. The great hall buzzed with energy, but his focus remained on Lachlan.

"Prosperity through new life," Lachlan affirmed, straightening as if the word carried the clan's future. He glanced around, ensuring their privacy in the middle of the hall's commotion.

Brodie's mind raced, trying to decipher Lachlan's cryptic words. "New life? I don't follow."

Lachlan's eyes narrowed with concern. "The wee bairn, Brodie. 'Tis common talk now." His frown implied that he assumed Brodie already knew.

"The child," Brodie murmured, understanding dawning on him but leaving more questions unanswered. Lachlan's dedication to his family was evident. It was that same loyalty that made him think Brodie would be informed about such a crucial matter.

Brodie's thoughts raced ahead, grappling with the implications of this newfound knowledge.

Brodie's frustration simmered as he left the great hall, the revelation unsettling him. He navigated the corridors of McAfee Keep, focused on confronting Moira.

He paused at the door to her chamber before entering. "Moira," he started, his voice steady. She stood by the window, morning light outlining her figure. "There is talk of a child."

The tension between them was palpable.

"Aye, there is talk," she responded, not facing him.

"And the father?" he insisted.

Her eyes held an inner fire as she turned toward him. "Is it the identity of the man or the potential scandal that concerns you?"

"Both," he said without hesitation. "For our families and the clan, we must be prudent."

"Prudence," she said with disdain. "Know this—I am not a problem to be solved."

"Moira, I do not see ye as such," he replied softly but firmly. "But we cannot ignore the ramifications of this secret. It is bigger than either of us."

Their gazes met in silent understanding, unspoken truths hanging in the air between them.

"Ye think to judge me?" Moira's voice cut through the thick air. Her stance was unyielding and commanding respect. "I'll not be tethered by whispers or weighed down by expectations of men who know naught of my life."

Brodie watched defiance flicker in her eyes, as fierce as Highland winds sweeping across the moors. "It's not about judgment," he said calmly, though her spirit threatened to ignite his temper. "It's about facing consequences together, for the good of all."

"Consequences," she spat the word, hands balling into fists. "As if I haven't considered them! I am no bairn cowering before a storm. I stand ready to face whatever comes."

"Moira—" Brodie began, attempting to bridge their misunderstanding.

"No!" She cut him off with a swift raise of her hand. "I've heard enough." With each word, her independence roared louder, echoing through the stone chamber like a battle cry. "Ye may strategize and plot, but ye cannot control life's course. Not mine."

Turning on her heel, Moira strode toward the door. Brodie watched as she marched away, embodying the Highland spirit that coursed through her veins.

With each step, she carried an unwavering loyalty to her family and clan toward solace found in the embrace of her sisters—those who would understand her struggles and share burdens without stifling confines.

The heavy wooden door closed behind her with a sound that reverberated through Brodie's core, leaving him in the shadows grappling with unresolved tension that hung in the air like mist over lochs. The confrontation had ended, but silent echoes lingered—a prelude to battles yet unfought.

Moira's boots echoed against the cold stone as she hastened through the dimly lit corridors of McAfee Keep. Her breaths came in short bursts, painting the chilly air with the fog of her exertion and defiance. She didn't need to knock; the door flung open as if by her will alone.

"God's teeth, Moira," Ailis remarked, noticing her younger sister's flushed face.

"Close the door!" Moira snapped, and as she turned around to secure it, her sisters exchanged concerned glances.

"Out with it then," Fiona said, her voice steady. "What did Brodie want?"

"Want?" Moira scoffed. "He wanted answers. About the babe." She paced like a caged animal. "But I'll not be cornered and questioned as if I'm some misbehaving bairn!"

"Ye're carrying a child," Ailis reminded gently. "People will have questions."

"I am married to my bairn's father. There should be no questions! Especially from him," Moira shot back. "My child will be raised a McAfee, strong and free."

"Did he threaten ye?" asked Fiona, rising from her seat.

"Nay," Moira stopped pacing and faced them squarely. "But he's asking questions about the bairn's parentage when he should be rejoicing with me that we're having a child together."

"Ye've naught to be ashamed of," Ailis said firmly. "Ye have always been brave and true. Ye wouldnae think of dallying with a man who wasnae yer husband, and this entire clan kens it."

"We stand with ye," added Fiona. "If ye cannae stay with Brodie after these accusations, we'll help ye raise yer child. He has no right to question ye that way!"

"Thank ye," Moira breathed out, feeling warmth from their solidarity.

A moment of silence filled the room until Ailis stepped forward and said, "We'll face whatever comes together."

"In the stronghold of my sisters' arms," Moira stepped into their embrace, "the world outside seemed inconsequential."

Moira stepped back, her gaze meeting each of her sisters' eyes—a mirror reflecting their shared resolve. The embers of defiance ignited within her.

"Ye ken I'll stand my ground," Moira said, her words firm and strong. "Brodie McClain may think he can sway me with his quiet ways, but I am not so easily moved."

Ailis nodded, her expression glinting with pride. "We ken well the mettle of yer heart, sister. It would make no sense for ye to back down now. If ye do, he'll think he can treat ye any way he chooses, and that cannae be the way he thinks."

"Besides," Fiona added, a mischievous twinkle softening the moment, "if Brodie dares cross ye again, he'll have all of us to reckon with."

Moira's lips twitched. "I'd like to see him try," she replied, the challenge in her voice palpable.

"Enough talk of McClains and confrontations," Ailis declared. "Tonight, we dine together, just us sisters."

Moira conceded with a nod, though her thoughts strayed to Brodie—his deep brown eyes always watching and calculating. She could almost hear his steady voice asking questions she wasn't ready to answer.

"Moira?" Fiona asked, concern on her face.

"Apologies," Moira said, shaking off Brodie's shadow. "I was lost in thought for a moment there."

Ailis teased lightheartedly about ghosts and Sinclairs on their land. Despite the laughter it brought, tension still lingered around Moira.

As they left the room together, Moira glanced over her shoulder—feeling the weight of the confrontation with Brodie like a tartan draped across her shoulders. The path forward was shrouded in mist and uncertainty but Moira's resolve remained unshakable.

With unwavering support from her sisters, Moira stepped out of the room. Yet beneath their solidarity, an undercurrent of unrest promised more challenges to come.

CHAPTER THIRTY-TWO

MOIRA'S BOOTS ECHOED through the silent war room as she entered. The vast chamber, typically filled with strategists' voices and the rustle of parchment, was unnervingly quiet save for the crackling hearth. A shiver chased down her spine, not from the Highland chill but from the knot of trepidation tightening in her belly.

The weight of her father's expectations felt as heavy as the claymore she had been trained to wield. As she approached Duncan, she prepared herself for the clash of wills that awaited her.

Duncan stood at the head of the room, his towering frame anchored by broad shoulders that bore their clan's legacy. Surrounded by maps, missives, and weighty tomes of heritage and law, he lifted his gaze from a scroll and acknowledged Moira with a subtle tilt of his head. His features softened slightly upon seeing his daughter before him, but there was no mistaking the gravity written on his face.

"Moira," he said, voice steady with authority. Duncan's hand paused over a map detailing their lands and lifeline. With a meaningful look, he beckoned her closer, signaling a conversation requiring more than their usual exchange.

Within the stone chamber, father and daughter stood on the precipice of decisions that could alter their lineage. Moira drew in a breath of fire-warmed air and braced herself for what was to come.

"Father," Moira's jaw tightened as she looked at the map between them. "I understand the importance of clan, but is love not meant to be free?" She fought to keep her voice steady and respectful, knowing she couldn't ignore her duty toward their people.

Duncan observed her stormy eyes, empathizing with her struggle. "It's not just about your heart, Moira. Our alliance with the McClains through yer marriage to Brodie secures our people's future. With all three of my daughters married to three sons of Laird McClain, we cannae risk the alliance being severed."

Moira stood still, outwardly calm while inwardly questioning if her happiness was worth sacrificing for political alliances. She knew leadership came with burdens, but accepting that truth was harder when it involved her own fate.

Moira wrestled with her thoughts. Duncan studied the parchment before him, his gaze locked on the inked boundaries representing more than mere land.

"Moira," he said, his voice echoing off the stone walls, "we must mend what has been torn asunder. The McClains are our kin now, and they must be treated as such."

His eyes met hers with an intensity that conveyed his unwavering dedication to their people.

"Da'," Moira countered, her distress evident, "Brodie and I— our union—it's not a simple matter of mending fences or signing truces. He has asked if the bairn I carry is his child. He doesnae trust me, and that cuts me to the core. I cannae stay married to a man who thinks I would stray!"

"It doesnae matter what he has said. Ye need to make amends with yer husband, and he will return to sleeping in yer chamber with ye tonight. There will be no more delays for hurt feelings. I refuse to see me daughter act so stubborn with her husband."

"And just who do ye think taught me to be stubborn?" she asked.

"And I would do it again. Now, bury yer stubbornness and invite yer husband back to yer chamber and bed. Me grandbairn will be raised by both of his or her parents, and ye will not quibble with me about it!"

She clenched her fists, feeling the weight of tradition bearing down upon her. "'Tis my life! I cannot simply feign affection where there is conflict."

Duncan's voice softened. "Ye are the lifeblood of this clan, and yer happiness matters. But we must stand united for the sake of all who look to us for leadership in these uncertain times."

Her breaths came in shallow gasps as she teetered between duty and desire. His unwavering sense of duty cast a long shadow over her yearning for a life chosen instead of assigned.

"But—"

"Enough, Moira." Duncan's hand rose as if to offer a comforting touch from across the room. His voice was gentle yet unyielding, like Highland heather and stone. "Love is not a fortress to be stormed or a battle to be won. It is the foundation where we stand together."

Moira listened, her fiery spirit tempered by her father's wisdom.

"Love bridges hearts," Duncan continued. "Understanding is what holds it fast. We cannot let pride or hurt destroy what we've built."

Moira felt the weight of history pressing upon her. Her father bore that burden with an air of inevitability.

Her thoughts tangled like thistles in the wind, caught between duty and her own dreams. Despite her conflict, she bit back her words out of respect for her father.

"Moira," Duncan's voice grounded her. "Your choices impact us all. I trust you'll find the path that honors your heart and our name."

An unspoken understanding passed between them—an acknowledgment of shared strength and the complex tapestry of duty binding their lives.

Moira stood silent, absorbing his words while grappling with loyalty to her father and her need to forge her own destiny—a destiny entwined with the wild beauty of the Highlands that had shaped her spirit.

"Love and understanding," she mused, the ideas melding like stones in a stream. Shadows danced with her wavering thoughts, torchlight flickering.

The stone walls of the war room closed in around Moira as her father Duncan's firm voice broke the silence. "Moira, by nightfall, ye must mend what's been torn asunder for the McAfee clan."

His decree left no room for objection. Moira clenched her fists, feeling his heavy expectation. The embers of rebellion within her flickered brightly.

"Father," she said steadily, "I'll meet with Brodie, on my terms."

Duncan met her gaze with unwavering intensity. "Aye, your terms, so long as they lead to peace by dusk."

"Peace by dusk," she echoed, accepting the challenge for her clan and for Brodie.

Duncan repeated, "Peace by dusk," standing like a steadfast sentinel. Duncan's nod was subtle, yet Moira felt the weight of its significance. She straightened her spine, fueled by her father's trust in her abilities.

Swallowing her resistance, Moira turned away and strode down the corridor. She would meet with Brodie on her own terms, guided by the wisdom inherited from her father. As the Highland sun cast shadows across the castle grounds, Moira knew it was a race against time and stubborn hearts. Bearing the blood of warriors, she was determined to face this challenge head-on.

She thought of the McClain stronghold nestled among craggy peaks and Brodie, steadfast like the mountains. But she knew his hidden tenderness that called to her heart.

Passing flickering torches, Moira resolved not to bend to mere commands; she must balance clan loyalty with fierce independence that pulsed through her veins.

Tales of love overcoming strife whispered in Moira's

thoughts, inspiring her strategy to bridge McAfee honor with the yearning of her soul.

Brodie would listen if she spoke from a place of honesty and acknowledged their shared past and potential future. It required precision and grace, but Moira wouldn't falter.

Approaching the castle entrance, each step brought her closer to destiny and perhaps the fate of two clans. "Peace by dusk" echoed in her mind as a challenge—one Moira intended to face with courage and cunning.

The cool air of the stone corridor brushed against Moira's cheeks as she strode forward. Tapestries depicting battles and unions lined the walls, pressing upon her the weight of her lineage. Echoes chased her thoughts with each footfall, a reminder of the task at hand.

"Peace by dusk," she murmured, steeling her back and squaring her shoulders. She would confront this challenge squarely and without fear, as Granny had taught her—with a spirit as indomitable as the mountains that cradled their home.

She stopped beside a window that looked out over the courtyard where he was training with the other soldiers. She placed a hand on the cold stone, drawing strength from its permanence.

With a deep breath, Moira pushed away from the window. The landscape had offered silent counsel, renewing her conviction. She would meet Brodie on her terms, weaving personal truth into the tapestry of the clan's needs.

Moira released her grip on the window ledge and turned away from the view. The rough-hewn floor whispered beneath her tartan dress as she strode down the empty hall. Her heart pounded, but her spirit remained unbroken.

With a clear path ahead, Moira prepared to face Brodie, another soul molded by their harsh and beautiful homeland. Their entwined fates demanded a delicate touch that only honesty could provide.

"Let him hear my truth," she murmured, a prayer to the ancient spirits that guarded her people. She knew her words must cut through layers of misunderstanding like mountain streams finding fertile ground.

She reached for the door handle, its cool iron grounding her thoughts. Breathing in deeply, she stepped into the fading light of early evening. Sunlight cast golden hues over the landscape, painting shadows like reaching fingers onto tomorrow's promise.

Moira McAfee faced her decision with unwavering conviction: to confront Brodie McClain not as a pawn but as a Highland woman—proud, fierce, and free. This night would determine her marriage and place within the clan while affirming her role in her people's history.

CHAPTER THIRTY-THREE

MOIRA'S BOOTS THUDDED against the training field's compacted soil as she closed in on Brodie, his sword arcing gracefully through the air. As she approached, she thought about just what she needed to say to Brodie so they could make peace.

The metallic clang halted when Brodie sensed Moira's presence and turned to face her, tension evident in his posture. Sliding his sword into its sheath, surprise morphed into anger that had been brewing since their last encounter. His deep brown eyes mirrored the tumultuous Highland skies.

Undeterred, Moira met his eyes. Both knew this confrontation meant a clash of indomitable wills. Bound by honor and past grievances, neither would yield easily.

Moira halted, maintaining a deliberate distance. "Brodie, we need to talk," she said, urgency in her voice.

Her rigid posture and expectant eyes fixed on him, allowing no refusal.

The world seemed to pause as Brodie studied Moira's face, his hand resting on his sword's pommel. His eyes narrowed, not in suspicion but in an effort to understand her message.

For a moment, they remained motionless, engaged in a silent battle of wills. Finally, with a curt nod, Brodie stepped forward and fell into step beside her. Their boots crunched upon the grass as they headed toward the forest trail, leaving the sounds of clashing steel behind.

Moira navigated the forest trail, sunlight and shadows creating a shifting mosaic on the ground. Memories of laughter and secrets whispered in this place clung to her thoughts as she moved through the trees. This forest was where she'd fallen in love with Brodie, and it was now here where they would have to make peace—if only for appearances.

She cut a determined path. She moved with grace, familiar with every root, stone, and bend that spoke of clan legacy and Highland valor.

Behind her, Brodie maintained a respectful distance, his guarded expression betraying nothing of his inner turmoil. He observed Moira's hair capturing beams of light—a nod to the fierce spirit he had thought he knew so well.

Silence stretched between them, filled with unspoken words and confessions yet to be aired. In the middle of the ancient trees, the complexities of their bond lay bare, waiting to be unraveled or knotted tighter still.

Amidst the forest's hushed serenity, Moira halted and turned to Brodie. "Here is as good a place as any," she declared resolutely.

"Moira—" Brodie began, but her stance silenced him.

"I've been told to make peace with you," she stated, her voice straining against her frustration. "Peace, but not without conditions." She stood tall, embodying the dignity of her clan position.

"Ye can return to my chamber," Moira conceded. "But ken this, Brodie McClain—there will be boundaries that ye dare not cross." Her voice remained steady and unyielding.

Brodie met her gaze, his eyes reflecting the shifting light but hiding his thoughts. He understood the weight of Moira's words and the shared uncertainty of their future.

Brodie's hand rested on the hilt of his sheathed sword, revealing the warrior beneath the strategist. Moira's words resonated among the ancient trees, each syllable a ripple in Brodie's composure. He listened, jaw muscles tense, as Moira issued her demands.

"Ye're not to lay a finger upon me," she declared, her voice steady like the Highland glens. "That is my first condition."

The air stilled, even rustling leaves pausing to hear her decree. Brodie's pride smarted; such a stipulation chafed at his honor. Yet, he held his tongue, silence stretching between them.

"Consider yerself fortunate," she continued, fire igniting in her eyes. "For if I had surrendered to my rage… Well, it's yer good fortune I dinna run ye through with my blade."

Moira's lips barely curved into a sardonic smile or a snarl— the seriousness undeniable. A testament to her restraint and the fierceness of McAfee blood—a warning clothed in mercy.

Brodie absorbed her words, silently watching her. The weight of their history surrounded them in the quiet forest trail, and for a moment, something akin to regret flickered in his eyes. But he remained silent as Moira's resolve stood firm before him.

Brodie's breath hitched, ready to unleash the storm of words behind his clenched teeth. His deep brown eyes, skilled at reading situations and enemies, now betrayed his inner turmoil. Anger sparked within them, ignited by Moira's admonitions, but beneath it lay hurt and unmistakable regret.

Before he could speak, Moira's hand rose—swift, decisive. "Nae yet," she interjected with commanding authority. Her gesture symbolized the walls she had erected for necessity and self-preservation.

"Listen to me, Brodie McClain," Moira began anew, her voice a sharpened blade. "What we had… it cannae endure under deceit and discord.

"Ye ken as well as I that unresolved issues and resentments simmer between us. It will burn us both if we dinnae attend to it." Her hands gestured passionately. "We must forge a new path forward, together or apart, clear and open-eyed. Can ye respect that? Can ye honor my boundaries without trampling them beneath yer pride?"

She stood her ground like a fierce McAfee warrior, demanding respect through her unwavering spirit. The question hung between them, a challenge and an invitation—their bond teetering on the precipice of his response.

Brodie exhaled, his breath vanishing in the cool Highland air. He took a step closer to Moira, shoulders tense.

"Moira," he murmured, voice heavy with inner turmoil. "I've been…adrift in a storm of emotions I can't yet fathom. I need time, Moira. Time to understand the depth of what has passed between us."

In the quiet, Brodie sought understanding in Moira's eyes. She gave a slow nod, her gaze intense but softened. "Aye, Brodie," she said, voice tempered with strength. "Ye've always been a man of thought, one to weigh each word and deed like a blacksmith balances his blade."

She stepped forward, resolute. "I won't pretend this will be easy or treat it lightly. But if ye are willing to meet me in earnest—to work through this mire—then I am willing too."

As Moira extended the olive branch of truce, they stood on the precipice of change amidst the wilds of the Highlands.

Brodie's gaze carried unspoken words, bridging the once insurmountable distance between them. Their breaths mingled in the cool Highland air before fading away like their lingering resentment, making room for something delicate yet brimming with potential.

With a subtle shift, Brodie broke the stillness and Moira faced him. Their eyes locked, and an unspoken promise crystallized between them. It was a tentative beginning, woven into their lives as the setting sun cast long shadows on the ground. Hope kindled within them—a glimmer that might one day ignite into a fire as fierce as the Highland spirit itself.

CHAPTER THIRTY-FOUR

MOIRA APPEARED IN the doorway of the chamber, dimly lit by the fire in the hearth. Fiona's fair head turned toward her first, while Ailis's darker expression held anticipation. As Moira entered, the space seemed to widen, her presence demanding attention.

She paused on the threshold and drew in a deep breath, bracing herself for the news she carried. "Father insists on reconciling with Brodie for clan unity," she said, her voice sharp. Her green eyes were like a turbulent sea during a storm.

"I've agreed to allow Brodie back into our shared bedroom," she continued, each word deliberate and heavy with resolve. "But hear this: he returns on my terms.

"There will be boundaries," Moira asserted, her stance strong and unwavering. "My independence is non-negotiable. It is my right, and I'll ensure it within me own quarters."

Fiona's gaze did not waver, and Ailis took in Moira's declaration thoughtfully. Silence hung heavy for a moment, broken only by the fire's crackle.

"Boundaries," she repeated to herself, as if fortifying her will against any future challenge.

In the chamber among sisters bound by blood and shared trials, Moira stood firm amidst a world that never ceased its relentless turning.

Fiona nodded slowly, the motion heavy with unspoken understanding. Ailis reached over and grasped Moira's hand firmly.

"Ye ken we stand with ye," she whispered.

"Your courage lights the way, sister," Fiona added softly, pride evident in her gaze.

"I cannae imagine what it would be like to tell Lachlan I was expecting and have him questioning who was the father. I think I would be forced to draw me dagger!"

Moira felt their support strengthen her resolve. "I was cut...too badly to think of me sword, but now that you mention it..."

Her sisters both laughed, and Ailis hurried forward to embrace Moira. "Dinnae let me put terrible ideas into yer head!"

BRODIE PACED RESTLESSLY in the dimly lit chamber. Shadows clung to corners as he battled turbulent emotions, struggling for control.

He paused before meeting Lachlan and Alisdair, seeking their counsel about his turmoil. Surrounded by whispers of clan legacy and silent judgment from ancestral portraits, he carried the weight of tradition on his shoulders.

The door creaked open, signaling an end to solitude and the beginning of the guidance he so desperately needed.

The door groaned shut, and Brodie faced his brothers. Lachlan stood by the hearth, firelight highlighting his rugged features, while Alisdair leaned against the stone wall, eyes locked on Brodie.

"Moira," he began, voice strained with emotion. "She's set boundaries within our own chambers." He paced, frustration evident in each step. "I am her husband, but she negotiates terms as if we were rival clans."

His fists clenched, anger seeping through his words. "She claims her space like a sovereign nation, leaving me feeling like an intruder in me bed."

Lachlan's brow furrowed, flames glinting off his thoughtful eyes. Alisdair's empathetic expression held steady beneath the shadows of concern that crossed his face.

Brodie stopped pacing, the tension thick as he met their gaze. "I know not how to bridge this growing chasm," he admitted, anger fading to vulnerability. It was clear that Brodie's struggle lay not only with Moira, but with the traditions shaping his marital expectations—expectations now crumbling like ancient ruins across their land.

Lachlan leaned forward, shadows casting depth to his determined expression. "Brother," he began, "marriage, like forging swords, requires both heat and temperance." He gestured toward the flickering hearth. "Understanding and compromise are what tempers it."

Brodie's grip tightened on the chair before him as Lachlan's words echoed in the chamber. "Our traditions teach respect for the fire within a person's spirit. Moira has this fire; tend to it well."

Alisdair stepped away from the wall, placing a supportive hand on Brodie's shoulder. "Moira's strength and independence bind her to the land and her people—traits to be admired, not quelled."

He let silence linger briefly. "Reflect upon yer actions, brother, and decide whether they fan flames of discord or soothe them into embers of peace. Yer choice shapes yer marriage's future."

Brodie looked between his brothers' earnest faces in the firelight. He felt the weight of his decision pressing upon him; there were no easy answers, only the necessity of reflection and change.

Alisdair took a deep breath. He obviously had something to say, but was unsure how to say it in a way that Brodie would accept. "Ye have accused Moira of being a wanton woman. She has shown ye nothing but love. She is friendly, and she talks to others because she is one of the hostesses. Her sisters are ready to rise up against ye as well as all McClains. They are angry at the way ye have treated their sister, and I fear they will not forgive ye."

Brodie's jaw clenched, the muscle twitching as he turned from his brothers. The flickering hearth cast shadows across his face, reflecting the struggle between pride and the need for a compromise in his marriage. He traced the wooden table thoughtfully.

"She has flirted with men right in front of me!" Brodie protested.

"Has she?" Lachlan countered. "Or has she shown hospitality that yer jealous mind has turned into something more than it rightly is?"

"I must think about this," he murmured to himself. After a moment of silence, Brodie strode from the chamber, steps lighter but filled with uncertainty.

MOIRA STOOD BY the narrow window in her private quarters, gazing at the dusky landscape and watching a lone falcon fly overhead. Embracing herself, she tried to chase away lingering anxieties caused by recent conversations. Night descended, doubt creeping into her thoughts like mist over the glens.

"Can strength alone mend what's torn?" she whispered, determination rekindling within her. Moira reminded herself of her clan's legacy and prepared to face Brodie with unwavering fortitude.

In darkness, she lit a candle and readied herself for confrontation, embodying the fierce Highland spirit.

She sat by the hearth, her thoughts drifting through her troubled marriage to Brodie. Her fingers traced the pattern of her tartan, reminding her of the bond they once shared.

Brodie had continually found the worst in her...or what he considered the worst. She'd saved his life, and he'd gotten angry. She'd been the best hostess she could be, and he'd gotten angry.

She no longer knew how to communicate with her husband.

Moira recalled their first meeting. There was a palpable connection at the Highland Games which had seemed to hold strong through war and politics. The laughter that had been so easy between them now seemed like a distant brook, its melody smothered beneath discord. Yet, memories of love stubbornly clung to life.

"Ah, Brodie," she sighed, allowing a moment of nostalgia.

A knock broke her reverie. Brodie's arrival was imminent, anticipation thickening as he entered the room. His deep brown eyes met hers, a silent exchange filled with emotion. In that gaze, Moira sensed his frustration, hurt, and reluctant hope.

Invisible yet insurmountable boundaries stood between them. They found themselves at an impasse, separated by pride and misunderstanding.

"Moira," Brodie began, his voice steady as the calm before a terrible storm.

"Ye ken why I'm here," Moira replied, her tone as firm as the mountains surrounding their home.

Moira straightened her spine, the candlelight casting a warm glow that intensified her resolve. Brodie closed the door, the soft click breaking their silence.

"Ye'll be sleeping on the far side of the bed," she said firmly. "And naught but slumber will we share until trust can be rebuilt." She sighed. "Or should I say, ye must learn to trust me. I've always trusted ye."

Brodie's jaw tightened slightly as he replied, "Understood, Moira." His eyes revealed contemplation—a man unaccustomed to compromise now faced with change.

They performed their nightly rituals, maintaining distance while sharing brief glances and gestures. In bed, an expanse of linen and wool separated them. Moira faced the wall, steadying her thoughts. Brodie stared up at the darkened beams above, his mind calmed by his brothers' counsel.

As dawn crept through the narrow window, it illuminated

two figures united not by warmth but by a fragile, unspoken agreement—the first step upon a path that she hoped would lead them back to each other, and not further apart.

CHAPTER THIRTY-FIVE

HOOVES THUNDERED AGAINST the damp earth, shattering the misty silence of the McAfee estate.

Moira's heart raced as the messenger dismounted, his cloak billowing. The family gathered in the great hall, whispers and the scent of peat thickening the air. Even before the wax-sealed parchment was presented, Moira felt an oppressive weight of impending news.

Her father, Duncan, stood at the head of the clan, eyes sharp as his dirk fixed on the missive. The fire crackled in the hearth, casting a warm glow but failing to dispel uncertainty.

"Let us see what tidings this dawn brings," Duncan said, his voice steady yet laced with concern. The family drew closer in anxious anticipation.

Duncan broke the seal with unyielding hands. Moira held her breath, knowing the contents would have consequences for both their clan and the balance of power in the Highlands.

He unfolded the parchment; each line he read aloud etched gravity onto his face—silent stories told by furrows and creases. His eyes remained focused on their fate while kin listened intently, expressions weaving a tapestry of hope, fear, and resolve.

In flickering light, Duncan McAfee shared the queen's will with his clan, each word rippling through their lives like stones cast into still waters.

"By royal decree," Duncan announced, "the queen declared

the fate of those captured here. All shall die by blade on the morrow, except Callum Sinclair, whose bloodline grants him mercy."

The McAfee family gasped as the decision's weight settled upon them. This act threatened to ignite a political firestorm throughout the Highlands. Sparing Callum hinted at hidden alliances and power struggles, endangering clans like the McAfees. When her father read on, Moira realized he'd been spared for the sake of the remaining Sinclairs.

Ailis stood amidst murmurs, her green eyes mirroring the hearth's flame. Her usually steady hands trembled. The news wounded her deeply. In sparing Callum, the queen burdened him with the guilt of what his family had done to deserve retribution—a fate some deemed worse than death.

Pressure etched lines of worry onto Ailis's features as her father folded the missive. She was familiar with Highland politics, but its harsh reality left her shaken. In the silence that followed, Ailis's turmoil mirrored the imminent grief befalling the Sinclair family.

Later, Ailis stared at the fading embers, lost in thoughts of Arran Sinclair's fate. The missive's words haunted her, and she struggled with her sense of responsibility. She was the one who had been first tasked with deciding how to punish them, but she hadn't done what she'd been asked. And now people were dying. As a healer, she couldn't think of anything worse than killing.

"Come away, sister," Moira urged, gripping Ailis's arm, while Fiona offered silent support as they walked through McAfee Keep's stone corridors. In a secluded alcove, the sisters tried to comfort Ailis.

"It was out of yer hands," Fiona reassured her.

"Arran took part in the Stewart's betrayal of our queen," Moira added firmly. "Justice grinds without favor."

Ailis acknowledged their words but couldn't silence her inner turmoil. She contemplated the fragile threads of fate that spared one life and ended another's.

In the dim alcove, Moira crouched before Ailis and asked what troubled her. Ailis wondered if she could have changed the queen's judgment had she fought harder.

"Arran made his choices," Fiona said, placing a comforting hand on Ailis's shoulder. "We cannot change the past or stop justice from being served."

Ailis questioned Callum's survival compared to his father's death, but Fiona reminded her that justice and politics often intertwined, especially when dealing with deceitful acts like those of the Sinclairs.

"Callum's life serves as warning and opportunity," Fiona said, her hair catching a beam of light, "a chance for peace on favorable terms."

"Peace bought with blood," Ailis whispered, mourning the cost of stability in the Highlands.

Moira's hand instinctively found her dirk. "Ye need not carry this alone, Ailis," she said firmly. "The Sinclairs betrayed our trust, spilled our blood. Justice is no burden for ye to bear."

Ailis turned toward Moira, feeling the certainty in her sister's voice. Moira's gaze held only unwavering Highland justice.

"Ye ken well the cost of mercy in these times," Moira continued, embodying McAfee lineage pride. "Laird Sinclair answered for his crimes. 'Tis the way of our land."

Ailis sighed, accepting the strength offered by Moira's resolve. "Your heart speaks with the courage I sometimes lack," she admitted.

"Courage resides in ye as much as any McAfee," Moira responded, resting a hand on Ailis's arm. "Different we may be, but equal in strength, my sister."

Ailis met Moira's eyes and felt their shared bond. "Thank ye, Moira," she murmured. "For your fire when my own falters."

"Always," Moira replied softly.

Together, they stood in the great hall as kin, fortified against the coming storm. With Moira by her side, Ailis knew they would face whatever the Highlands held in store.

The sisters' conversation intertwined loyalty and concern, interrupted by Granny McAfee's quiet entrance. Her petite frame contrasted the strength emanating from her.

"Ah, my bonnie lasses," Granny said, her voice like smooth pebbles found beside a river. "Ye bear the weight of the world on yer shoulders."

Ailis felt lighter in Granny's presence, the old woman's eyes brimming with humor.

"Yer eyes are storm clouds, Ailis," Granny observed. "But even the fiercest tempest gives way to clear skies. Sit with me a spell."

In a quiet nook with walls that had witnessed generations of solace-seeking McAfees, Granny held Ailis's hand.

"Let me tell ye a tale, child," she began, her voice echoing ancient Highland storytellers. "When I was a lass, our clan faced discord like a black fog over the moor." She recounted her brother's accusation of treachery and the clan's division.

Granny locked eyes with Ailis. "We weathered that storm because we held fast to each other. We found justice not in retribution but through understanding leadership and the price of peace.

"The true measure of courage is ceasing wars within ourselves. Trust your leader's soul, Ailis." The older woman wrapped her arms around Ailis, trying to give her some comfort. They all understood Ailis's guilt, and wanted to ease it any way they could.

Granny's words settled upon Ailis like a cold yet pure first snow upon mountains. In Granny's wisdom, she found hope that the clan would endure even in dark times.

"Thank ye, Granny," Ailis whispered, more connected than ever to her land and legacy. "For reminding me of who we are."

"Who ye are," corrected Granny gently, "is exactly who ye need to be."

Ailis clasped Granny McAfee's hands. "I'm grateful for your wisdom—and for all of you." Her gaze connected with Moira and

Fiona, the bond between them palpable.

"Ye needn't thank us," Fiona said, her warmth comforting. "We stand together."

Moira nodded fiercely, her spirit undimmed. "The Sinclairs struck our heart, but it's a heart shared by many."

Ailis rose, feeling supported though uneasy, ready to face what lay ahead. They left the alcove, the grand hall now somber instead of expectant.

Duncan addressed the clan, his voice heavy. "We cannot alter the queen's decision or ignore its implications. Our path forward must be tread with caution and unity."

Ailis joined the circle as they discussed strategies and future risks. Duncan concluded, "The strength of the McAfees lies not just in sword and shield, but in the courage of our convictions. We shall navigate these troubled waters with honor."

As tasks were assigned and carried out, Ailis felt renewed unity within the clan. The keep stood as a testament to her people's endurance. She was ready to play her part as a McAfee and would not falter.

Ailis stood by the hearth, watching the embers dance and crackle in the dimming hall. The McAfee clan surrounded her, faces etched with resolve as the stone walls of McAfee Keep absorbed their determination.

"Through unity, we have withstood storms," Duncan proclaimed. "And united, we shall face this."

Ailis felt the weight of her father's words. Across the room, Fiona consoled a younger clanswoman with compassion and silent promises. Granny McAfee shared wisdom with an elder in her comforting voice.

"Tomorrow, we rise with the dawn," Duncan said. "We will meet our fate with fortitude that has defined the McAfee name for centuries."

Ailis touched the cool stone wall, feeling its unyielding solidity beneath her fingers—a reminder of her legacy and spirit.

"Let us rest tonight in the knowledge that we are one clan,

one family," Duncan finished.

The McAfees dispersed with singular purpose etched into their hearts. Ailis lingered, eyes tracing shadows on the stone floor that hinted at challenges to come.

CHAPTER THIRTY-SIX

BRODIE MCCLAIN SAT in his chamber, staring into the hearth. His brothers' words echoed in his mind, reminding him of his corrosive jealousy that threatened his bond with Moira—the woman who held his esteem and affection. And his love. All of his love went to the stubborn woman.

He paced the room, gaze falling upon the sword against the wall—a symbol of honor and protection he feared he had compromised. How could he have been blinded by baseless suspicion?

Highland air swept through the window, cooling his shame. Trust was essential to his alliance with the McAfees—trust he must embody once more. He muttered, "Enough," feeling a resolve well up within him. Brodie knew an apology was owed and chose his words carefully.

He approached the door, determination growing. A warrior stirred within him—not to fight an enemy but for the love and respect of Moira. With her name on his lips like a promise, he committed to seeking forgiveness in the shadowed courtyard where she practiced her swordsmanship.

Taking a deep breath, Brodie McClain stepped out of his chamber, a new chapter beginning as the door closed behind him.

IN THE COURTYARD, Moira McAfee's sword clashed against steel with precision and grace. Her red hair was a tight braid that swung with each pivot and lunge. The afternoon sun cast shadows on her focused expression as she delivered each strike to the practice dummy.

Moira's movements were sharp, mirroring her inner turmoil. Brodie's jealousy smoldered within her, fueling her swordplay. She channeled her emotions into energy, severing invisible bonds of doubt in their relationship.

Brodie watched from the entryway, his brown eyes following her fluid form. Hesitant, he moved forward, knowing well he was about to navigate a different kind of battlefield—one where words mattered most.

As he approached Moira with caution, the unspoken apologies and hope for forgiveness filled the space between them. He paused, gathering his thoughts before calling out softly, "Moira." His voice betrayed vulnerability as he waited for her to face him and start mending their strained bond.

The clang of steel ceased as Moira turned, her gaze holding a lonely intensity that met Brodie's. The silence hung between them, heavy with unspoken emotions.

"Moira," Brodie began, his voice trembling. "I've come to apologize." He swallowed hard and continued, "My actions, driven by jealousy, have wronged us both."

He stepped closer, each word deliberately chosen. "I know my doubts had no place between us. Ye've been loyal to our clans and to me. I am deeply sorry."

His confession lingered in the damp Highland air as he searched her eyes for absolution.

Moira's grip on her sword loosened, and she slipped it into her scabbard. Her brows lifted slightly, her stance relaxing as she considered his words. She let out a slow breath and spoke, "Ye've given me much to consider, Brodie."

There was a pause filled with distant birdsong before she continued. "Hearing yer apology…it gives me hope that perhaps we might move beyond this." She spoke calmly, but her heart felt as if it had been mended. An apology was all she'd wanted from him. She needed hope for their future and for the child she bore.

Moira stepped forward, her arms encircling Brodie's shoulders with a strength contrasting the tenderness of the moment. Her embrace conveyed relief and love.

"Ye have always been me anchor in the wildest of storms," she whispered, her breath warming his neck. "To have ye doubt me rattled me spirit." She met his gaze with intensity. "But yer words now, they are like a medicine that has healed me, Brodie."

He stood motionless, careful not to shatter their fragile peace.

"Trust is our foundation," Moira said, her voice steady. "I need yer unwavering faith as the Highlands are ancient and unyielding." Her eyes, mirroring the fierceness of the glens, held his own. "Can ye trust in me loyalty and love?"

Brodie's voice resonated with newfound clarity. "Aye, Moira, I can, and I will." The weight of his past misgivings lay bare in those words. "My jealousy clouded my judgment. 'Tis a fault I deeply regret. Ye've done nothing to betray me, and I think I have just worried that ye dinnae really love me."

He reached up, cradling her face, thumbs caressing away uncertainty. "Ye are the heart of me. This, I swear this to ye. And going forward, I will be better. I will do all I can to keep ye and our bairn happy."

Moira sighed softly, leaning into his touch. In the quiet courtyard, they found solace in each other's presence.

Brodie wrapped his arms around Moira, pulling her close. Her head rested against his chest, listening to the steady drumming of his heart—a rhythm that spoke of enduring strength.

"Whatever comes," Brodie murmured into her hair, "we'll face it together."

"Aye, we will," Moira affirmed. She was thankful he finally understood, and they could be together. She said a silent prayer that his jealousy would never take over again.

The Highland air carried the distant echo of a piper's melody, winding through glens and over heather-strewn hills. Brodie held Moira, absorbing the serenity around them.

"Listen," Moira breathed. "The Highlands sing for us."

Brodie nodded, aware of the rustling leaves, soft murmur of water from a nearby loch, and the call of an eagle. Releasing her, he took her hand and together they faced the ivy-covered castle walls.

Their steps matched in a silent dance as they approached the heavy oak doors. Brodie glanced at Moira, whose eyes were reminiscent of the sky overhead. Her spirit burned brighter than ever.

"Moira," he said, "I vow to stand by ye, to honor yer strength and meet it with me own."

"And I will hold ye to that promise, Brodie McClain," she replied firmly. "Together, we are unbreakable."

Hand in hand, they crossed the threshold, carrying memories of their surroundings with them.

Torches flickered, casting a glow on Brodie and Moira's faces as they exchanged meaningful glances.

Brodie squeezed Moira's hand and said, "The trials we've faced have forged us anew—stronger than steel or these walls."

Moira nodded, her green eyes ablaze with determination. "Fire-tested, we emerged tempered. The Sinclair betrayal, the Stewart conspiracy…it led us here."

"Here," Brodie agreed, pausing beneath an archway leading to the great chamber. "Our clans united against any challenge."

"Like entwined oaks outside these walls," she added, admiration in her gaze.

Their hands clasped as they entered the chamber where kinsmen greeted them enthusiastically. A shared glance between Brodie and Moira held an ember of hope for their future.

Their love would serve as a guide through life's storms— bound by trust.

As Brodie and Moira stepped outside the castle walls, the cool Highland breeze carried scents of pine and wild thyme. The land stretched before them like an untamed canvas under the late afternoon sun.

"The Highlands await us," Moira said, her voice harmonizing with the wind.

"Aye, lass," Brodie murmured, fingers intertwined, "our tale is far from over."

Moira challenged, "Race you to the stream," and sprinted forward, her hair trailing like a flame in motion.

Brodie followed, laughter filling the glen as they ran toward their future, both of them content with the knowledge the other loved them.

"Whatever comes," Brodie vowed, his voice steady as the mountains, "we'll face it side by side."

"And win," Moira said. At that moment, everything in her world revolved around her husband. She knew it wouldn't be long before they had a houseful of children, and then they would be her focus.

In this quiet moment, the future lay rich with mystery and magic of the Scottish Highlands—an endless horizon of hope and possibility for the couple whose hearts beat fiercely as the untamed land they called home.

EPILOGUE

Scotland—1600

B RODIE AND MOIRA guided their steeds through the wild Highlands toward the McAfee keep.

The oaken doors of the keep swung open to reveal their kin. Lachlan stepped forward with brotherly affection in his gaze. Ailis' dark hair and green eyes mirrored the forest, Fiona emanated gentle strength, while Alisdair's presence reassured.

"Welcome home!" Lachlan boomed warmly, embracing Brodie firmly.

Moira met each family member with a determined tenderness. "It's good to be back with ye all once more," she declared.

Stories and laughter filled the reunion, shoulders relaxed, and smiles came easily as they reconnected.

Outside the keep, children played boisterously on lush grasses. Watching them, Brodie found renewed purpose in protecting the future generations. Moira's fierce demeanor softened into a smile reflecting pride and promise as they stood side by side, leading together.

The late afternoon sun cast a golden hue over McAfee Keep as Brodie McClain prepared to share troubling news. His family encircled him, their faces aglow from the reunion.

"Kin," Brodie began, "there's news from the court—King James VI has set his sights on witch hunts across the land." The group stilled, as if holding its breath.

"Trials and burnings?" Lachlan asked, his voice mirroring the hills surrounding them.

"Aye, brother," Brodie replied. "Many innocent lives may be lost to fear and suspicion. We must stand vigilant."

Moira grasped Brodie's hand firmly, an unspoken pledge between them. The adults exchanged grave looks as laughter faded into memory.

Brodie continued, "There is some good news—Boyd and his wife and children leave for a voyage to the New World. They cannae risk being branded as witches."

Surprise flickered through the gathering. "The New World?" Fiona inquired with concern.

"Aye," Brodie said. "A chance at a new beginning, far from our troubles here."

Moira added with pride, "An adventure grand enough for any McAfee or McClain."

"Boyd will take our blessings and prayers for success," Brodie assured. "His courage will pave the way for future generations— our bloodline will flourish in realms anew."

"May the old ways guide him," Ailis whispered, her gaze drifting toward the children.

"May they ever do so," Brodie agreed. As they watched their grandchildren play together, their bonds felt stronger than ever, even while bracing themselves against the oncoming winds of change.

As Brodie's voice rose above the Highland breeze, he announced the new laird of Clan McClain, the fourth eldest brother of theirs, Grant. Lachlan squared his shoulders, Alisdair's face softened with pride, Fiona whispered a prayer, and Ailis squeezed her husband's hand in support.

"A clan requires a leader who can navigate these treacherous times," Brodie stated firmly.

"We stand united beside him," Alisdair added, asserting unity within the clan.

Their attention turned to the children playing beside the keep, laughter filling the air. "They are the reason for every difficult choice we make," Moira confided, eyes glistening. The others silently agreed, reflecting on their sacrifices for a brighter future.

"Generations hence, they'll speak of these days," Alisdair mused. They voiced their beliefs: love and loyalty from Fiona; courage and faith from Ailis; and strength of family from Moira— all pillars that defined the essence of the Highland Clans.

Brodie's gaze shifted toward his family, noticing mixed expressions of pride and concern. "The New World," he said. "It's a land full of dangers and opportunity."

"Boyd has the heart of a lion. He and his kin will forge a new destiny there, out of the witch hunts' shadow," Moira added.

"Their strength will be enough," Alisdair said softly. "And with Boyd there, all will go well. Is Grandfather Colin going with them?"

Brodie looked sad as he shook his head. "With Boyd's son being a healer, Grandfather Colin will stay behind and stop healing himself to extend his life."

Alisdair looked as if he'd been hit. "I suppose he's lived a good, long life. And it's his time. Though, it hurts me."

"Courage isn't the absence of fear, but its mastery," Lachlan declared. The group murmured assent.

As hooves clattered nearby, Laird Callum Sinclair and his advisor Lucas Gordon arrived on horseback.

"Laird Sinclair, Lucas, welcome," Lachlan greeted, shaking hands firmly.

"Thank you," Callum responded, dismounting gracefully. His presence commanded attention.

Lucas followed, nodding at his friends, who had once been his competitors.

"Moira, Brodie," Laird Sinclair acknowledged them. "Times are changing. We must adapt or be swept away by the tide."

"Indeed," Brodie agreed. "The Highlands stand ready to face what comes."

"Let us hope that unity prevails," Lucas added.

With greetings over, the adults settled in the expanded circle while the children continued playing, unaware of the shift in dynamics as influential figures joined the gathering.

"Changes are afoot," Laird Sinclair announced, scanning the gathering. "We stand at the precipice of a new era—one that may redefine Highland life."

Brodie McClain leaned forward, meeting Sinclair's gaze. "We must consider how best to navigate these currents." His voice held certainty.

"King James' pursuits cast shadows upon us all," Moira interjected, her red hair glinting in the dying light. "The McAfee will not falter under scrutiny or superstition. We must protect our own."

"Protection requires unity," Laird Sinclair murmured, nodding at Moira's resolve. "Yet unity is fragile when met with ambition and fear."

"True," Brodie agreed, "but through understanding our shared traditions and fostering alliances, we can fortify against threats. The Highland code of honor binds us."

Lucas Gordon conceded reluctantly, "Wisdom must be paired with vigilance. The landscape of power shifts treacherously."

Moira scanned the faces of her kin. "Vigilance has long been our way. The McAfees do not yield to treachery. Our ties give us strength."

"Strength that will serve as we face whatever sort of witch hunt that ensues," Brodie added, casting a glance toward their stronghold—a looming threat. "We must anticipate their moves, counter when necessary, and always protect our people."

Laird Sinclair acknowledged their commitment with a look of respect. "It is this resolve that will see us through the challenges ahead."

"Challenges we shall meet head-on," Moira affirmed, her eyes unwavering. "Together—one family, one clan, one united force within these Highlands."

As silence settled among them, each leader contemplated the

future beyond the safety of the McAfee keep, ready to guide their clans through whatever storms lay ahead.

As twilight descended upon McAfee Keep, stories and laughter filled the glen. Brodie stood with Moira, observing their clan's glee by the firelight.

"Remember Seamus leaping into old Mairi's arms at Beltane?" Alisdair roared. The group burst into laughter at the vivid memory.

"And Fiona outsmarting the Sinclair scouts?" Ailis added with a mischievous grin.

Lachlan nodded, "Her cunning is legendary."

Moira beamed, "Our history is full of courage and cleverness, like our plaids."

Brodie replied softly, "These moments unite us in spirit as well as blood."

Later, Brodie sought solitude near the keep's stone wall. Moira joined him, leaning against the rough blocks. "Much has changed since we first stood together," she said.

"Aye, but some things remain steadfast—our bond," he replied, taking her hand.

"Yer counsel has guided me," she admitted.

"Ye've always been fierce," he countered. "Yer fire lights our way."

Moira chuckled softly. "You've tempered my tempestuous nature with patience and foresight."

"As one, we'll face all challenges," Brodie affirmed, his deep brown eyes conveying love and admiration.

"Always," Moira agreed. Their shared silence spoke volumes—an unspoken pledge binding them together.

The setting sun cast a warm glow on the McAfee keep as the family gathering wound down. Laughter faded to murmurs and farewells, with the scent of pine and hearth fires weaving through the air.

Moira stood, taking in her loved ones' faces. She breathed deeply, feeling her concerns for the future ease within her.

"Look at them, Brodie," she said softly, gesturing toward the children playing in the fading light. "They are like young saplings…strong and flexible."

Brodie joined her side, his eyes filled with pride. "Aye, they'll grow tall and steadfast," he agreed as they watched a boy help a girl to her feet. "Our roots—our stories and values—will nourish them. It's the legacy we leave behind."

Together, they watched the children chase twilight, silhouettes dancing along shadow and light. A young lad scaled a low stone wall, arms raised in triumph as others cheered him on. Life persisted, vibrant and indomitable.

Moira recalled Granny McAfee's words: "Every new generation is the clan's hope reborn." The truth resonated within her.

"Hope is a powerful thing," Brodie whispered, drawing Moira close. "It's a flame that never dies. Our children and grandchildren will carry it forth long after our time has passed."

As night fell over the Highlands, stars twinkled like distant torches lit by ancestors long gone, guiding the way forward.

As the evening chill crept in, the children's laughter echoed through the glen, framed by the rugged Highlands.

The day had been a whirlwind of emotions, but Moira and Brodie found solace in each other. Hand in hand, they turned back toward the keep.

"Until the morrow," Brodie whispered to both Moira and the land.

"Until the morrow," Moira replied, her heart swelling. Their joined shadows stretched behind them like a single entity. Ahead, the children played on—silhouetted against the fading light—a testament to life's unyielding march and their family's enduring legacy.

THE END

ABOUT THE AUTHOR

USA Today bestselling author Kirsten Osbourne knows how to write. Each book is an experience that transplants the reader, indulging them in decadence, intense emotion and sweeping love.

Kirsten was born in Wisconsin, and now lives in Idaho, but she's lived in Minnesota, Texas, and Louisiana along the way.

She writes contemporary and historical romance, venturing into the realm of paranormal romance and women's fiction. She invites you to join her in her world of fantasy, love, and make believe, no matter the location, where there is always a happily ever after at the end.